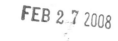
THIS IS A BUST

THIS IS A BUST

A Novel by Ed Lin

 Kaya Press

All thanks to my first reader and universal partner Cindy Cheung. Many thanks to my parents, Doris Lin, Daniel Kim, and Melody. Grace Elaine Suh's incredible eye and support were invaluable. So was Sunyoung Lee's chipper way of chipping away at problems. Detective Thomas Ong, NYPD (retired); Detective Yu Sing Yee, NYPD (retired); KFL; and GCC all put up with my nagging presence and were overly generous with their time. Corky Lee is the man. Chez Bryan Ong is kid dynamite. Thank you, Julie Koo, Thaddeus Rutkowski, Jessica Hagedorn, Han Ong, Henry S. Tang, Jen Chou, Pritsana Kootint, Rika Koreeda, Terra Chalberg, Tasha Blaine, Jin Auh, and extra special thanks to Anthony Rapp.

www.edlinforpresident.com
www.myspace.com/edlinforpresident

Published by Kaya Press, an imprint of Muae Publishing
New York City
www.kaya.com

Book design by spoon+fork.
All photos by Corky Lee back in the day. Mural by City Arts Workshop.

Manufactured in the United States of America.

Distributed by D.A.P./Distributed Art Publishers
155 Avenue of the Americas, 2nd Floor
New York, NY 10013
(800) 338-BOOK   www.artbook.com

ISBN 978-1885030450
ISBN10 1-885030-45-2

This publication is made possible in part by state funds from the New York State Council on the Arts, a state organization; an award from the National Endowment for the Arts; and the support of Hong Yung and Whakyung Lee, Minya and Yun Oh, Jungmi Son, Gabriela Jauregui, Joseph Goetz, Amelia Wu, Kate Durbin, and others.

For all the blue guys.

Chapter 1

January 20, 1976. The Hong Kong-biased newspaper ran an editorial about how the Chinese who had just come over were lucky to get jobs washing dishes and waiting tables in Chinatown. Their protest was making all Chinese people look bad. If the waiters didn't like their wages, they should go ask the communists for jobs and see what happens.

Here in America, democracy was going to turn 200 years old in July. But the Chinese waiters who wanted to organize a union were going directly against the principles of freedom that George Washington, Thomas Jefferson, and Abraham Lincoln had fought for.

Those waiters were also disrespecting the previous generations of Chinese who had come over and worked so hard for so little. If it weren't for our elders, the editorial said, today we would be lumped in with the lazy blacks and Spanish people on welfare.

I folded the newspaper, sank lower in my chair, and crossed my arms. I banged my heels against the floor.

"Just a minute, you're next! Don't be so impatient!" grunted Law, one of the barbers. A cigarette wiggled in his mouth as he snipped away on a somber-looking Chinese guy's head. When he had one hand free, he took his cigarette and crushed it in the ashtray built into the arm cushion of his customer's chair.

He reached into the skyline of bottles against the mirror for some baby powder. Law sprinkled it onto his hand and worked it into the back of the somber guy's neck while pulling the sheet off from inside his collar. Clumps of black hair scampered to the floor as he shook off the sheet.

The customer paid. Law pulled his drawer out as far as it would go and tucked the bills into the back. Then he came over to me.

Law had been cutting my hair since I was old enough to want it cut. He was in his early 60s and had a head topped with neatly sculpted snow. His face was still soft and supple, but he had a big mole on the lower side of his left cheek.

You couldn't help but stare at it when he had his back turned because it stood out in profile, wiggling in sync with his cigarette.

He looked at the newspaper on my lap.

"We should give all those pro-union waiters guns and send them to Vietnam!" Law grunted. "They'll be begging to come back and bus tables."

"They wouldn't be able to take the humidity," I said.

"That's right, they're not tough like you! You were a brave soldier! OK, come over here. I'm ready for you now," Law said, wiping off the seat. I saw hair stuck in the foam under the ripped vinyl cover, but I sat down anyway. Hair could only make the seat softer.

"I don't mean to bring it up, but you know it's a real shame what happened. The Americans shouldn't have bothered to send in soldiers, they should have just dropped the big one on them. You know, the A-bomb."

"Then China would have dropped an A-bomb on the United States," I said.

"Just let them! Commie weapons probably don't even work!" Law shouted into my right ear as he tied a sheet around my neck.

"They work good enough," I said.

When Chou En Lai had died two weeks before, the Greater
China Association had celebrated with a ton of firecrackers
in the street in front of its Mulberry Street offices and
handed out candy to the obligatory crowd. The association
had also displayed a barrel of fireworks they were going to
set off when Mao kicked, which was going to be soon, they
promised. Apparently the old boy was senile and bedridden.

"Short on the sides, short on top," I said.

"That's how you have to have it, right? Short all around,
right?" Law asked.

"That's the only way it's ever been cut."

If you didn't tell Law how you wanted your hair, even if you
were a regular, he'd give you a Beefsteak Charlie's haircut,
with a part right down the center combed out with a
Chinese version of VO5. I was going to see my mother in a
few days, and I didn't want to look that bad.

"Scissors only, right? You don't like the electric clipper, right?"

"That's right," I said. When I hear buzzing by my ears, I want
to swat everything within reach. Law's old scissors creaked
through my hair. Sometimes I had to stick my jaw out and
blow clippings out of my eyes.

The barbershop's two huge plate glass windows cut into
each other at an acute angle in the same shape as the
street. Out one window was the sunny half of Doyers Street.
The other was in the shade. How many times had I heard
that this street was the site of tong battles at the turn of the
century? How many times had I heard tour guides say that
the barbershop was built on the "Bloody Angle"?

The barbershop windows were probably the original ones,
old enough so they were thicker at the bottom than at
the top. They distorted images of people from the outside,

shrinking heads and bloating asses. In the winters, steam from the hot shampoo sink covered the top halves of the windows like lacy curtains in an abandoned house.

In back of me, a bulky overhead hair dryer whined like a dentist's drill on top of a frowning woman with thick glasses getting a perm.

The barbers had to shout to hear each other. The news station on the radio was nearly drowned out. The only time you could hear it was when they played the xylophone between segments or made the dripping-sink sounds.

If you knew how to listen for it, you could sometimes hear the little bell tied to the broken arm of the pneumatic pump on the door. The bell hung from a frayed loop of red plastic tie from a bakery box. When the bell went off, one or two barbers would yell out in recognition of an old head.

The bell went off, and Law yelled right by my ear.

"Hey!" he yelled. Two delayed "Hey"s went off to my left and right. The chilly January air swept through the barbershop. A thin man in a worn wool coat heaved the door closed behind him and twisted off his felt hat. His hands were brown, gnarled, and incredibly tiny, like walnut shells. He fingered the brim of his hat and shifted uneasily from foot to foot, but made no motion to take off his coat or drop into one of the four empty folding chairs by the shadow side of Doyers. He swept his white hair back, revealing a forehead that looked like a mango gone bad.

"My wife just died," he said. If his lungs hadn't been beat up and dusty like old vacuum-cleaner bags, it would have been a shout. "My wife died," he said again, as if he had to hear it to believe it. The hairdryer shut down.

"Oh," said Law. "I'm sorry." He went on with my hair. No one else said anything. Someone coughed. Law gave a half-

grin grimace and kept his head down, the typical stance
for a Chinese man stuck in an awkward situation. The radio
babbled on.

The barbers just wanted to cut hair and have some light
conversation about old classmates and blackjack. Why come
here to announce that your wife had died? The guy might
as well have gone to the Off Track Betting joint on Bowery
around the corner. No one was giving him any sympathy here.

Death was bad luck. Talking about death was bad luck.
Listening to someone talk about death was bad luck. Who
in Chinatown needed more bad luck?

"What should I do?" the thin man asked. He wasn't crying,
but his legs were shaking. I could see his pant cuffs sweep
the laces of his polished wing tips. "What should I do?" he
asked again. The xylophone on the radio went off.

I stood up and swept the clippings out of my hair. The bangs
were longer on one side of my head. I slipped the sheet
off from around my neck and coiled it onto the warmth of
the now-vacant seat. Law opened a drawer, dropped in his
scissors, and shut it with his knee. He leaned against his desk
and fumbled for a cigarette in his shirt pocket.

I blew off the hair from my shield and brushed my legs off.
I pushed my hat onto my head.

"Let's go," I told the thin man.

—

He led me through a garbage-strewn alley to a rear-
tenement building. It was built in the middle of a block and
enclosed on all four sides by other buildings. It was dark
back there, and the thin man pointed out where I should
watch my step and where I should watch my head. God

would have had to hold a magnifying glass under the sun to get any light into that building.

The smell was terrible. No tourist could take it. Imagine phlegm hacked out onto crumbly grout between bricks and damp, moldy hanging laundry that took days to dry out. It didn't bother me at all. I've eaten worse.

The thin man said his name was Yip. He and his wife Wah had been married for more than 50 years, 20 before they came over. They had never changed apartments.

Bald spots were worn into the carpet on the stairs. By the time we hit the sixth floor, hair clippings were slipping down my neck on trickles of sweat. I felt pangs for a drink.

Yip's apartment was at the far end from the common bathroom. The doors in the hallway looked as fragile as balanced playing cards.

Wah's body was lying in the sheets of a foldout bed. Her thin hair looked like fungus on a dead tree. She was even skinnier than Yip. You could fold the bed back up into a sofa and you wouldn't even feel a bump when you sat down.

I looked around the one-room apartment. A small stand on the sewing machine held a curly black wig that was going bald. Gaunt jackets slumped on the coat rack. Three pairs of shoes and two pairs of slippers lined up by the door. Three bumpy lemons huddled in the soap dish of the sink. The windowsill was crowded with empty halves of Tiger Balm tins.

Wah's color wasn't good, but I knelt down and checked her vitals anyway. Yip stood by the door and stared at her. I got on the radio to tell them to send the paramedics who would officially declare her dead. Then we needed the medical examiner to make sure there hadn't been any funny business. You can never be sure. I looked around for more details for my report. There wasn't much more to see.

In a few days, her body would be in the back of a hearse running through the tight and narrow streets of Chinatown. The traditional last ride around the neighborhood. The hearse's horn would blow and startled tourists would focus their cameras on the face of the woman in the picture tied to the front fender.

Honk! Honk! Honk!

Another chunk of money that had been saved to someday move out of Chinatown would go to the Five Fortunes Funeral Home. As much as Chinese loved to bargain, no one would dare to cheap out on the burial of a loved one. It would be bad luck.

Honk! Honk! Honk!

And then Yip would pick his way back through the alley to his apartment. He'd keep sleeping on his side of the foldout bed. His clothes would become tattered and rip at the seams. He'd stumble over steps because he didn't have a hand to hold on to.

I knew because I know lonely Chinese men. That's why I didn't bother to talk to Yip.

He took a seat at the small dining table and put his hands down flat in front of him.

I hooked my thumbs into my pockets. It could take a while before the ambulance showed up. I had never realized how much of a cop's job was wasting time until I was in uniform.

I went over to the sink and stared at the just unfurled 1976 calendar from the Mei Wah Restaurant.

In the previous year, the city had fired the 5,000 cops with the least seniority, not because of performance issues, but because of fiscal mismanagement. That was one sixth of the force. Morale had already been lousy, what with Frank Serpico's book and movie smearing shit on our badges in the public's eye. Maybe Serpico had seen himself as a muckraker, but how many muckrakers make millions from a book and movie and move to Europe?

Bruce Lee was dead.

Vietnam was going to be completely communist. It was just a matter of signing the papers. That situation didn't go over well with the NYPD, either. Apart from having to deal with war protests, a lot of cops and their brothers, fathers, and cousins were walking around carrying gook shrapnel, if they were still walking.

You can imagine what they thought about me. They didn't know that I had fought on their side.

My name is Robert Chow. I had grown up in Chinatown before it became my beat. And it was the last place in the goddamned world I wanted to be.

Chapter 2

I headed over to the Five Precinct on Elizabeth for the 0800 to 1600 shift. It was a cold January morning, but I was sweating. Something didn't feel right. I chomped down on a Tic Tac and toyed with my right collar.

The street was filled with high-school kids heading to the subway. After school was over, they'd head off to college-prep classes and/or piano lessons. Saturdays were for Chinese school and Sundays were for Chinese church. Chinese kids learned how to cram, or they learned how easily their skin bruised.

The kids stared at me as I walked by. I could see they were worried that if they didn't get into a good college, they'd end up with a dumb, low-paying job like mine. That was the Chinese attitude about it. I smiled and said, "Good morning," to the kids closest to me as I went up the steps.

"Good morning," the kids said to their socks.

The Five Precinct is an old brick building in the middle of the block, on the west side of Elizabeth Street between Canal and Bayard. The Five was built in 1881, and being in there is like taking a trip back to those days. There's no elevator and no modern heating. Someone was always on duty to shovel coal into the furnace in the basement. The giant iron hook on a chain at street level hauled out bins of coal ashes, but all the parents told their kids the hook was for hanging criminals.

When you first come in the door, the C.O.'s office is to the immediate left. There were only two reasons you'd be called in there: if you were in trouble, or if you were in big trouble.

The commanding officer was a small, thin Irishman named Sean Ahern. He had short reddish-brown hair, without a spot of gray although he was well into his 50s. His clear blue eyes twinkled when he looked directly at you, which was deceptive, because he was never nice to anyone, and the last thing you'd ever want to do was block his view of his closed office door.

The C.O. favored heavy-soled shoes that he liked to stomp, even when he was sitting. In his chair, he liked to hunker down, pound his fist on the table, and look up at you, as if you were some bully out of his childhood that he never got to settle the score with.

His right eyebrow was missing hair about the width of a pinkie right in the middle. When he raised his voice, his eyebrow went up and you could see the muscle in that hairless part flex. That was why we called him the Brow.

The Brow kept a woodcut print framed on the wall above his head. A British soldier in a Revolutionary War uniform stood with one foot raised on a step and one hand brandishing a sword over his head. In front of him was a defiant teenager in rags holding up a dirty elbow to block the soldier's blow.

I'll never forget my first day at the Five and my first meeting with the Brow. I couldn't believe I'd gotten assigned to Chinatown. It was the last precinct I'd wanted, and everyone else from my class had been assigned elsewhere. Funnily enough, everyone else wasn't Chinese.

By the time I walked into the Brow's office for the first time, I was already having second thoughts about what I was doing there. The reek of gun oil filled my nose and mouth while resentment throbbed in my heart. In the Five precinct I'd be dealing with people who knew me and my parents. People who would ask about the war, my father, and other stupid questions. I'd even considered putting my badge on the table and saying, "That's all, folks!"

Instead, I stared at the British soldier woodcut. There wasn't much else to look at apart from the Brow's face. He followed my stare to the woodcut and spoke.

"That dirty little boy is Andrew Jackson, the first Irish President of the United States," he said. "That's him being slashed for refusing to shine that bloody English officer's shoes. Carried that scar on his arm to the grave. Now let me make something clear to you, mister. I don't shine anyone's shoes, either!"

He looked at me expectantly.

"Yes, sir." Apart from being a sign of respect, it gave me something to say.

Then he exhaled slowly and stretched his arms a little.

"I understand, Mr. Chow, that you're one of our boys from Vietnam. A good soldier follows his conscience. A good policeman, too. I'll bet you're wondering why you're here and how we selected you for our rather exclusive house." The Five had a rep for being one of the safest precincts in the city, with great cheap food. It was a nice place to work 20 years and then retire at half pay.

"Yes, sir."

"Well, it just so happens that you're a very special person to this house, don't you know? As a Chinese cop, you're very important to our image in the community."

"Yes, sir."

"In fact, from time to time, I'd like to ask you to represent us at community functions and other gatherings. Just talk to people. Smile. Show them you care."

"Sir, I'm not one of the more experienced men. . ."

"But, son, you've got the right look." I felt honored to be asked to represent the house, but at the same time, I was being asked to be the resident wok jockey. I leaned back on my heels and stared at little Andrew Jackson.

"You really like that woodcut, don't you? That little lad Jackson stood up to that English bastard, and he went on to become one of the great Presidents of the United States of America." The Brow squinted his eyes at me before continuing. "He's the only Irish President I care for. That Kennedy was a dirty, dissolute man who got everything he deserved."

"What do you think about McKinley, sir?" I asked. I knew that William McKinley was Irish because in grade school I'd gotten stuck writing a profile about him.

The Brow's brow went up.

"I don't think about McKinley!" He pounded the desk and cocked his head at an angle. "And neither should you, mister! There are crimes being committed right this second! Now go do something about it!"

But of course, he didn't really mean it. Well, sure he did want me to go write up tickets to bring some more money into the city. But he didn't want me to seriously fight crime at large. That was for the real policemen.

I was the guy who proved that the NYPD could get along with people with sing-song names and black hair. I went to graduation ceremonies, new restaurant openings, and Chinese New Year celebrations.

It was great at first, but then I got to feeling like I was a teddy bear in a police uniform for the kids to hug, a prop for the newspaper photos. Once in a while they would let me handle a domestic complaint, the kind that broke up as soon as I rang the doorbell and resulted in nobody willing to press charges.

The other blues thought I was a joke.

In time I got to hating what I was doing and, worst of all, hating Chinese New Year and the rash of ceremonies I had to attend before, during, and after. That holiday used to mean a mouthful of candy to me. Now I was gritting my teeth through it. The NYPD liked us Chinese, all right. As long as we didn't try to be more than a lowly beat cop.

Most daytours and nighttours would end with me drinking my fucking eyeballs dry.

—

Directly opposite the C.O.'s office, the desk sergeant sat up in his pulpit. The muster room for roll call and assignments was farther back inside, where it was always drafty. The door to the staircase going down into the backyard and the rear tenement would never stay shut. The back wall of the muster room had an RC Cola machine and a candy machine. The holding cell for patrolmen was off to the side.

When you trudged up the wooden staircase to the second floor, you'd come across the detective squad and their holding cell. The third floor featured showers, lockers, and the most diverse collection of Hanoi Jane stickers in the world.

The fourth floor was called the lunch room, but the lights were off for the most part because cops on the turnaround and some old-timers liked to nap there. The place stank of cigarettes. The volume on the black and white TV was broken, probably on purpose, and the screen would bathe the sleeping cops in a fizzy light. The open and empty pizza boxes and crushed Coke cans on the table made the room look like a teen sleepover party that had run out of steam.

I was glad that I lived close to the Five. When I was coming off the 1600 to 0000 I could go home and sleep, then come back for the 0800 to 1600.

The only reason I'd go to the fourth floor was because, like a lot of the newer guys, my locker share was there. It was a big deal to get a share on the third floor when one opened up — a big enough deal to get into a pushing match.

It never mattered to me because I lived in a walkup and my legs, numbed to climbing, could take it. One more floor wasn't going to change my life. But if you were planning on doing 20 and out, one more floor every day for the next X number of years could drive you to murder. If a share on the third floor ever opened to me, I'd trade it for season Rangers tickets.

I got changed and got down to the muster room on time. I slept with my eyes open through most of roll call. They were telling us to look out for delinquent youth activity. But kids weren't stupid. I'd been in a gang when I was a kid. Cops might as well look for signs of witchcraft. You weren't going to catch anyone in the act of anything here.

I thought about my old partner, a guy named John Vandyne. He had moved on, and was now running with the detective squad of the precinct, so he didn't have to stand for roll call anymore. Just before the layoffs and cutbacks kicked in, Vandyne and I had lost our sector car, but he'd found a way to pick up investigative assignments. He'd been on the job a year longer than me and the extra experience must have helped him.

They'd told me to walk a footpost to get in touch with the community. Yeah, that was how they put it. In one way, they were right. Most cops on the footpost sulked around, chatting more with tourists than with the Chinese.

The way the Chinese felt about it, talking in English to an American cop could only invite misfortune, like how visiting an American doctor can only cause you to become sick or start an entire chain of events to get you deported.

They'd let Vandyne work in plainclothes and someday soon he was going to have a detective's gold shield. That was what I wanted, but I was too valuable as a Chinese face in uniform. I got to collar bad guys, but most of them were older Chinese men who frankly were no match for me.

Roll call droned on. I yawned into my fist through the last bit. Then I hit the street.

Right away, I had to stop for someone's car that had gotten scraped by a tofu truck off of Baxter. I lifted up a flattened cardboard box on Bowery and told the guy under it to move on now that he'd had a full night's sleep.

It was still cold, although the sun was bright as hell. My eyes felt raw and red. I rubbed them a little. I did a quick circuit of my footpost, just to make sure everything was set for the time being before heading for Martha's Bakery. You don't want buildings to burn down while you're out for coffee.

Martha's makes iced coffee by pouring old coffee into a foam cup, mixing in condensed milk from a can, and spooning in sugar like it was healthy to have. They stir it before they add in the ice. After they put on the lid, they turn it upside down and give it a few good shakes.

Two women at the counter handled several hundred customers in the morning rush hours, and neither was named Martha.

If Lonnie is making my coffee, I'll take two hot-dog pastries fresh from the oven and damp with steam inside the wax-paper bag. A hot-dog pastry is a unique Chinese American invention. They use the same dough as for the custard buns and taro buns, only they wrap it around an Oscar Meyer hot dog. The ends stick out like horns on a Viking helmet. They're good.

Lonnie was young, only 20, but very good-looking, and not too skinny. Well, how skinny can you stay working in a bakery? She had thick black hair that looked pretty okay by me. Sometimes she'd tie it up with a plastic hair loop that helps women style hair that perms can't curl.

Lonnie would shake my coffee upside down and say, "Officer Robert, how are you today?"

I'd say, "I'm fine, Lonnie," and ask how her classes at Borough of Manhattan Community College in midtown were going. Lonnie was a business-communications concentration because she wasn't sure what she wanted to do. She was thinking about journalism. She once showed me her review of an Alexander Fu Sheng movie for the college newspaper. They'd spelled her last name wrong, but she had that clipping laminated. Of course, non-Chinese had no idea who Alexander was. We saw him as the new Bruce Lee, only with a sense of humor.

If Dori ended up making my coffee, I'd take three hot-dog pastries. Dori is in her 40s, unmarried, and not real eligible.

She looks like the Pillsbury doughboy with a wig and talks at you, not to you. She'd slap my change on the counter so I'd have to pick up each penny.

I take that extra bun because Dori always made me think of what I had to look forward to in a few years. She made me not care what I looked like or what people thought of me.

One day, some other woman with about the same physical characteristics as Dori was behind the counter. But it was Dori. She wasn't wearing any makeup and looked like she hadn't showered. The collars of her uniform were wrinkled. I had to ask for my change that day. Lonnie told me later that Dori's mother back in Hong Kong had died. Dori had been devastated about not making her mother a grandmother. But that didn't stop her from coming into work. They got no sick days at Martha's Bakery. A day out was a day with no pay and no free mistake pastries.

—

After getting two hot-dog pastries from Lonnie, I went back on the footpost. I checked meters and wrote out some parkers.

It was Monday, so I stopped by the toy shop on Mott to see if Moy wanted to have lunch. I've known Moy since second grade, when his family came over. He had wanted me to teach him English, but I'd referred him instead to "Hawaii Five-O." His parents had opened a laundry at first, but they went with the toy shop when hula hoops got really big. His parents were good at picking up on trends. Their store was the last place in New York you could get the sold-out G.I. Joe dolls with the special Kung-Fu Grip, marked up in price, of course.

It was just the two of them now, Moy and his dad. His mother had died of cancer when we were in high school.

The lumpectomy hadn't worked. She was nice.

Moy worked at the store almost 12 hours every day. His father never trusted anyone else to get behind the counter except me.

After Nam but before I got my head on right, Moy's dad was nice enough to give me a job unpacking toys from boxes from Hong Kong. I couldn't believe how much money kids had to spend. They were either skimming from their family businesses or selling fireworks to the tourists.

The work was pretty mindless, but it kept you busy. Two years went by like that, and, like Moy, I didn't meet any girls there.

Like a lot of guys, I hadn't had sex until I got to Nam. Some of the girls didn't know what to make of me, but they took my money and let me go at it. It was five minutes of humping and 10 minutes of shame. I haven't had sex since I came back to the world in 1972. I haven't killed anyone since 1972, either. I kind of associate the two.

Moy had never had a girl ever, and sorting out spaceship models and monster replicas doesn't sharpen social skills. He was average looking and at 26 he was only getting older. Like me.

The big problem with Moy was the hearing aid in his right ear. He was born with some kind of defect, but until he saw a doctor about it, he'd gotten hit on the head by various balls in gym class. Even now when you talked to him, Moy would cock his head and point his good left ear at you.

I popped my head into the toy store.

"Moy, you up for lunch?"

Moy leaned back against a glass case that showed off

astronaut figures. He had freckles like Howdy Doody and bushy eyebrows shaded his watery eyes. Moy reached up with one hand and played with the wire that ran from his ear to the shirt pocket of his dark blue t-shirt.

"I'm hungry," he said, "but I can't leave. Dad's at the post office and we're getting a shipment in soon."

"What's coming in?" I asked.

"Models of robots and Godzilla."

I left, got some noodles from a sidewalk cart, and walked them back to the toy store. We were almost done eating when Moy's dad came in. He was wearing a worn felt beret and holding an orange plastic bag and a cane with side legs and a tiny seat that a folded out into a tiny stool. He looked like Moy, but with about 25% less fat, and had a voice harsh enough to tear through a sheet of Reynolds Wrap.

"You idiot, I said I would bring lunch! Why did you waste your money on that?" Moy's dad growled.

"I'll eat what you brought. This is just noodles," said Moy.

"How are you, Uncle?" I said to Moy's dad. "You've made enough money here. Time to move to California." He frowned as he took plastic soup containers out of the orange bag.

"What for? Everything I ever knew about America is right here. I still have my friends here," he said. Little bits of saliva sprayed on the glass counter as he talked. "I like it here. Don't have to change anything."

"You have to find a wife for your son," I said. He laughed while Moy put his head down. I jabbed Moy's arm. It felt a little flabby.

"Only thing I have to do is stay away from blacks," Moy's

dad said. "When you see a black face around here, you better watch your wallet. They can slip it out of your pocket and you won't even feel it. The only places they know how to behave are on the basketball court or in jail." Then he laughed like he was saying, "It's funny but it's true!"

I stayed quiet. What can you say to a guy who was old and ugly, and had such a heavy accent when he spoke English it would make the white guy in "Kung Fu" cringe. He just wanted to be surrounded by Chinese faces for the rest of his life, which wouldn't last much longer. Let him die like that.

—

After the 10-minute lunch, I left and walked to Columbus Park. A dark-skinned black man with a medium build was leaning against the iron fence. He was wearing a brown leather jacket with a ripped vest pocket and a Yankees hat with the brim curled down as far as blinders. He was watching men playing Chinese chess and frowning.

"Chow," he said, and clapped my back. We did a one-arm embrace.

"Vandyne," I said.

"I got a message for you from that Willie Gee. He said he wants police protection from the protesters. And he said he wanted to talk to a Chinese cop, because I wouldn't understand the cultural subtleties of running an honorable business." Vandyne was smiling like he could prove someone wrong.

"Yeah, I'll stop by later today," I said. My footpost was Sector Alpha, which took me past Jade Palace on Bowery, south of Canal. It was the biggest dim-sum place in Chinatown, and Willie Gee was the owner.

"What are we supposed to do about the protestors?" I

said. "They've got a permit. They're staying behind police barricades. They're not even that loud. And they only come out in force on the weekends for the dim-sum crowds."

A bunch of former Jade Palace workers and their families were picketing the restaurant for paying below minimum wage and taking waiters' tips. What was pretty dumb on the restaurant's part was that they had rounded up stool-pigeon dishwashers and bus boys to stage the management's own counter-picket, which they also had a permit for. That made the protest seem twice as large to tourists coming in for dim sum, because you had two groups holding signs in Chinese and yelling at each other in Chinese.

"You know what the protesters are doing now?" asked Vandyne. "They started a hunger strike. The *Daily News* picked up on it and the Jade asshole wants it stopped. He said nobody wants to eat in a restaurant while people are starving outside."

"What does he want? Someone to shove food down their throats? It's not illegal to not eat. If they're spray-painting the walls, then we can do something. You know, if it was white people demonstrating, they would've chained themselves to the doors, or something dramatic like that."

"Yeah, and if it was black people out there, they'd cover the whole block, shut that place down. They'd have to call the dogs out."

"I think I'm going to head over there now," I said, checking my watch. "You looking to get a game in?"

"I'm taking on the midget next," he said, pointing to a four-foot-tall man sitting on an upturned bucket that used to hold bean curd. The small man pointed back, making a gun with his thumb and forefinger and pulling the trigger.

The midget had thick, half-opened eyelids, making him look eternally sarcastic, which he was. He kept his face unshaven, as if he were conscious of looking too much like a kid. His smooth, combed hair was shiny like wet licorice.

Vandyne had picked up Chinese chess from a book and from playing against the midget, who had tipped off Vandyne about an upstart heroin ring a year before, when he was starting investigative assignments. Helped him a lot.

The midget was a small guy, but no one had bigger eyes, ears, or brains. A game against him was all in good fun, because everyone knew that no one had ever beaten the midget at anything.

I swung out from the park and walked up Bayard.

Something somewhere in Chinatown hummed. It could have been sewing machines in a sweat shop. It could have been old Chinese in freezing apartments trying to clear their throats.

—

The gaudy gold characters on the awning of Jade Palace hit you when you were about two blocks away. If you were driving to Manhattan from Brooklyn on the bridge, you'd see it flaring in the distance like a comet streaking over rooftops cluttered with TV antennas and crooked brick chimneys. I never understood why they wanted to use gold letters. Why not make it the "Gold Palace"? Or if they didn't want to rename the place, they should've made the sign as green as Oz.

The customers didn't care what the place was called. They knew the clams in black bean sauce were the cheapest around. They knew the place was big enough so that the wait for a table — even for four people who'd driven in from Long Island or New Jersey — would never be longer than 10 or 15 minutes. And that was all they cared to know about the place.

Of course, I'm a little biased about it, because my father had been a Chinatown waiter. It was fifty cents an hour and he was only allowed to keep half his tips.

He came home enough times with nothing in his pockets but fingers blackened with ink from the racing forms. Luckily, my mother had a job sorting punch cards for Chemical Bank, and we'd survived on her pay alone. But good Chinese people don't want to merely survive — they want each successive generation to have more.

—

In front of Jade Palace, two hunger strikers, a man in his late 30s and what looked like a college girl, were sitting on flattened cardboard boxes. They had bilingual signs in their laps. One said, "Jade Palace Steals Our Tips," in English and, "Jade Palace Drinks Our Blood," in Chinese. The other, held by the girl, said, "Your Dim Sum Dims Our Hopes," in English and, "Jade Palace Worse Than Communists," in Chinese.

I walked by them and found three frosted glass doors at the entrance of the restaurant. I picked one and swung it open.

Two escalators went up to Jade Palace dining room. A discreet elevator to the side went straight into the offices. A big, bored-looking man leaned against the closed elevator door, his eyes pointed like ICBMs at the hunger strikers outside. His bangs gave him a boyish look, but it would take two strong thumbs to make that face smile. He had on a suit tailored to accommodate his muscles without making him look too much like a monument.

"I'm here to see Mr. Gee," I told him.

The big man tucked in his chin and grunted into a bulge in his shirt pocket. He waited a few seconds before opening the elevator with a key and stepping aside. I slipped in and rode up. The doors opened directly in front of a giant rosewood desk.

"You see that sign out there?" exploded Willie Gee even before the doors were completely open. He was in his late 50s, had hair that swept in a helmet around his head, and wore prescription shades. He looked like an evil Roy Orbison. "They're calling us communists! They're calling us murderers! My father gave all people a chance to work here! I still offer a job to anyone who wants one! Now they're calling me this? You should take them to jail now! If they want to starve, have them die in jail, not out here! They don't deserve to die here!"

Willie's office was adorned with photographs. Willie with Mayors Robert Wagner, John Lindsay, and Abe Beame. Hong Kong singers and movie stars with Willie. A signed Cosmos jersey from Pelé. Willie and Barbara Streisand. A photograph of the grand reopening of Jade Palace (after the installation of some wall ornaments and fire sprinklers) featuring Willie in the middle of a chorus line of smiling, happy people. The jerk in the cop hat was me.

Willie twirled a pen in his left hand and squeezed his right hand until there were red and white stripes across his fingers. I looked around for a chair on my side of the desk, but there wasn't one.

"Mr. Gee," I said slowly, "They have every right to protest here. They have a permit. They don't have to eat if they don't want to. There's nothing illegal going on..."

"They are liars! They are liars and they're going to hell!

They can eat misery! They can eat their lies!"

"Mr. Gee, if you have a problem with their signs, you can sue them in court for slander. Get your lawyer and file a claim. I can't do anything here."

"You're a policeman! You're Chinese, too! Whose side are you on? How can you support the law when you let those goddamn liars sit out there in the street? You know how bad this looks for the Chinese people?"

I scratched my thigh. Don't let the Chinese people look bad is beat into the head of every young Chinese kid. But the truth was that we made ourselves look bad, and look worse whenever we tried to make ourselves look better.

"We're all Chinese here," said Willie, even though we were the only two sitting in his office. He lowered his voice. "We could arrange something mutually beneficial."

I took the elevator down and sauntered out of Jade Palace. King Kong took two steps after me and then withdrew and stood still as the front door closed in his face. I continued up Bowery and took a quick glance back at the strikers, trying not to look sympathetic. A little less food never hurt anybody.

—

On Tuesday I was on a 1600 to 0000. Ice coffee and hot-dog pastries are as good in the afternoon as they are in the morning. Maybe a little less fresh. Lonnie was at the counter trying to open the wax-paper bag with one hand, but she ended up ripping it.

"Lonnie, goddammit, you keep ripping bags! You're so clumsy!" growled Dori as she snatched the useless bag and tossed it somewhere under the counter. "What a waste!"

"That bag wouldn't open, I think it was defective," said

Lonnie, who looked away from Dori.

"It's defective now!" said Dori. "What a disgrace you are. I think we need to have a training program here. Now watch me, little girl!"

Dori whipped her arm and snapped a new bag into a crinkled pyramid. "See? Easy!" She extended the opened bag to Lonnie, who ignored it and grabbed her own.

Lonnie shook the next bag open and looked like she was going to cry. Dori called out to the person behind me.

"What do you want? What!" Dori yelled. Her face couldn't have been more defiant if she were holding a battle flag in one hand and a grenade in the other.

"See what she does to me?" Lonnie asked in a voice ready to shatter. "Every time, every day, it's like this." She stuffed two hot-dog pastries for me into the bag.

"Lonnie, you don't need this," I told her. "You can get a job anywhere else." She creased the bag shut, put it on the counter, and turned around to make my iced coffee.

Here was the girl for the lead role for the Hong Kong remake of "Cinderella." The hag for the wicked stepmother was here as well.

Dori was at the other end of the counter, reaching into a rack of sponge cakes for her customer.

"Job doing what?" Lonnie asked, with her back to me.

"Doing hair, doing nails? Another bakery? There's always going to be bitter, old women who hate everyone younger than them. Stupid, old, ugly women who don't know how to do anything else. Don't even know how to speak English. I'm not going to end up here the rest of my life."

Then to Dori she said, "I'm graduating college in a year!"

Some of my coffee spilled over onto the counter when she slammed it down.

"Hey college girl, wipe off that counter!" yelled Dori. "I can't be responsible for all of your screw-ups!"

On my way out, I saw a few kids hanging out on the tables near the door. A few of them were smoking, and one boy with spiky hair lifted his head up and nodded at me with a leer on his face. Two other boys twisted their heads to each other and laughed. One girl turned and spat on the floor.

I thought to myself, These kids are a waste.

—

I came into the Five and saw the thin man Yip sitting in a chair by Detective 1st Grade Thomas "English" Sanchez's empty desk. A cane lay flat on the floor between Yip's feet. His wife had died only two days ago, and I'd never expected to see him again. I pumped two Tic Tacs into my mouth before going up to him.

"Yip, what are you doing here?" I asked.

"The police told me to come. I couldn't understand what they were saying. I'm not like you, my head was born in Canton."

"I'm going to find out what's going on." I checked with the desk, but all he knew was that English had wanted to talk to Yip. I left to look for English and told Yip to stay put.

English was a light-skinned Latino who looked Italian and loved that he did. He was about my height, with a meaty and heavily pockmarked face. Parts of him were bulky but he wasn't fat overall.

He'd gotten his name because one day, when they were looking for a Spanish speaker to talk to a hysterical man on the phone, someone had asked English if he were a native speaker and he'd said he was. But when he'd gotten on the phone, his face had slowly turned red.

"No habla Español," he'd said awkwardly into the phone.

After that, someone had said, "I thought you were a native speaker!"

"Of English! English!" Sanchez had said.

I ran into English outside the head.

"Chow," said English. His hands were wet and he wiped them across his stomach. "I was looking for you."

"English. What's going on with the guy you brought in?"

"Can you translate for now? The community-board person never showed up. The medical examiner ran a random blood test on his wife, uh, Wah, and found what could be poison. It's a suspicious death, and now they can't release the body for the funeral." We went back to English's desk.

I looked at Yip. He was looking at me, expecting me to tell him what was going on. His fingers worked at his knees.

Did Yip kill his wife? Motivation? There was no way. I thought about it, and then I felt sorry for myself. Here I was trying to think like a detective. I should have been on the detective track by now. I wouldn't have needed a translator. English had started talking to me again so I snapped back to the situation at hand.

"Chow, can you tell him?" English said. He faced Yip and said, "Your wife Wah died from poisoning."

I turned to Yip and began with, "I'm sorry to tell you, something terrible has happened."

"Was Wah working?" asked English.

I translated back for Yip: "She worked as a waitress at Jade Palace even though she had arthritis. She pushed a cart of dim sum around six hours in the morning every day. She liked to play mahjong sometimes. Her head was always itchy, but she never wanted to get a new wig."

"Do you work?" asked English.

"I work as a dishwasher at night at a small restaurant so sometimes we'd go for a few days without seeing each other awake. I made her breakfast before she woke up because her arthritis was so bad in the morning."

"What did she do at night when you were gone?" English asked.

"She liked to take a nap or read some books."

"Can you give me a list of her friends?"

"Her friends were all the people she worked with. Go down to the restaurant, talk to them. She liked her friends' children. She was sad she never had any."

"Was she feeling depressed about it?"

"She wasn't happy."

"Is there anything else you want to tell me?"

Yip's eyes grew unfocused and watery.

"I'm also sad she never had children. We were saving and saving, and we grew old. Turns out all that money was for nothing. Why did we come here?"

When it was time for Yip to go, he said he was fine walking by himself even though I offered him a ride.

"I don't have to hurry anywhere," Yip said.

"Are you okay?" I asked.

"I still have my job, my health, and my apartment," he replied. I picked up his cane.

"Did you hurt your leg? You didn't have a cane the first time I saw you."

"It's nothing, nothing. I'm old, Officer Chow. Things like this happen."

"You have to be careful," I said.

Yip got up and took his cane. "Thank you, Officer Chow. Don't worry about me." He sighed and tapped his cane. "Just let me bury my wife." I gave him my home number.

—

"Who would want to kill an old woman with no money who lived in a busted-up tenement?" I asked English.

"Why would anyone want to kill someone else?" he said, rubbing his nose. "You been where I been, you see kids killing parents, parents killing kids, people killing parents and kids. So what the hell. Anyway, thanks for handling that, I'll take it from here."

"You need me to go to the restaurant with you?"

"Nah, I'm going to call up that community-board translator and chew his ass out and get him to go with me. Thanks again, Chow."

"Anything else I can do?"

"I've got nothing for you. Thanks."

"Sure, detective."

There's no formal process to get on the detective track. You could do a decade on a footpost and never get on it. Basically someone higher up had to hand you investigative assignments before you could be on your way to a gold shield.

I shuffled back up the stairs to my desk, took a pen out of my vest pocket, and chucked it into the corner. Then I tore open my brown bag and bit off half a hot-dog pastry.

After a while, I threw out the second hot-dog pastry. On my way back, I got my pen back off the floor and chewed on it.

I wasn't getting anywhere thinking about the possible homicide or my career, so I put them both out of my mind. I ran a quick check on my pad and cuffs.

It turned out to be a slow night. I handed out two parkers and one mover. I watched a plastic frog swimming in circles in a tub of water at a vendor's stall. I wondered how long those batteries lasted.

—

To get to my apartment, you have to go east on East Broadway until you don't see any other Chinese people. It's about an eight-minute walk from Bowery. I live in a slouching walkup just past the southeast corner of Seward Park. At the turn of the century, it had been an all-Jewish neighborhood, but now a lot of Spanish live there. I took the apartment because we weren't allowed to live within the boundary of the precinct we served, but it was still close to the job. The building was a lot nicer than anything in Chinatown, anyway. The subway was right there, too.

My mail was cooking on the radiator when I got back home. The mailman was so lazy that instead of sorting out letters by mailbox, he'd slap the entire building's mail on the lobby radiator.

I guess you couldn't really blame him. About 20 beat-up, wall-mounted mailboxes at varying heights were crookedly nailed into the wall, their dented lids jutting out like shrapnel. You'd cut yourself sooner or later trying to fill all of them.

Most of the stuff was junk mail. Sometimes I would get something good, though. I lived for that. I liked getting sample-sized toothpaste or cereal. Once there had been a package of tapes from the Columbia Record Club for someone in another building. The guy's name was Robert Chew, so I figured I had dibs on it. That was like the best day of my life.

I climbed four flights of shabby stairs that only fit one person going up or down at a time. I put a key into the battered lock to #5A, and I was home.

My apartment was a sizeable one-bedroom that got too hot in the summer and even hotter in the winter. I had to leave one of the windows partially open all the time. I was lucky not to have a window that opened up to a shaft. Instead, I got to see East Broadway in all its squalor by daylight and by street lamp.

As soon as I had my shoes off, I pulled a can of Sapporo beer from the fridge and popped it. Japanese beer was pretty cheap in Chinatown because it was shipped in from a Chinatown in Japan. The busiest trading routes in the world were navigated with Chinese hands.

A Rangers replay game was on, and the blueshirts were down two goals in the last period. They skated like tin men in need of an oilcan. The goalie, John Davidson, was caught out of position, and the goal light lit up. Now they were down three goals. They were strong contenders this year — not for the Cup, but for the basement of the division.

I switched to the communist Chinese station on UHF. As the frame slide down and centered on the screen, I saw that it was an old civil war movie. "Heroic Bravery on Luding

Bridge" or "Brave Heroics on Luding Bridge." Something like that. It seemed that there was a movie for every little skirmish in the whole damn war.

The Taiwan station was airing an interview with a famous Buddhist monk.

"Is it ethical," began the cute and unemotional female interviewer, "for people to eat tofu and gluten formed into substitute meat and still say that they have a vegetarian diet?"

The monk sucked in his lips and nodded. "No. Absolutely not," he said. "While those people are not actually eating meat, they are still eating in the spirit of consuming flesh. It is definitely wrong."

Both the communist and the Taiwan stations were originally recorded in Mandarin, but were dubbed in Cantonese for the New York City market. Everything was subtitled in Chinese characters so that everybody could read what was going on.

I spoke Cantonese almost as good as a native speaker but my understanding of Mandarin was shaky at best even though both dialects used the same written language.

I settled in and drank five more beers. Pretty soon I felt the urge to shift my body over and realized that my eyes were closed.

Chapter 3

My year with Vandyne, 1974 to 1975, was spent driving from
crisis to crisis. When we had creeps handcuffed in the back,
we liked to stop the car short so that their faces would slam
into the glass divider. We only did that when they took
swipes at us first, though, or if they really deserved it —
purse-snatching punks from Canal Street and men who had
beaten their children badly.

The murder rate was soaring through the rest of the city,
but being in Chinatown was like being in the rear in Nam,
away from the front, with few homicides to speak of. We
were relaxed, but always alert to trouble. Some nights
nothing happened, and we would just talk.

Still, the Brow was worried for my safety, me being the
precinct's little public-relations poster boy. He made sure
to keep the two of us in mostly backup positions. When
Vandyne moved onto investigations, they shifted me to a
footpost that was as tame as a chihuahua.

The best thing about my friendship with Vandyne was
that we always pretended that we were hearing the same
stories from each other for the first time. Sometimes it
would be like you were hearing the story for the first time,
because the other person would change around the details
or make up new ones. We would even take details from
each other's stories and tell them as if we had lived it. It
was the right attitude to have, especially when we talked
about Nam.

"How many Negroes do you think there are in New York
City?" Vandyne had asked the first time we ate together.
I think he was feeling me out, to see if I was cool or not.
We were at Katz's on Houston Street, and Vandyne had cole
slaw on his face.

"There aren't any Negroes. Lot of blacks, though," I said.

"I like that answer. I like that a lot," said Vandyne.

"How do you feel about being in Chinatown?" I asked, looking at him straight on.

"I feel good about it. I have a lot of respect for the Chinese people and their culture."

"You good with chopsticks?"

"Pretty good," he said. I found out soon enough that he'd poke his eyes out if you didn't watch him closely. "You must be happy to be in Chinatown. You get to be amongst your own kind and do something for the community."

I dropped my voice. "Honestly, it's lousy. I mean, I can already see the resentment in the people's faces, like I've been co-opted. I'd rather be in Harlem."

"You don't want to be in Harlem," said Vandyne, looking down as he wiped his hands with a napkin.

A few hours later, we were parked on the corner of Grand and Elizabeth.

"I don't support Jane Fonda's message," said Vandyne. "I support her right to say it, but it was wrong for her to fly in and then fly out. Maybe if she moved to North Vietnam and lived there, then that would have been different."

"The message that we were killing kids?"

"Yeah, like that."

"Vandyne, I killed a kid in Nam. I mean, one that I'm sure of."

He was quiet for a little bit.

Then he said, "Oh yeah?"

I started talking.

"We got the orders to go from village to village, interrogate people, burn the hooches down. I mean, I wanted to take the backseat to all that, leave it to the gung-ho guys to do the interrogations. But then as we were going from village to village, I'm feeling all the hatred of the Vietnamese directed at me. They knew I was Chinese — they can tell, man. And they hate the Chinese there."

"Because the Chinese are the merchant class in Southeast Asia. They control the economy."

"Not only that. The Chinese have charged full retail for centuries. You have to expect the customers to resent it a little."

Vandyne shook his head and chuckled.

"So I tried to cover my face up with shades, some mud, but they'd always zero in on me. Old women would throw rocks at me. Little kids would try to kick me. You know they'd never do this to anyone else in a uniform, black or white."

I waited for Vandyne to nod. Then I gave up and went on.

"This old man came up to me and said in Cantonese, 'Excuse me, are you Chinese?' I said, 'Yes.' I was sort of relieved, because here's this guy trying to be almost friendly with me. Then he opens up his mouth wide, and he's got like seven teeth and he says, 'You fucking Chinks have sucked our blood for too long! Ba tàu! You're worse than the French and Americans put together! We're going to kill all the Chinese in Vietnam!'

"I just snapped. I kicked that old man to the ground. I was the quiet guy in the company, and no one else knew what he was saying, but they knew it had to be pretty bad to get me like that."

"Did you kill him?"

"Hurt him bad. They told me it could have been a good kill. After that, I was one of the lead interrogators in the company. I pushed pregnant women around and twisted their arms behind their backs, just waiting for some excuse to shoot them in the head. Being in Nam made me learn to hate Asians. Seeing another Asian face made me want to reach for my gun. Especially when I heard Vietnamese. It sounds like that mint, 'Tic Tac.'"

"So how did you kill that kid?"

"We were walking down this road when this kid with a ball comes running over to us. He's got a rubber ball with him, but it might be filled with explosives. You really don't know."

"So you shot him?"

"I shot him in the head and heart."

"Was it a bomb?"

"It was just a ball. But the worst thing was that I never even told him to stop. He should've known not to come running at us, though, right?"

Vandyne was quiet. After a while, he said, "I killed a kid, too."

"What happened?"

"We were camped out, sitting quiet," said Vandyne. He was talking slow. I couldn't look at him. I turned my head and watched steam come out of the gutter and curl into nothingness. "All of a sudden, shots are going out all over the place. We couldn't figure out where they were coming from. Then I saw a little flash coming from this tree, you know, the trunk of the tree itself. I'm thinking, the VCs are training fucking trees to shoot at us? I shot that tree up. Then it didn't fire no more and blood was coming out of the holes. I was scared out of my mind when I saw that. We got shovels and dug up the roots of the tree, and found a tunnel and the body of a little man, still holding his gun. In fact, the gun was bigger than him. He'd dug that tunnel under the tree, then hollowed out the tree from the inside and crawled up in there and fired at us. He'd killed two and wounded five. They told us later it wasn't a little man—it was a 12-year-old boy."

I waited for a few minutes. Then I asked, "How do you feel about it?"

"I don't feel anything about it, man," Vandyne snapped. "I don't care if it's the Easter Bunny. If it's got a gun pointing at you, you shoot it."

I wanted to ask him if he ever saw that little boy again, but I decided I not to. I didn't want him to think I was crazy the first day.

Sometimes I dream about that little boy I killed. He still runs in at me, only I don't have my gun anymore. If he gets close enough before I wake up, he explodes in my face.

—

My phone rang loudly, foreign and yet familiar. I checked the clock. It was 14 minutes after 1000. That meant it was okay to answer. I even considered opening my other eye.

I have this rule about answering the phone: Never pick up the phone when it rings on the hour or half hour, because it probably means bad news. Whenever someone has to make a tough phone call, they delay it until the hour or half past, because they're reluctant and need a deadline. Maybe they turn on the TV and then resolve to make the call when the show is over. That's what I do.

When there's something good to say, people can't wait to call you, so they tend to call at odd times. Six after. Forty-eight after. Fourteen after.

I picked up the phone and waited to hear who it was.

"Officer Chow?" said a thin voice.

"Yip, how are you?" I asked, surprised and suspicious.

"Did I wake you up?"

"No. I'm usually up this early on Saturday."

"I was calling to see if you wanted to join me for a late breakfast." A vision of me having a beer before heading downstairs came into my head and then faded.

"Sure, yes. I'll meet you. I'm allergic to seafood, though." I had to tell him that because nearly every dim-sum dish has some shrimp squeezed into it. He gave a heavy sigh. No one has any patience with food allergies. Chinese think it's all in your head, even when you're covered in hives, struggling to breathe.

"Okay, no seafood. We'll go to a cafe," said Yip.

I met him at a coffee shop that only people who came over before 1943 go to. Those were the people who spoke the Toisan dialect. After 1943, they changed immigration laws, and Chinese who spoke Cantonese started coming in. Toisan and Cantonese are different enough so that the Toisanese stuck together and so did the Cantonese. Native Toisan speakers generally know Cantonese as well, but not the other way around. They didn't need to talk to each other, anyway. Each group had their own coffee shops to go to.

I stirred some more sugar into my coffee and looked around. An old man at the far end of the counter brushed crumbs off his lap. A lopsided booth held two other old men. And then there was me and Yip, sitting on chairs at a table where an old booth had been ripped out. Hanging on the wall behind the cash register were scratch-and-win New York Lottery tickets for sale. Those probably kept this joint in business.

"He can't eat shrimp," Yip said to the waiter, who didn't have a notepad and lingered only a moment. You didn't have to order here. Everyone got the regular. Then Yip said to me, "Have you heard any more information?"

"I'm sorry, I haven't. But you know it's not something I handle. It belongs to the detective squad."

"But you're Chinese. Shouldn't you be the one in charge of this?"

"It's not like that, Yip. I can't talk about the case. Actually, I shouldn't even be talking to you."

"They don't give you a high enough position. They keep you at a low-level job because you're Chinese."

"I don't like to think about it that way."

Yip sighed. "First time I came to this country, I got a job with this contracting company mopping office floors. I was the only Chinese. I was lucky to get such a high-paying job. I was working with Italians, Irish, Spanish, and some blacks. We all worked really hard. Overtime with no overtime pay. Then I voted for having a union. We won, but the bosses closed the cleaning company and started a new one. We all lost our jobs."

A waiter dropped off two coffees, two plates of steamed rice noodles with ground pork, and two small dishes of pork spare ribs with black-bean sauce.

"So that was when I started with the restaurant in Chinatown. I got paid less, but it was in cash and food was free." He paused to pick his teeth, then indicated he wanted to be close friends by asking, "Where is your father from?"

"My father's dead."

"I'm sorry."

"I'm still mad at him."

"What did he do to you?"

"He gambled away a lot of our money. My mother's the only reason we pulled through."

"I'm glad your mother was good to you."

"She was tough."

"Your parents came from a different time, a different place. But I'm sure they're proud that you became a policeman."

"That was when my father stopped talking to me. He wanted me to do something better."

"When I came here there were no Chinese policemen. The white ones all had bad tempers and hated the people here." Yip paused to finish his coffee. "I want you to know that I'm so proud to know that a Chinese can be a policeman. I'm so proud to know you," he said, patting my cuff.

"Thank you."

"So you married?"

"No."

"You're too picky. There are a lot of nice girls."

"And they all know a policeman doesn't make much money."

"Most of the girls don't think like that."

"Just the Chinese ones," I said.

Yip laughed and I bit my lip. What's so fucking funny, old man, I thought. His mouth opened wider and I saw black splotches on his molars. After he calmed down a bit, he asked, "How old are you and you're not married?"

"I'm 25."

"You have to think about your children."

"I'm not sure I want to have children. I'm not even sure I want to find someone to love to have children with."

"Someday you will." I nodded and didn't say anything because I didn't want to keep talking along these lines. I became aware of an older Chinese woman standing near our booth. She was clutching a small beaded purse.

I leaned into Yip and said, "I think you got a friend here."

"She's Wah's shift supervisor. She wanted to talk to you."

"I told you before, it's not my case. I'm not handling it," I said. That cued the woman to approach us directly.

"Hello, Yip," she said. "How are you doing?"

"Officer Chow, this is Lily."

"Hello, Lily," I said. She took a seat and squeezed Yip over to face me directly.

"I wasn't just Wah's supervisor," she said. "I consider myself a friend of hers. We worked together almost 30 years." She dropped her voice a few octaves before going on. "I have never talked to the police before about anything. I've tried to live my life honestly and never get the police involved. Never wanted any trouble." She brought her face in close. Lily's hair was in a tight, smelly perm. She tried to cake makeup into the lines around her face, but she didn't use enough. A red scarf was draped across her broad shoulders.

"Sometimes the police have to get involved," I said. "We don't like it any more than you do. But we've got good men on the case already."

"You're the only one I can trust," she said. "I start trying to speak English and the stupid white cops roll their eyes at me."

"If you have something to report about Wah, we can get you an interpreter at the precinct. This is not my case. Someone else is handling it. Did Yip tell you to come here and meet me?" I looked at Yip, but he had his head down and his hands around his tea cup.

"I told Yip I had to meet that Chinese policeman and talk to him," Lily said.

"What do you want to tell me?"

"I know who killed Wah."

"Look, if you know something, you have to go down to the precinct or at least call it in."

"I don't want to! I have to tell you! No one else understands!" It was no use talking to her. I felt waylaid by the old woman. I resented Yip for making me come out. I glared at him, but Yip didn't make a sound.

"Okay," I said. "What do you know?" She smiled.

"Wah was one of the best workers at Jade Palace. She could always convince people to get two or three extra dishes. She knew all the customers by name and what they liked. There are two groups of waiters and waitresses at Jade Palace — the young and careless, and the old and bitter. She had the energy of the young people and the old people's connection with regular customers. But Wah was being paid the same as everyone else."

"And she expected to get paid more."

"It's even worse than that. The younger people were geting angry that the management was taking part of their tips. They started holding meetings to see if they should start a union. The old people already knew that this was the established practice and accepted it, but Wah went to some meetings. They told her she should be paid at least 20% more, based on her seniority. Then when the younger workers decided to go on strike, Wah went to the upper management. You know, I'm just a low-level manager. I'm only one step above the workers. I told her not to, that they would laugh in her face."

"And she didn't get her raise."

"She got the raise!" Suddenly Lily dropped her voice. "And a month later, she was..." Lily pursed her lips and flipped her hands to show her palms. "It must have been a jealous co-worker, one of the younger people."

"Who?"

"I don't know."

"You said you knew who killed Wah!"

"No! I didn't say that!"

"You said you thought you knew who killed Wah."

"I didn't say that!"

"Yes, you...oh, never mind. I think it's time for me to leave." I was getting too bogged down with useless information. Some dry Japanese beer would help clear the chalkboard.

"What are you going to do now?" Lily asked.

"I have go match up some stray socks. I'm sorry I can't help you."

"But Wah is dead!"

"If you think one of her co-workers killed her..."

"I never said that!"

I lazily scratched at my face and turned to Yip. "What do

you know about this?"

"She told me about the raise, but I didn't know anything about the meetings. We never talked very much about work. We only wanted to talk about the good things in life."

"Lily, you're going to have to go to the precinct and make a statement."

"No, I can't! I don't want any trouble!"

I stood up and dropped a few bills on the table.

"Officer Chow! You cannot pay! I invited you out today!" Yip exclaimed.

"Yip, I can't allow you to pay for me. Nice meeting you, Lily."

"Nice meeting you, officer."

The dim-sum crowds on the sidewalks were getting louder, but no tourists came into this cafe. I walked to the door and hit the street. I thought about a little coffee shop that had catered to people who came over in the 1920s. They spoke a dry, sharp Shanghainese you almost never hear in Chinatown anymore. That cafe's a pharmacy now.

I got off the sidewalk and onto the street, hugging the parked cars. It was the easiest way to get through Chinatown, since the sidewalks were crammed with tourists and vendors. I put my hands in my pockets and thought about people who were dead, places that were gone, things that had changed.

—

I was born into a batch of kids that Chinatown just loved. Because of the War Bride Act, Chinese women of a child-bearing age had finally been allowed to come over in significant numbers. Before then, a lot of Chinatown consisted of groups of old men getting older. And these old men would stand on a corner all day just to get a look at a Chinese woman, maybe glance at her legs, too. This guy I called "uncle" whom I wasn't related to at all told me the best place was Mott and Bayard because there were markets nearby, and you'd see the women doing some shopping.

When the Chinese women started coming over in numbers, it prettied up the scenery. It also increased the sound volume — newly born Chinese kids wailed from their makeshift cribs all night every night. For the first time ever, you could smell diapers in the streets.

Nobody complained, because us kids were miracles. The Chinese community wasn't going to die out. Nearly every merchant had loose candies to hand out to us.

I was born in 1950, the year after my mother came over and married my father in a deal that his boss helped fix. I still don't know exactly what happened. He was a 40-year-old waiter and she was 20. She was expecting the Wizard of Oz, but she got the scarecrow, my dad. They named me after Robert Mitchum, this American B-movie chump my mother liked.

I had a great time as a kid. Everybody older was "uncle" or "aunt." Nobody ever hit us. There were no grandmothers or grandfathers to guilt us into doing anything. No older brothers to slap us around or older sisters to snitch on us. Birthday parties every day. The only thing we were forced to do was say, "Thank you," when we got little candies. Everybody knew Cantonese, but we spoke English to leave out our parents.

Things started changing when I was around 10. The older kids were shoplifting, smoking, and ripping off dusty bottles of gift booze their parents had forgotten.

Two gangs set themselves up in different parts of

Chinatown. You had to be in one or the other. The group I was in was the Continentals. We used paint scrapers to hack off the metal emblems from Lincoln Continentals. You had to get eight to join. The rival group was the Darts. I joined the Continentals only because those cars looked cooler. Moy was in the Darts, but he was still my friend.

I guess the Continentals and Darts weren't really gangs, because when they met up in Columbus Park, something like a softball game would break out. It was tame. Fellow group members were as likely to come to blows (for striking out or missing a catch) as people from rival groups. The only fights we had were against the Italian kids from across Canal Street and the Spanish kids on the east side of Bowery. They'd come into Chinatown and try to steal stuff from stores, or maybe eat in a restaurant and run out on the check.

The Continentals would hang out in Cathy's, this soda joint on the south end of Mott, right by the fancy Port Arthur restaurant. The Darts hung out at Rocky's, which was down at Chatham Square and Bowery. The two hangouts were about two blocks away from each other, but we stayed away from each other's hangout.

After Cathy's closed to become a hair salon, the Continentals and the Darts both shared Rocky's and the rivalry died. The older kids had gone off to college, and new kids were coming over from Hong Kong. The American-born kids were finding themselves in the minority. Me and this other guy started going to the Police Athletic League events for the free McDonald's meals and ice skating.

Then in 1969 the draft came to Chinatown. I didn't care about getting out of it. I had finished high school and was drifting. But I knew how bad it was in China, and how we should be grateful for the better life we had in the U.S. I knew that serving was the best way to prove how much I loved America. We had to stop Communism.

Some other guys I knew were making up crazy stories to get out of the draft. They were now Buddhist vegetarians who believed that ending another creature's life was against their religion. One guy took a post teaching English in a Navajo school out west. Fuck them, I thought. If you're not willing to fight for the freedoms of this country, you shouldn't be allowed to live in it. Hell, your parents shouldn't have been allowed to come over.

I was real stupid and innocent back then. That was before we were in basic training and the instructor pulled me out of line, faced me to the company, and said, "This is what a gook looks like. He's the complete opposite of you, and he's out to kill you. What are you going to do about it?"

—

After I got my shield and piece, I ran into an old buddy of mine from the Continentals, this guy named John Lo who was also in Nam. He told me that some of the vets were getting together at Rocky's on a regular basis and that I should come to the next meeting.

I went to a meeting and John Lo pulled out some pictures. Vietnamese girls in short skirts. Street kids flashing peace signs. A smiling John Lo in a ricepicker hat, tied up on the ground with a bunch of white GI's pointing bayonets in his face.

"John, what the fuck is this?" I asked him.

"What? That's just having fun with the guys. Tell you a story, I got the hat from a boom-boom girl."

"They tied you up like a VC and that's funny?"

"What are you getting so worked up about?"

"What kind of fucking idiot are you?"

"You need a shrink, Robert. The war's over."

"Too bad for you. You wanted to dress up like a dink some more."

"It was just a joke!"

"Why don't I go into your house and rape your mother and shoot your father and say it was a joke because I thought they were VC?" I stopped myself there, because I was getting to be known with my press photos. It didn't look good for me to be talking like that. I kicked my chair back and left.

—

I understand that the group only met a few times more. Guys dropped out one by one.

Chapter 4

After two days on the 0000 to 0800, I was on the day tour again. The turnaround was always tough. If the job duties alone weren't bad enough, there was always the interruption to your sleep cycle to sprinkle more sand in your shell.

It was three days before Chinese New Year on January 31 and I figured I should be drinking more to get me loose enough for the holiday.

I was feeling kind of carefree after my morning beer and a Tic Tac chaser, so I decided to drop in and have a little talk with the Brow.

"Mister Chow," said the Brow, folding his hands into a pile of dry twigs. "Always a pleasure."

"Hello, sir," I said.

"Something on your mind? Please. Have a seat."

I looked down at the only other chair in the room. The varnish was rubbed out of the seat from people squirming in it. I sat in the center of the light spot.

"I understand," said the Brow, "that you have another one of your events to attend tonight."

"Chinatown Girl Scouts, sir."

"Do they sell Girl Scout fortune cookies?"

"I don't know, sir."

"I want to thank you once again, as always, for your help. The Department congratulates you heartily."

"Well, I appreciate that, sir. But I wanted to talk to you

about something."

"What is it, mister?"

"Sir, I don't want you to think that this is all I can do. I could really contribute in a lot of other ways."

"Mister Chow. You don't think we're limiting you by having you attend these little gatherings, now, do you?"

"I understand how the Five wants me there for the photographs in the Chinese papers. . ."

"Not just the Five, Mister Chow. You represent every policeman in the city. When the Chinese people pick up the newspaper, they don't just see someone from our house. They see a member of the Police Department of the City of New York."

"Sir," I said slowly, thinking of how to put it. "It's not a hard thing to do."

"But Mister Chow," the Brow said, putting his thumbs on the edge of the desktop. "You are in fact the only one who can do this."

"Sir, I want to be on the detective track. I want investigative assignments. Think of how my language skills. . ."

The Brow was shaking his head.

"Mister Chow. We are in a fight right now for the hearts and minds of the people. We're slowly winning them back. And we're winning them back because of you. The trust is once again, ah, rising between us and the community because of you."

"There are other ways we could help rebuild that trust, sir."

"This is the best way. Through the press, in their own language. They need to see how integrated we are with their people."

I thought about how sick I was of going to see Chinese people get awards for being smart, rich, or beautiful. A Chinese cop in the background was just another prop in the play.

"We're not providing enough of a challenge for you, are we Mister Chow?" the Brow asked, leaning back so he could look down at me.

"I just think I could do more, sir."

The Brow nodded and chewed on the inside of his left cheek.

"Mister Chow, do you know how lucky you are? Do you know how many blueshirts would trade places with you if they could?"

"Why would they want to, sir?"

"You're getting your picture in the papers. You're getting free food. You're getting attention from your people. And you're getting extra money." He held up his hand immediately. "I know you're getting money from these things, and it's only fair that you do."

"But I'd rather spend the extra time on investigative assignments, sir. If I keep doing these events, I'm never going to get a gold shield."

"And so what if you don't? Who wouldn't want to walk a beat, make friends, and get their pictures taken? Think of all the people you meet and the goodwill you spread. The Chinese people love you, the police administration loves you — you have the best of both worlds. You'll have the easiest 20 years of anybody. You'll retire and you'll have a department pension and probably be named to several community boards."

"I was thinking that I could be more than a 20-and-out kinda person, sir."

"My boy, please be practical about this. Think of all the detectives and lieutenants who grow bitter and end up hating the people they're supposed to protect. And that hate is mutual! The community here admires you! In a few years, you could practically be the mayor of Chinatown!"

"That's all fine by me, sir, if you want me to keep attending community events, but I don't want to keep walking a beat."

"You realize that with the cutbacks, we're understaffed and underbudgeted. We don't have the luxury of letting people do what they want, Mister Chow. Everybody has to do what is best. But I'll let Mister Sanchez know that you're ready for any investigative assignments that happen to be available. Not that there are any."

"I appreciate it, sir."

"In the meantime, I don't want you slipping in your duties. I expect at least 30 movers or parkers a month."

"That won't be a problem."

"Now consider yourself dismissed without prejudice, Mister Chow."

I left the house and got onto the footpost. I looked down at my feet. If I had been born smarter, instead of stupid, I wouldn't be stuck like I was. I could have had a lot more options. America was all about living out your dreams, but I had blown it and it was all my fault. There was nothing I could do now, except 17 more years. Then I could get my stupid pension.

—

I went up Bowery. When I hit Canal, I had to wait before the light changed. There were about 20 people on the corner waiting with me, but that didn't stop them from spitting and jaywalking. I could fine them for crossing against the light, but that law was practically unenforceable in New York. I might as well write up people for being Chinese.

To the right was the Manhattan Bridge, which connected Manhattan to Brooklyn. The entrance to the bridge was forever under construction. Canal Street traffic poured directly into an assortment of plastic mesh fences, concrete bunkers, and orange plastic barrels. This week, the lower roadway was shut off. Next week, the upper one would be closed.

To the left, Canal sloped down past Broadway into the Holland Tunnel. Shadows from taller buildings cut the sunlight into diagonal strips. Jewelry stores glittered on the northern side of the street. They looked a little trashy because the floors were littered with crumpled strips of newspaper, which functioned as a sound alarm in case someone got the idea to tiptoe behind the counter when the store was crowded.

A large tractor-trailer going up into the Manhattan Bridge entrance grunted like it was hungry. It blew out exhaust that passed through us at about eye level as we stood on the corner. No one even blinked. The light changed and a stray car shot through the crosswalk at the last second. I looked at the decals on the rear window and let it go. It was an off-duty cop.

I continued north, passing grocery stores and giving a few limp waves to the storeowners. Soon, I was under the awning of one of the four movie theaters in Chinatown, the Music Palace. The other theaters were the Pagoda on East Broadway by Catherine, the Rosemary on Canal, and the Sun Sing under the Manhattan Bridge overpass.

All of them ran double features for two bucks, and you couldn't argue at that price. Sometimes it would be Bruce Lee. Sometimes the movies bordered on nudicals. Lonely Chinese guys went there to disappear in the dark. I didn't do it too often.

My favorite theater was the Sun Sing. Its lobby had a virtual shrine to Linda Lin Dai, an actress who had killed herself at the height of her popularity. She'd always played the woman who was betrayed by the man. A lot of Chinese women could relate to that. Linda took a lethal dose of sleeping pills before her last film debuted. Then she truly became that woman in the movie poster behind the glass case that no one could ever touch.

By contrast, here at the Music Palace was a poster advertising yet another iron-fist-themed slapfest. I could tell by the bad photography alone that it was one of those movies where you could see the guy receiving the pulled punch clap his hands or slap his thigh to make the sound effect.

I turned away from the theater and almost stepped on a toy dog on a plastic tube. It yapped at me, then flipped back into the ranks of cheap Hong Kong toys in the street stall.

Holding the pump end of the dog's tube was a dusty old man sitting in a dirty plastic chair. A portable heater on an extension cord hummed at him. He smiled at me and nodded his head. A wind-up toy dolphin wriggled frantically against the edge of a half-filled tub of water. I leaned over and saw a smaller tub in the shadows filled with baby turtles.

I pointed at the turtles and shook my head.

"You can't sell those," I said.

"They're just my own pets," the old man said, laughing. "I'm not selling them, officer." He picked up the small tub and set it down behind his chair.

I turned and left. I bet I wasn't more than five feet away before he brought out the turtles again.

I got to the corner of Grand and Bowery, one of the smelliest intersections in the world. Slime runoff from ice-filled racks of seafood dripped into a sewage drain already clogged with soapy restaurant grill grease poured in the night before. Homeless white men piled up on the sidewalk like bleached driftwood between seafood stands. On a hot day, you could pass out from the smell. Luckily, it was still winter.

I was done for the day, but I still had time to kill before the Girl Scouts thing. I went back to Columbus Park to see the midget. He was sitting on his upside-down bucket as usual, smoking and chatting to an old male fortune-teller. The midget flipped the cigarette around his fingers like he wanted to make sure the smoke got into every knuckle.

When he saw me, the midget screwed up his face and said, "I'm glad you're here, Officer Chow. I'm looking for one more win for today. That would make it 25!" I smiled and sat down on the bench across from him. I nodded at the fortune-teller. He returned the gesture but remained silent, waiting for the midget to introduce him first. He stroked the part of his face that was trying to be a beard and stayed quiet.

"How about some checkers?" I asked the midget.

He nodded his head. "Yes, officer. Anything you say, officer. Are you going to arrest me if I win?" He reached into his knapsack on the ground and pulled out a bag of black and red checker pieces. He knew how to play every board game, Chinese and American. He even played steeplechase with plastic horses. Two crushed plastic bottles of herbal tea bowed at his feet. I subconsciously willed him to throw them away before he left the park.

"You want to be black or red?" I asked the midget.

"Doesn't matter to me," he said. "What's your favorite losing color?"

I snickered. The midget liked to dish it out, but he wouldn't do it in English. Even an old friend like Vandyne would only get, "Good move," "I'm sorry," or "Play again?" The fortune-teller smiled some more and shifted in his seat, but the midget ignored him so I did, too.

The midget grabbed fistfuls of checkers and planted them around the board. He gave me the reds so I moved first. I tried to make a bridge with two columns of pieces, but he cut it apart like a sword through straw. He toyed with me a little and I ran out of captured pieces to crown him with. It was as if he had a bonus move every turn.

He was having trouble holding all the captured pieces or maybe he was rubbing them against each other to annoy me. The midget tapped his foot three times and tilted his head up at me. I looked him in the eyes and he tapped his foot again.

"Okay, I give up," I said.

"Twenty-five!" the midget yelled. Then he chuckled and swept the pieces back into the bag. He folded up the board and put it into his knapsack.

"This is Wang," he said, finally introducing the fortune-teller who I'd seen around doing odd jobs, but whose name I hadn't known. He didn't need me to introduce myself. I was famous from the Chinese newspapers.

Wang looked about 70 years old, but seemed to be in pretty good health. His skin had shrunken and was taut against the bones in his face, wrists, and elbows. Wang's peppery hair was thick and clumpy and looked like an art project with cat fur.

"Let me tell your fortune," he said, taking my hands.

"I don't believe in that kind of thing," I told him.

"Just let him do it," said the midget with faked irritation.

"Give this old man something to do."

He noticed a mahjong game breaking up at the benches by the water fountain. "Hey, ladies!" he yelled, "Come and hear the fortune for Officer Chow! Maybe he'll marry one of you!" They cursed the midget, but they still came over to listen.

"You have a very lucky face," Wang said to me. "Luckiest I've seen in a long time."

"I'll bet you say that to all the boys," I said.

"This is going to be a very lucky year for you. I can tell."

He placed my hands together in a finished clap and shook them three times before opening them. His moist eyes flitted as he looked at the lines in my palms. "When were you born?" he asked without looking up.

"December 2, 1950."

Wang reached inside his vest pocket for a pile of sticks and singled one out.

"You're married."

"I'm not married."

"Umm. You're not married." Some of the women giggled. I recognized them as the second-shift workers at a garment shop on East Broadway. They all looked as if they had kids to cook for at home. "You have a girlfriend."

"No, no girlfriend."

"You don't have a girlfriend." He opened his mouth and

then closed it. He nodded and then asked, "You have a boyfriend?" The women laughed and the midget kicked his heels in the air.

"No, I don't have a boyfriend." Wang waved his hands.

"Doesn't matter, doesn't matter." He looked at the stick and read the characters, blocking out parts with his thumb and forefinger. "You're going to have a son this year," he said.

"How can he have a son without a wife?" asked one of the garment workers.

Wang ignored her. "Your life will be changed."

"Just tell me if I'm going to be rich or not!" I joked. Chinese people pray for riches more than world peace.

"I can tell you that now!" said the midget. "As long as you work for the city, you won't be rich!"

"You're going to have a son," the fortune-teller repeated. "You don't have to worry about money, just worry about your son." I took my hands back and squeezed my knees.

"Okay, Wang. Thank you." He nodded. After a moment of hesitation, I pulled out two bucks and gave it to him. "If I don't pay you, the prediction doesn't come true, right?" I asked. Wang laughed and folded the bills up. The women shuffled home to make dinner. I stood up. The midget zipped up his knapsack but made no other motion to leave.

"There's still some daylight left," Wang said. "Maybe there are some fortunes left to tell."

"I'm still waiting for a good game of Chinese chess," said the midget. "I'm going to teach you how to play, officer. It's a shame you don't know how to play something Chinese."

"We're in America, not China," I told the midget.

—

The Chinatown Girl Scouts had their ceremonies in the Ocean Empress Palace on Bowery, down a ways from Jade Palace. One of the girl's fathers had a hand in running the place.

It was one of the nicer large Chinese restaurants, and the menus had English translations for everything. They must have paid decently and reliably because there was almost no staff turnover. When I walked in past the tied-back bead curtains at the entrance, I saw older waiters who had been old when I was young.

A short man with crooked teeth came up to me and grabbed my right shoulder.

"You! I remember you when you were this tall," he said, slapping his thigh and laughing. He was completely bald on the top of his head, and the white hair he had left looked like a toilet brush from my point of view.

"Hello, uncle," I said. "How are you doing?"

"I remember when we had a going-away party here for all of you who were going off to the war. We were so proud of all of you. Say, where did they all go? I never see any of you anymore."

"I don't know."

"Well, the communists couldn't have killed all of you, right? You can't all be dead."

"I'm really a ghost."

"Don't try to fool an old man, now. I've seen you in the newspapers. You're the Chinese police captain."

"I'm not a captain."

"You must be important, I see your picture all the time!"

"I'm only a low-level cop."

He screwed up his face.

"Agh, you think I'm just a lousy little waiter. You don't think I'm worth your time." I watched him walk back to the kitchen with a slight limp. The sounds of mothers fussing over their little girls got to me and I headed to the other end of the dining room.

Freestanding wall sections on wheels separated the Girl Scout event from the regular diners. As I went around the far side of the wall, I came face to face with someone I hadn't seen since high school.

The moment I saw her, I felt the sudden jab of a sharp childhood memory.

"Barbara," I said.

"Robert! How are you? I was thinking you might be here."

"How come?"

"I've been seeing you in the papers! You really get around!"

I did a nervous fake-laugh and looked at a freckle on her neck. She shifted and I looked up and into her bright eyes. Was this really the fastest runner in the class? Was this really the first girl I had ever kissed?

"I'm here and then I'm there," I said, fake-laughing some more. God, how stupid did that sound? "So, you help out around here?"

"I'm here for my youngest sister. You know I have three sisters, right? My parents never did get that boy they were trying to have."

"She's going to win one of the prizes tonight?"

"She dropped out of the awards ceremony. This is the last

thing she volunteered to help organize. I have to help out because she couldn't make it."

"I don't like it when people just throw in the towel, you know? Kids today aren't as diligent as we were."

"She got into Barnard early," Barbara said. "She's already auditing classes."

"Only Barnard, huh? She wasn't the smartest cookie in the jar," I joked.

Barbara wasn't smiling.

"Robert?"

"Yes?"

"You were in the war, weren't you?"

"Yeah." I felt the air getting thin. Barbara grabbed my wrist.

"Hey," she said. "I've got to round up the girls for their presentations, but maybe we can chat later on tonight. After."

"Sure, sure."

I made my way over to the front table and sat down with the Girl Scout's head girl and a committee that was lobbying for the creation of a Chinatown YMCA.

Something really bothered me about Barbara. She was one of the beautiful people. Always had been. One of those people who never got a pimple, never got called a "chink," never had a bad day or night ever.

She had gone to Harvard. Free ride. Everybody knew about it. People were in awe of Barbara and her three younger sisters. They walked through Chinatown like four princesses. Even in their plastic sunglasses and flip-flops, they were the best-looking things south of Canal. When those girls left for college — and of course, they would all go to college — they were leaving Chinatown and never ever coming back.

I didn't need to hear about how rich Barbara was. How rich and white her stupid husband was. And you knew he had to be white. How she was expecting twin boys and how they were going to win the Heisman Trophy and the Nobel Prize.

Barbara and I weren't even people to each other anymore; we were only visions of what could have been in each other's respective worlds.

When the event was over, I got out as soon as I could, even though I knew Barbara was still tied up backstage. I wasn't sure what I was scared of.

A waiter on the way out handed me a brown paper bag. He just missed giving me a clap on my back as I blew past him.

A few blocks later, I found that the bag held a red envelope and a bottle of Cutty Sark. It was 2215. Drinking time.

Chapter 5

Forty-eight hours to Chinese New Year. Time was slowing down. No one in Chinatown is ever in a rush, which pisses off native New Yorkers when they come down here. Chinese people like to walk slowly, and ideally, side by side. They always run into people they know coming from the opposite direction. Then they all stop, creating a logjam.

The holiday just made it worse. Canal Street was more crowded than the subway. With foot traffic at a near standstill, I had enough time to read the front of every red holiday card stacked on folding tables that crowded the sidewalks even more. "Prosperity" was the most common single character for wishes in the year of the dragon.

I saw a break open up. I jumped through it and turned off onto Elizabeth Street.

Two unchaperoned kids, a boy and a girl who looked too young to talk, were lighting up fireworks on a manhole lid.

I grabbed them by the backs of their jackets and made them sit on the curb. They started crying when I took away their fireworks and lighter.

"You're going to blow your fingers off!" I yelled at them. They cried as if no one had ever yelled at them before. It was likely. Probably spoiled by a grandmother while the mother and father put their souls to the grindstones at work.

I took two Tic Tacs from my pocket and stuck them in their mouths. It's amazing how quickly children can lurch from miserable to happy. Candy to keep them happy in Chinatown. Cigarettes in Nam.

I felt ready to go to Martha's and see Lonnie. It turned out that I got doughy Dori instead.

"How are you doing, Dori?" I asked.

"I'd tell you to eat less because you're getting fat, Officer Chow, but that would be bad for business. Hot-dog pastries in the morning." She was shaking her head.

"Hey, you bake them this early, why can't I eat them? My uniform's feeling pretty loose on me, anyway."

"That's because you're not as fat as the average policeman. But don't worry, you'll get there soon. Hey, take your change. I don't take tips."

I muttered something under my breath that made her smile.

—

Vandyne had left a message on my desk. We weren't official partners anymore, but it was as if we were forever bonded, having been each other's first. I've heard plenty stories about cops who are closer to their old partners than their new ones.

The message said that Willie Gee had called for me again. The tabloids had been hammering at him for a while, but the *New York Times* had just reported that the State Attorney had filed charges against Jade Palace, citing the restaurant's apparent short-changing of its workers. If Willie Gee didn't like it, he should call up the state or the newspaper, or better yet — pay his workers, already. I crumpled up the message and tossed it. Three points.

I wondered if Willie Gee had known Wah personally, or if she had been just another worker bee for his hive. Her asking for a raise surely would have drawn some attention. I didn't want to think about it too much, though, because I couldn't do anything to help.

English was being a prick and obviously wasn't going to let me get a fingernail in on the case. And I didn't want to charge in, because my old partner was on the case. So I decided to do something that was within my power.

I swung out onto Bowery intent on finding five or six parkers or movers. There isn't any quota, but there is a "suggested minimum" of 30 parking tickets or moving violations per month. Even Stevie Wonder could find 30 cars parked wrong in a month. Even a marginalized cop like me could do it.

Some people get passive-aggressive about it. I've seen cops duck into storefronts when they see someone parking in front of a hydrant. They fill out the whole ticket and wait for the guy to leave before planting the ticket under the windshield wiper. I always wondered why the hell people like that wanted to be cops in the first place if they were so scared of confrontation.

I hadn't gone five feet before I found my first parker: a beaten white van that read on the side, "Jin Fook Flushing Queens," spelled out with pieces of duct tape. The van was parked halfway in a bus stop zone.

The next one was a little tougher. A middle-aged woman came running out of a market with a baby in her arms and gave me some grief as I was slipping a ticket under the windshield of a black Duster.

"Hey, what's that for? What did I do?" she cried.

"See that?" I asked, pointing to the 'No Standing Anytime' sign.

"But I left my emergency lights on!" She shook the baby a little. It had a rice candy stuck to the back of its right hand.

"That doesn't matter. You can't leave your car in this zone."

"How am I supposed to know what 'standing' is supposed to mean?"

"You took a driving test, didn't you?" After no response, I asked again, "Didn't you?"

"The sign's not even in Chinese, how am I supposed to read it?"

"Please," I said, tipping my hat and walking away.

I gave more tickets to a Plymouth Fury, a Bug, and a Gremlin at expired meters. I walked by Jade Palace and saw that the protest had gained more steam. I didn't look too long. I gave a nod to the two cops by the barricades. They were busy but they nodded back.

I felt a hand pull my arm rudely, and I instinctively shot my elbow back. It was Willie Gee.

"You don't return my calls," he said through gritted teeth as he rubbed his stomach where I had jabbed him.

"Because I don't work for you," I said.

"I want to know why the police department sends two lo fan officers to protect the protesters. They don't even send the Chinese officer. How are they supposed to know what to do?"

"Everyone who comes out of the academy knows what to do. Including how to handle a protest. A legal protest. Something that's protected under free speech in this country."

"It's not free speech — it's free lies," hissed Willie.

"Say Willie, did you know this woman named Wah?"

"Sure, she died. I knew her. I even gave her a raise. I already told that darkie."

"You watch it, Willie."

"What? What? She was old, she died! What did I do wrong?"

I turned to go.

"Wait," he said, reaching for me and then withdrawing his hand suddenly. "Come up and talk to me in my office."

"You got problems, you talk to these officers right here," I said. A tractor trailer on Canal trumpeted like an elephant out for revenge and I didn't hear what Willie shouted after me.

—

I found myself daydreaming at the Kiwanis Club dinner. The photos were already taken. Now it was time to stuff my face and listen to the speeches and awards throughout the night.

"We have to fight for the human and spiritual welfare of our children," said the president, holding up an open palm. "Not only here, but also in our homeland, which is now in the grip of the poison that's infecting much of Asia and Africa. Earlier tonight you saw our own brave hero Robert Chow on the stage here. You may not know that he personally fought for freedom in Vietnam. Please, let's now recognize him."

A round of applause around the room brought me back slightly. I started clapping, too. Then he droned on and I slipped back into the mud.

Is this what I became a cop for? Back when I was working in the toy store I thought I was lucky to have a job. I didn't hate it and I sure didn't have a better idea about what to do with myself. One day, I'd been in the subway, stuck between stations. Everyone had looked pissed off or sleepy except for three black transit cops standing around a pole. They were joking around and laughing.

Right away, it brought back my experience in Nam. It seemed they had the kind of close love under the gun that I hadn't realized I missed until that moment. Sure they were having a good time, but if there was trouble, you could tell they were ready to swing into action. I wanted to stand up, walk over, and put my arms around them. That's how close I felt to them.

—

In August of 1973, I had been back to the world for nearly two years – as long as my active service. My father and I were sitting on the roof, drinking. For some reason, whenever I look back at this scene, the sun is up and there's a glare in my eyes, although I know for sure that it was after midnight. I almost never saw my father by daylight.

"When are you going to think about going to college?" my father asked me. "You're not going to stay at the toy store forever, right?"

"I haven't thought about it yet."

"Maybe you should find one that's far away from here. California, or maybe Texas. If I had the chance, I'd travel more, see more of this country. You just send me postcards from wherever you are. You can go anywhere with the GI bill, right? Don't let it go to waste."

"Dad, I have to tell you something. I think I'm going to skip college." I was on my fifth beer and feeling loose. I felt ready to say what I had to say. He wiped his mouth with his fingers, then rocked back and forth in anticipation.

"What are you talking about?" he asked.

"I'm thinking about becoming a cop. I have a good shot at getting into the police academy, and my military record will give me seniority once I'm out."

"What!" he spat. He shot out his legs, kicking roof gravel

loose. "A policeman! You're a fucking stupid idiot! This isn't China! You're supposed to make money in this country!"

"You're right, this isn't China. It's America. Being a cop is a good job."

"I worked this terrible job for years for your benefit, and you piss on me by deciding to become a policeman! You should be studying to be a lawyer or a doctor! A cop! Completely useless! You might as well become a garbage man or a teacher! At least nobody's going to shoot you!"

"I knew you wouldn't understand."

"I understand! You're stupid! I just never realized how stupid you were! You understand English, you were born in this country, and still you want to throw your life away! What did I save my money for? I could have just flushed it down the toilet!"

"Or maybe you could have gambled some more, or gone to more whorehouses," I said. "Mom knows all about it, anyway!" While I was away, before I'd gotten back to the world, he had slipped back into his bachelor-days habits.

There was a twitch in the side of his scowl.

"I don't have to listen to you! You're never going to live as hard a life as me! Now stop this stupid idea and apply to some good schools!"

"I already got into the academy, Dad."

—

I was at the toy store when I got a call from my mother later that week. My father had fallen off the roof. They found out later his blood-alcohol level had been three times the level of being legally drunk.

It was a closed-casket ceremony. His face had hit a non-functioning fire hydrant on the sidewalk. They drove him around in a hearse that had a bundle of lit joss sticks clamped in the passenger-side window.

They gave me the option to defer enrollment at the academy, but I said I wanted to go now.

—

After forever, the Kiwanis dinner was over. I stood under a tin awning on Mulberry Street. It was about 28 degrees outside, but the heat had been on full blast inside. My sweat was still leaking out and I could feel loose Tic Tacs melting in my damp pants pocket, making my thigh tingle.

I used to keep a small tube of toothpaste in my pocket to squeeze into my mouth and cover up my breath. Then I had trouble finding the travel size, and when I did, it was almost the same price as the regular, so I said to hell with it. I wasn't going to pay the same price for something less. That was against the laws of economics and, therefore, against Chinese culture.

Now I keep some loose Tic Tacs in my right front pocket with the keys. I don't like the sound of them rattling around in the little plastic box. When I'm running low, I lick my finger and run it around the inside of my pocket to pick up the pieces.

"The cold doesn't stop the mailman, why should you people be any different?"

I looked down at the midget. He was smoking.

"Mailmen take breaks, too," I said.

"Who has a more important job, a mailman or policeman?"

"In Chinatown? People love the postman. Could be bringing a package from Hong Kong. Could be bringing a sweepstakes winner. When they see a policeman, he's only bringing trouble."

"Everybody doesn't think that way."

"You tell me who doesn't. I can tell just by the way they look at me."

"You get used to the way people look at you," said the midget. He tossed his cigarette into the street. "You can learn how to use it."

—

I went into a drugstore on Henry Street off of Catherine. I had been on my way back to my apartment, but I was out of toilet paper and using the cheap napkins I had piled up from over-rice joints were the stuff that nightmares are made of.

It was a small store, probably only 12 by 12. The floor was half worn-out carpet and half tile where the carpet had been torn out. Most of the floor was covered up by dented wire shelves filled mostly with hammers, plungers, and other light hardware. The guy who ran the store never said much and sat slumped against the counter, seemingly oblivious to the transistor radio chittering from somewhere unseen under the counter.

I only went there to buy toilet paper because it was the cheapest place in Chinatown for it. I picked up a four-pack of Charmin and brought it up front.

"I don't have any shopping bags left," the slumping man said.

"So that means I get a discount, right?" I said.

He frowned. It was the most expressive I'd ever seen him.

"You don't think my prices are cheap enough?"

"Hey, come on now, I was only kidding." His face resumed its stony look when I took my money out and paid him.

I walked out of the store with the toilet paper shoved under my left arm. It didn't stick out much, but I managed to ram it into the chest of a woman walking towards me.

"I'm so sorry — Barbara."

"Robert! Nice to see that you're taking care of yourself."

"I certainly am."

"Hey, where did you go after the Girl Scouts thing? How could you walk out on me?"

"I guess I could ask you the same question, regarding a certain dance."

She pushed her lips up into her nose. It was an ugly thing to watch.

"That was 10 years ago," she said. "More than 10 years ago!"

"You take a girl out, you think you have some sort of bond with her. I'm not saying boyfriend-girlfriend thing, but, you know, something."

"Oh, Robert, I was so much higher on life back then."

I looked over her left shoulder.

"Can I buy you a drink?" I asked.

"Yeah. You can."

We went over two blocks to Wilson's on Oliver Street, a dark and quiet place. It was no place for a date, but if the cigarette fumes were fading from your clothes and hair, the bar was a great place to get a touchup. We slid into a booth and got two Michelobs on tap.

"Why the hell are you back in Chinatown?" I asked her.

"A lot of reasons."

"Let's go through them."

"For one, I work here now."

"In Chinatown?"

"In New York. Midtown East."

"What do you do?"

"I'm a low-level associate for the American Trade Council for U.S.-China."

"What the hell is that?"

"What we are, really, are consultants who specialize in business and political connections between the U.S. and Taiwan."

"I thought you said it was the council for China."

"Yes, Taiwan as in the 'Republic of China.' America doesn't have official trade links with mainland China."

"How is business?"

"Not good, and getting worse."

"Why's that?"

"Basically the fact is that sooner or later, probably sooner, the U.S. is going to switch allegiance and recognize the mainland instead of Taiwan."

"If they are going to fucking recognize a communist country, then why the hell did they send us over to Nam?"

"What happened in Vietnam is a part of what is going to lead to the decision on Taiwan. If we had been able to wipe out North Vietnam, then there's no way we'd even think of abandoning Taiwan. We'd probably be helping them launch an attack on the mainland."

She looked calm, professional, and even a little bored.

My beer was already gone and I had nothing to cool down the anger that was building in my chest.

"Must be nice to just sit back on your cushy Harvard ass and write about whatever pops into your head."

"Robert... "

"I was there, Barbara! They sent us into hell and wanted to forget us when we couldn't win!"

"I know how you feel."

"You don't know how I fucking feel! You have no idea!"

"My husband served in Vietnam."

"Drafted?"

"Enlisted. Finished one tour and then re-enlisted."

"When did you get married?"

"Senior year."

"That's early."

"If it feels right, you do it. I'm the oldest of four. I get older at a faster rate, too."

"Do you feel like your husband cares about you?" It was a hard question for me to ask.

"He doesn't care about anybody anymore."

"Two tours of Vietnam will do that to you."

"He's dead. He was killed in Khe Sanh."

"I'm sorry, Barbara."

"It was years ago. I thought I could just stay in Boston and move on with my life. But in reality, I was falling apart. My parents were going back to Hong Kong, so I figured I'd move back into the apartment."

"Is everything working out OK?"

"I used to know everybody. Now I feel almost like a stranger here. Everyone you knew back then, are they still around?"

"They're all gone for the most part," I said. "I'm pretty far gone, too."

"I knew you when you were a kid."

"Well, I knew you, too."

I had another full pint in front of me. At some point, refills had come to our table without us noticing.

"I didn't graduate from Harvard, Robert."

"You didn't finish school?"

"No, I went to college, but my certificate says I went to Radcliffe. Harvard is the degree men receive."

She looked at me and gave her glass a half turn.

"You know, Robert," Barbara said. "The girls used to call you 'Cracker Jack.'" She smiled for the first time in a while.

"How come?"

"You used to be so, I don't know, pro-America and anti-Communist. You wouldn't shut up about it. So we said you were like that sailor on the Cracker Jack box with his perpetual salute."

"God, I think was."

"What was I like?"

"You don't remember? You were like Miss Chinatown."

"It seems like somebody else."

I was halfway done with my drink.

"Barbara, I used to think we could've been something."

"We were something, Robert."

My glass was empty now.

"I took you to that Chinese New Year dance and I kissed you," I told her. "Then you kinda avoided me for a while. You went to Stuy in tenth grade and we never said much to each other after."

Stuyvesant was one of the city's special schools for gifted children. You had to take tests to get in. I wouldn't have even qualified to mop the floors there.

"Robert, I studied my brains out. Right through college."

"I thought everything came to you naturally."

"No, way! I was always reading. In fact, I had to stop taking classes the summer before sophomore year in college."

"Most people stop taking classes in the summer."

"I was trying to get a double major done. Economics and English. You know, one degree for my parents and one for me. So one day, I started hearing voices. I had some therapy sessions. The funny thing was they were paying me because it was an experiment."

"They gave you LSD?"

"No! It was all about talking. I talked everything out and they listened."

"What did you talk about?"

"Believe it or not, I talked about you a little bit."

She gave me a knowing look that made my leg twitch.

"Aw, bullshit."

"No, I swear, I still have the transcript!"

"Is it in your apartment?"

"It's in a box in the kitchen. You wanna see it?"

"Sounds like a good-enough excuse," I said.

I swung my arms back and stuck them into the sleeves of my coat. We slid out of the booth.

—

I had never been to Barbara's house. Back when I had taken her to the dance, I had met her at the pinball parlor on Pell that's a dumpling joint now. Like most Chinese parents, Barbara's mom and dad hadn't liked the idea of her dating before college.

We went into the vestibule of her apartment on Madison. The outer door was missing, and the inner metal-plated door looked like the hood of a Datsun after UAW workers had gotten to it with sledgehammers. I looked down at the floor as Barbara fumbled with her keys. The ceramic tiles were wet and dirty.

"This goddamn lock," Barbara muttered.

"Lemme see," I said. I shifted the pack of toilet paper to my left arm and took over. I rattled her key the way I rattled mine and the cylinder turned. "I win."

"That's nothing. I'll race you upstairs," she said.

"No."

The apartment was on the third floor, behind a door that was mummified with opaque cellophane tape and bits of red paper from 30 years of Chinese holiday decorations.

Down the hall, past two tricycles, Neil Young was singing "Cinnamon Girl."

Barbara got her door open and I followed her in. We were immediately in the kitchen.

"This apartment's laid out really funny," she said. "A long time ago, they knocked down a few walls and put up another."

She turned on the bare light bulb in the kitchen and it lit up the entire apartment.

"How the hell," I started, "did all of you fit in here?" There was a kitchen, a living room, and a closet bathroom.

"We had cots set up in the kitchen and living room. All of us never slept at the same time. Our parents slept during the day." She fumbled around with a kitchen drawer.

"Drink red wine?"

"Yeah."

She got on her toes to reach for a bottle on top of the refrigerator. Her short sleeve fell away to show the hump of a muscular shoulder.

"How'd you get that?" I asked. "You're like a marine."

"I keep a five-pound barbell in my desk at work. A couple of reps a day helps me deal with stress."

She got us two coffee mugs and poured wine to the brim, which was risky because both of them had chipped rims.

"Hey, watch it!" I said. "Don't spill any!"

"Well, don't dribble!"

I quickly drank my mug down an inch.

"I had thought that out of everybody down here, you would never come back, Barbara."

"Why?"

"You're beautiful. And you're smart."

"What's that supposed to mean, Robert?"

"It doesn't mean anything here."

"I didn't plan on coming back, not this way, anyway. Goes to show, you never know what life will deal you." She leaned forward on her elbows and put her face up to mine. "I didn't think I'd see you again."

"Did you want to see me again?"

"I don't know, but it's so good to see you. Really, it is." Some pink was getting into her eyes. It was either the drink or she was about to cry.

I wasn't sure what to do, so I drank. A trickle of wine slipped through a chip and traced down my neck. She put her fingers on the back of my neck and rubbed her thumb slowly against my throat. It felt tingly, slippery.

"Don't rub the lamp if you don't want the genie to come out," I said.

"I get three wishes, don't I?"

I gently nudged the table and drinks aside. Then I pulled Barbara into my lap.

Chapter 6

I propped myself up against the headboard, which was the back of the foldout sofa. My head was hurting. There wasn't much light coming in, but it was about eight.

Tomorrow was Chinese New Year.

I slid out naked and staggered to the refrigerator. I found a bottle of Bud on its side under the crisper. I came back to the bed and sat on the edge. I picked at the cap with the tine on my belt buckle. I finally worked it off, but the bottle cap landed in Barbara's hair.

She moaned, then brushed her ear. I took the cap away with my free hand.

"Robert, are you drinking?"

"Yeah, got a beer out of the fridge."

"Argh, I was saving that for cooking." After a few minutes, she asked, "Do you always drink in the morning?"

"Only when I'm up before noon."

I took a few deep swigs.

"Hey, that was really nice last night," she said.

"What do you mean?" I asked. I finished the bottle and put it on the coffee table.

"What are we doing? We're crazy!"

"This is not the first time for either of us."

"But this is the first time. For us!"

"Let's celebrate with breakfast."

"I'm so hungry." She pushed half her face into the pillow.

"And there's nothing to eat here."

"How about some pastries?"

"Yeah, let's go to Martha's!"

"Oh, whoa, no, not Martha's!"

"It's the best bakery in Chinatown!"

"It gets too crowded in there."

"It's crowded because it's good and it's on the way to the train."

"That woman there gives me the evil eye, you know, the one who looks like she shovels gravel?"

"It takes a tough woman to make a tender pastry. C'mon, let's get moving!"

—

When we came in, the morning rush was already over and Lonnie was by herself behind the counter. Dori was sitting in a corner, smoking a cigarette and reading the Hong Kong newspaper. They both stared at us. I became very conscious of the fact that we looked disheveled, more so than usual for me.

Three teenage degenerates hugged the walls in the corner. The one with the spiky hair smiled at me and picked his teeth.

"Looks like the cop finally saw some action last night," he said out loud to his friends. I wanted to put a bullet in his head, but he wasn't worth the paperwork I'd have to do after.

Dori smirked. Lonnie put on a very serious look.

"How are you today, Officer Chow?" she asked.

"I'm doing well, thank you."

Lonnie gave me an expectant look.

"Oh, Barbara, this is Lonnie. Uh, she works here."

Barbara smiled and said, "Hi."

"More hot-dog buns, today?" asked Lonnie.

"You eat those, Robert?" asked Barbara incredulously. "It's kid food!"

"Sometimes I feel like a kid," I said.

"Every day," said Lonnie.

"That's a lot of calories!"

"It's not so bad," I said. "I mean, I walk it all off."

"I think I'm just going to have a plain bun and a hot coffee," said Barbara.

"And you?" Lonnie asked me.

"Just an iced coffee."

Lonnie turned and put the plain bun into a paper bag.

"Can you put that on a tray, Lonnie? We're going to eat here."

"Actually, Robert," Barbara said, "I'm going to get that to go. I have to go back and do some work. But you stay with your friends here."

"I, uh, sure. OK."

She grabbed her stuff and left without even waving. I was dimly aware of getting my iced coffee from Lonnie. I leaned against the counter and drove a straw into the lid.

"Is she your girlfriend?" Lonnie asked.

"Oh no, no, no. She's an old friend. We grew up together."

Dori spoke up.

"That woman, she could do a lot better than a policeman. She doesn't even want to be seen in public with you, Officer Chow."

"She just likes her privacy, like me."

Lonnie cleared her throat.

"So, you don't have a girlfriend?" she asked.

"I'm not really the type to have a girlfriend," I said.

"Lonnie!" shouted Dori. "You have to clean off the counter!"

"It's already clean."

"Clean the part Officer Chow is on when he leaves. He probably got it greasy."

"I'm leaving," I said.

"Bye, Officer Chow," Lonnie said.

If I had stayed, I might have left a bigger mess for Lonnie to clean up. I glanced at those punk kids but they were completely ignoring me.

—

Then, suddenly, it was my least favorite day in the world. Chinese New Year and its endless photo ops for me. The actual celebration goes on for two weeks in Chinatown, but on the legitimate first day, they hold the parade with the lion dances. 1976 was the year of the dragon — it was supposed to be a year of tumultuous change.

The Brow sent us off with his annual remark: "I don't want to see you put in for holiday differential on this one. This is no American holiday."

On the footpost, I walked by a seafood restaurant on

Bowery whose big windows were crowded on the bottom with tanks of fish, crabs, prawns, and lobsters. The rest of the window showed off the crowded dining room and the all-you-can-eat buffet that was only open to people who could read the characters in the sign above it.

I saw a family sitting there, two parents and a daughter and her boyfriend. I knew he was the daughter's fiancé because she was showing her parents the engagement ring on her finger while he sat back and sipped his water. I didn't break my stride, and I only saw them all for two seconds, but it brought home how removed I was from regular life in Chinatown. I used to wish that they'd left us in the war longer so that I could have gone on fighting until I was dead.

Then this thing with Barbara had happened. Maybe there was something out there for me. Not today, though. Barbara was tied up with some relatives for the day, and I had to go see my mother, so we would miss each other today.

—

Ten thousand small firecrackers, each representing a year of prosperity, had been strung across Mott Street in front of the Greater China Association's office. The president of the association and several other community businessmen stood together where the firecrackers dipped at their lowest point. I stood at the edge of the group. Whenever a press photographer wanted to shoot a picture, I was pulled into the frame. A dozen cops circling us kept the crowd at bay.

Although I had smiled for the pictures, I was irritable. Every time I heard firecrackers go off in the crowd, I looked around for someone to slap.

"Why so jumpy, Chow?" asked Peepshow, a cop who was off to my left. "You people live and breathe firecrackers, right?"

How the hell Peepshow had managed to keep his shield through the layoffs was beyond me. He was lazy and incompetent. He had a lower-ass rip in what was apparently his only pair of jeans. That's how he got his nickname. No one ever told him to get it patched up. His real name was Geller. People forgot his first name.

I said, "Not only are fireworks illegal, but they're dangerous."

"To hell with that talk," Peepshow said. "The Chinese have a religious and cultural right to bear them. What would Chinatown be like without firecrackers? We got to keep the visitors entertained."

———

One of the honorees was a guy from the Chinatown American Legion, a decorated World War II vet. His hair was off-white and crisp like his khaki slacks. His shoes were in bad shape. He probably couldn't see them over his bulging stomach.

When it was time for more pictures, I got up on the stage next to him and gave a plastic smile.

"Hey, Chow," said the vet, "you were in Vietnam, right?"

"Yes, sir."

"Can I ask you something?"

"What?"

"How did you lose?"

I stared at him for a little bit.

"We were let down," I said.

"You guys didn't have it in you to fight. You were coddled too much when you were kids. Color TV. Rock music. Your generation doesn't have any real men in it. You guys are a bunch of pussies."

"I guess real men plump when you cook 'em," I said, pointing to his gut.

"Oh, yeah, I'm an old man now, but I paid my dues. I was in France, Chow. I helped achieve our goals. Goals of the free world. You and your bullshit attitude remind me of the lousy soldiers who lost China."

"You think you could have stopped communism in Vietnam?"

"Hell, yeah. We stopped Hitler, didn't we?"

"Weren't you fighting on the same side as communists against Hitler?"

"We just had the same enemy back then."

"Weren't you allied with communists, old man?"

We were both smiling as cameras flashed. We talked out the sides of our mouths.

"Hey, Chow, you shut your mouth."

"Aren't you a fucking commie, old man?"

"I'll tan your goddamn hide for saying that."

"I already have a tan. From Nam."

When the pictures were over, I glared at him, then stepped away.

—

At 1300, the president of the association took a red plastic lighter from his shirt pocket, flicked it, and lit the firecrackers. We were quickly enveloped in clouds of sparks, sound, and smoke. Burnt firecracker paper settled dreamlike over the cheering crowd. It was tough to see for a few minutes, and I gagged on the smell of gunpowder.

I waved my arms around until I saw Peepshow again.

"Hey, everything's cool, baby," he said. "Just relax." He gestured at the throngs of tourists breathing dim-sum breath.

I couldn't take it easy because I knew trouble was going to start once the parade got underway. It was the first one since the death of Chiang Kai Shek, who was the head of the Kuomintang in Taiwan.

The KMT had lost the Chinese civil war to the communists and retreated to Taiwan. But the party still held power in Chinatown. It was no secret that the KMT poured cash into the Greater China Association and paid the salaries of its board. The association was an umbrella group for Chinatown's many smaller family associations. Most business owners paid lip service to the KMT and bankrolled the parade to show what great communism-fighters they were.

The parade prominently featured the KMT flag, held in triumph, as if they had won the war. And if you weren't there on the sidelines cheering and blowing kisses, you might be branded a pinko by the neo-McCarthyites in the community.

"Kuomintang and the Chinese people for 10,000 years!" screamed a little girl with a megaphone at the front of the parade. Everybody cheered. She stomped on red firecracker paper shreds as she started her march. I shifted my weight and balanced my right hand at my hip.

A dissident group of merchants who were aligned with the communists had put up posters throughout Chinatown that by dawn had been ripped down by their rivals. A tourist walking by one of these posters wouldn't notice anything different between it and the numerous other signs offering money-wiring services, get-rich schemes, and apartment listings. But anyone who ate rice and was even semi-literate would see:

ONE TRUE CHINA FOR THE CHINESE PEOPLE!
BURY THE CORRUPT CHIANG KAI SHEK!
BURY THE CORRUPT KMT!
RAISE OUR VOICES AT THE PARADE!
COMMITTEE OF UNITED CHINESE

The committee was mostly made up of mainland Chinese affiliated with old warlords who bore grudges against the KMT and had passed them on to their kids.

Resentment runs deep in Chinese people. Forgiveness is not a Chinese value. We pray for fortune, luck, a long and happy life, but never for the redemption of our enemies; we want them to die a thousand deaths. Chiang Kai Shek killed communists every chance he got, especially unarmed ones. The communists threw KMT soldiers and their families into re-education camps when the war was over. It was stupid to forgive because forgiveness meant you hadn't learned anything.

A few years ago, the U.N. had expelled the KMT-ruled Taiwan from its roster of permanent members, a move opposed by the U.S., which still recognized the KMT as the legitimate rulers of China. The U.S. had no diplomatic ties with so-called "Red China." But Americans didn't know that the color red has always symbolized China to all Chinese, whether they followed Chiang, or Mao, or Dr. Seuss. Even the KMT flag is dominated by a red field. That red could represent all the blood of Chinese killed by other Chinese, whether at the collapse of every dynasty or in a gambling den.

When the elementary girls were done with their clumsy, mercifully short dance, Boy Scouts came stomping in. Instead of their traditional neckerchiefs, they were wearing the KMT flag. One kid with gold and silver arrow badges running down his chest played a bugle that jiggled a shaggy mane of yellow cords. He did a pretty good version of "Yankee Doodle," and then he played the KMT anthem. The crowd cheered, and when he was done, he saluted. Tourist cameras went off. The bugle boy led the scouts marching forward to make room for the next performers.

I saw some commotion in the crowd — eight men with baseball caps pulled low over their faces jumped into the opening behind the scouts. They lined up and unrolled a huge banner as wide as the street that read:

BURY CHIANG KAI SHEK / BURY CORRUPT KMT!!!

A small part in English read:

U.S. RECOGNIZE CHINA

The immediate crowd reaction was a mass contest to see who could hold their breath the longest. This brash display at a KMT event was shocking to everyone whether you agreed or not.

The only sounds came from the tourists and the cops, who had no idea what was going on.

"They didn't put a lot of thought into that banner, eh?" asked Peepshow, throwing an elbow into me.

Suddenly six men with their heads tied in red handkerchiefs charged out onto the street. Each held a deceptively thin bamboo pole that was strong enough to smash cinder blocks. The pole-bearers advanced on the men holding the banner. The Chinese people in the crowd took two steps back behind the tourists.

"Hey, it's a kung-fu exhibition!" said Peepshow, crossing his arms. I grabbed his right elbow and yanked him forward with me.

"Listen, yo-yo! This fight is for real!" I yelled at him.

I don't know who hit first. The guys with the bamboo poles were awkward, and their weapons were soon grabbed away. Baseball caps and handkerchiefs were yanked off. Pretty soon, you couldn't tell who was from which side, and bamboo poles were spanking anyone within reach.

None of us were ready for a riot, least of all the merchants who had opened special sidewalk displays for the parade.

"Grab anyone with a pole!" I yelled at Peepshow. I wrestled down a man who must have been twice as old as me and yanked the pole out of his hands. I was reaching back for my handcuffs when I saw a periscope rise out of the chaos and zero in on my face.

"It's a Chinese cop!" said the periscope. A hand reached out from the crowd and grabbed the bamboo pole on the ground that I had just taken away.

I twisted around and stepped on the hand. The man under me squirmed.

"Ouch!" said a female voice, and a woman tourist rolled forward onto the ground next to me. The periscope swung away, revealing a male tourist with a TV camera.

"What the hell are you doing!" the man tourist demanded to know.

"Don't touch that pole!" I yelled at the woman tourist.

"I just wanted to see what it was made of," she moaned.

"I'm going to report you!" threatened the man tourist. He swung his camera lens back at me. "I got your badge number and everything."

"Keep that shit out of my face!" I yelled at him. I heaved against the camera and felt him fall back. The man under me managed to scoot out and slipped into a sea of legs somewhere to the south. "Motherfucker!" I yelled to God.

"I can't believe you talk like that!" yelled the tourist woman. She was cradling her hand like it was a sick hamster.

"Go fuck yourself!" I told her.

—

We managed to get six men into custody with no reports of serious injuries in the crowd. We weren't sure who we had, and even though a few thousand Chinese had seen what had happened, no eyewitnesses would come into the house.

We gave the men warnings for disturbing the peace. They all seemed to know English.

"Can you believe it, those guys pushing for Red China?" asked Peepshow. He'd managed to get a bruise on his jaw. "Right when the Viet Cong are running all over. Those Red China protesters are right down there with Jane Fonda. They keep up at it, people will think they're gooks."

"People already think they're gooks," I said.

—

I went home, took a shower with a bar of sandalwood soap, and cut myself shaving. In the mirror, I saw that I had bruises in the shape of fingers around my neck. I didn't remember getting them, and they didn't hurt, so I ignored them. I got into plain clothes and went back out. The streets were flooded with tourists going in and out of the restaurants and shops. I headed for Columbus Park.

The rundown park was jammed with groups of Chinese people talking loudly while eating rice cakes, leading some to choke on too-big bites. Grandmothers spitting into their hands and wiping children's faces. Old men standing together, each adding another sentence to an imagined story about this guy they all used to know. Teenaged boys and girls slapping handballs around on the courts. Someone had a soccer ball, but with no field or goalposts in the park, the kids took turns trying to bounce it on their knees. Everyone was dressed in red or wearing something red.

A little boy sucking on a dry plum stared at me and I buttoned the second button to my red flannel shirt. When he spat the seed out, it would slip into the cracks in the asphalt, where there were hundreds of other seeds that had been spat out by his father and uncles.

I found the midget sipping sweetened soy milk from a plastic bottle. He nodded and said, "Officer Chow," without taking the straw out of his mouth. He was wearing a red cardigan over a t-shirt that had turned pink from being washed with the sweater. He was idly playing a game of Chinese chess against a little boy dressed in a suit with a red tie.

"I didn't see you at the parade," I told him.

"I don't have to go to the parade," said the midget.

"Aren't you proud of your culture?"

The midget took the straw out of his mouth.

"I'm very proud of the Chinese people," he said. "We invented soy milk, right? What a wonderful drink. Anyway, if you're talking about things like the lion dance, I don't support that. You know where that originated from?"

"There's that old fable about that guy who wanted to show how brave he was by playing ball with the lions."

"Yeah, there's that. But the whole ritual of dressing up dancers as lions and going around to businesses to collect red envelopes was just a big bribery scheme cooked up by government officials in ancient times. You give enough money to the lion, you buy some 'good luck.' Sound familiar?"

"That was a long time ago. It's not like that now."

"Well, they use more than lions now."

"If it were a crime, we'd have detectives on the case."

"I heard about the dustup at the parade today," said the midget. His soy milk bottomed out and he tossed the empty bottle over his shoulder into a trash can. "Fighting amongst ourselves is in our culture. Think about China's history. How many little countries were defeated and consolidated and broken up again over how many thousands of years?"

"A lot."

"Yes, a lot. Think of all the regional beliefs and traditions that each of those countries had, even before the Mongols and the Manchus colonized us. Everyone who's Chinese is really many different ancestries, with the blood of a hundred different nations that are now gone."

To the little boy in the suit, he said, "Take that piece back. That's a bad move. Very bad move." The boy sadly dragged his cannon back and bit his lip.

The midget went on. "All the Chinese people feel this internal struggle. That's why Chinese leaders are so terrible."

"Both the KMT and the communists are lousy," I said. "But you know, if Sun Yat Sen hadn't died suddenly, China would be farther along than Japan is now."

The midget blinked. "Sun, he would have ruined China if he had lived."

I was shocked that the midget dismissed Sun so easily. Both the KMT and the communists looked up to Sun. He was the one who'd kicked out the colonizing Manchus in 1911. Tragically, he had died before seeing his reforms put into practice. If you ate with chopsticks, you loved the man.

"You can't say that about Sun," I said. "He was the one who got China back on its feet."

"He was so vague about everything," said the midget. "No wonder both the KMT and the communists love him so much. If he had lived and headed the country, he would have been expected to be as ruthless as the old emperors, like Mao and Chiang are now — otherwise people wouldn't admire him. Sun loved Chinese people so much, he couldn't stand the thought of mistreating anyone. That's what killed him."

Life under the Manchus had been hard on China. The men had to wear their hair in queues to show loyalty to the Manchus and pay taxes to a Manchu emperor. Chinese weren't allowed to rise up to the highest military or government ranks, which were held by Manchus or Europeans. It had been almost 300 years of institutionalized discrimination against the Chinese. I wondered if the Manchus had allowed the Chinese cops to get investigative assignments.

"Okay," I told the midget. "You think Chinese people make lousy leaders and we all hate each other, then how come we all live together in Chinatown? Why do you come to Chinatown?"

The midget shrugged.

"I'm only in it for the soy milk," he said.

I shook my head and checked my watch.

"I gotta go see my mother," I said.

"Have fun in Brooklyn," the midget said with a wry smile.

"Happy New Year!"

"Whoopee."

—

Down the street, I bought a fresh green bamboo twig from a sidewalk salesman. It was cultivated in a nursery where it had been slowly twisted over a few months so it would grow into the shape of an undone wire coat hanger. More twists made it more lucky.

I stopped at Martha's Bakery. Lonnie and Dori both looked frazzled. To save time, boxes had already been packed with rice cakes and stacked up. I picked one up and threw my money at Dori.

"Happy New Year!" I told her. She glared at me, but held her tongue. It was bad luck to say anything mean-spirited on New Year's, since that day would set the tone for the rest of the year. In Dori's case, I couldn't see how it mattered. She was going to have a lousy year whether she talked badly about me or not. Still, we all followed traditions we didn't believe in. Like being a diligent son.

Lonnie gave me a searching look.

"Happy New Year, Lonnie!"

"You, too, officer!" she said, already looking away.

The Brooklyn-bound platform of the N train was packed with tourists heading for home. There were some Chinese, but almost none of them would be riding out as far as me to just past Bay Ridge.

I got on the train and leaned against the doors when they closed. I thought about how my mother wanted nothing to do with Chinatown any more and lived in a neighborhood where she was the only one who knew how to fiddle around with a wok. When I got out of the train, I walked down to her block, which looked like a suburban Little Italy. I was sure I was carrying the only rice cake for miles.

"Stupid, low-class Chinese culture," she said. I had just seated myself down on her couch, which was swathed in a multi-colored crochet cover with three God's eyes. Seeing me always reminded her of how she came to this country and ended up living and working with people she considered beneath her social status back in China. Understandably, she was always in a bad mood at first.

"I saw the little girls parading on television today. They use such cheap material, and they didn't dance in time with the drum. Then they had that fight. So disrespectful. Made me lose face," she said, swiping her cheek with a finger.

She leaned forward into me. "Hey Robert, what's this?" she asked, tapping at the nick in my chin. I was glad my shirt was covering up the bruises from this afternoon.

"Oh that? That's from a bullet, Mom."

"Shut up! It's from shaving!"

"If you know it's from shaving, then why did you ask me?"

"I just want to talk to you. You don't want your mother to talk to you? Maybe I need to get a ticket from you to say that you write to me." A whistle went off in the kitchen and she left to get the tea.

She owned this apartment, a one bedroom in an old brownstone on the ground floor. My mother did really well. A lot of women of her generation had to work as seamstresses.

But my mother's family had been one of the richer ones, and she already spoke enough English when she came over. She managed to get a job working for Americans in midtown, sorting and punching 80-column cards for the computers. Now she supervised the department.

The women who worked in the sweatshops weren't so lucky. When they got older, they slipped up more and got canned from the garment factory. They found themselves making dumplings for a penny each. Or giving foot massages on the sidewalk. Or worse.

"This tea comes from the middle of China. Not the cheap Hong Kong garbage," said my mother. She walked back into the living room with a lacquer tray. The teapot and two cups had a crack glaze finish that looked like lizard skin. A raised seal stuck out on each of the three pieces, the character for longevity, which looks like an old man bent over with cane. She also brought out a rice cake sliced into eighths on a small dish.

"What's wrong with Hong Kong, Mom?"

"Nothing wrong with Hong Kong! Did I say something's wrong with Hong Kong?"

"You called it 'garbage.' This isn't the way to start the new year, talking badly about Chinese people."

"When are you going to learn?" asked my mother, taking sips of her tea. She slipped a piece of rice cake into her mouth.

"Don't worry about 'Chinese people.' Just worry about yourself. You think people in Chinatown care about you? They all just want to make enough money to get out of there."

"How did you learn to hate Chinese people so much?"

"You think I hate Chinese people? Chinese people hate me!

You know how they treated me! After your father died, everybody turned their backs on me. I'm buying groceries in the street, the store owners don't even look at me until I give them money."

"But you still have Chinese friends. What about Auntie Two Big Girls and Auntie One Girl and Boy? You hate them?" I never knew the names of my mother's friends; as I was growing up, and even today, we just referred to them by their children.

"They are my friends. I know them. But most Chinese people are simple and unsophisticated."

"Now you're being racist against yourself, Mom."

"Robert, don't you hate working in Chinatown? Chinese people don't love you and you don't love them right back."

"You know, you sound like Dad going off on the communists. How can you hate people who look like you?" I bit off a rubbery chunk of rice cake and it instantly glued my mouth shut. I took a sip of tea to help break it up.

"Don't talk about the communists," she said, running out of steam. "You've never been to China, how can you talk about the communists?"

"I read the newspaper, I know about the political situation. The communists defeated the KMT so easily, they obviously had the support of the Chinese people."

My mother sighed and sipped more tea.

"The Americans are celebrating the 200th birthday of their country this year."

"It's our country, too. We're American citizens, Mom."

"You're American. I'm only American on paper. You know my English isn't that good. Anyway, China's history is more than

20 times longer than 200 years. You have no idea how old our history is. You think the communists are going to last? Even if the KMT had won, they wouldn't be doing better. Nothing lasts. Worry about yourself. That's history's lesson."

I thought about the reports coming out of some parts of China. The Cultural Revolution had destroyed the country in ways the Japanese could only have wished to do. Employees had killed their bosses, students had beaten their teachers, and cats had chased dogs up trees. The movement now seemed to be losing steam, according to reports in the Hong Kong and Taiwan papers, but you never knew for sure.

"What do you think happened to all the money that Dad sent back to China?" I asked. "It wasn't too much but we really could have used that money a few years ago."

"All of it was confiscated by the communists," sighed my mother. "Along with your dad's brother. The entire family was labeled 'class enemies' because of all the money your father had been sending them. But that's not the worst part."

"What could be worse than losing your money?"

"Well," said my mother, leaning back and speaking very slowly. "I never told you this before. Because your father was sending money back to China, he was under investigation for being a communist."

"Who was investigating him?"

"The FBI, but really, the old guard Chinatown organizations, the ones who loved the KMT. They were compiling information on everyone who was sending money back to China. They wanted to get them all deported. They didn't want anyone sending money to the communists."

I was stunned by this revelation.

"He hated the communists! How could he be accused of

being a communist?"

"When your father fell off the roof, some people said that it wasn't an accident," said my mother. Her voice had all the emotions squeezed out of it. "They said that it was a guilty man committing suicide."

"Motherfuckers," I said. "Who were they?"

"I don't know."

"What were their names?"

"Nobody knows. They only sent us anonymous notes in the mail."

"You never told the police?"

"What am I going to tell them? Huh? If I came into the police station, they would tell me to do their laundry. I didn't dare go there. Huh!"

"They wouldn't do that!"

"Tell me they wouldn't!"

I put my hands on my knees.

"We should really talk about good things, Mom."

She nodded.

"How is your job going?" I asked.

"Can't complain."

After a minute or two, we had the TV on.

—

I called up Barbara not too long after I got home. It was a few minutes after 0100. I didn't know if she'd be there.

"Yeah?"

"You answer the phone like a guy, Barbara."

"I can do everything a guy can do. Even more."

"Yeah, I know, I remember. Hey, what are you doing now?"

"Recovering from the worst Chinese New Year ever at
my aunt's."

"I gotta bottle of Seagram's. Wanna help me read the label
upside-down?"

"You have to come over here. My bra's already off."

Chapter 7

Somebody shook me and I opened my eyes.

Barbara had her coat on and was sitting on the side of the fold-out bed.

"Time is it?" I asked, turning on my side.

"Around 5."

"You going into work now? Today's my day off. I was thinking we could have some drinks and go back to bed."

"No can do. I have to finish some reading before a meeting today."

"When are you gonna get out tonight?"

"I'm not sure."

"How about tomorrow?"

"Robert." Her voice came out in a way that made me cross my legs and my arms. "Our time together has been really great. We really had a lot to get out of our systems. But I'm not ready to be in a thing now."

She'd obviously put a lot of thought into this. Her presentation was pretty good.

"The good times never last, do they?" I said. I could feel my center of gravity shifting from my chest to the bottom of my stomach.

"We can still get together once in a while."

"Once a week? Once a month?"

"Let's not put restrictions on it, Robert."

I leaned back on one elbow.

"I see how it stands," I said.

"It's not just me. It's us. We both need to work on things."

"Things? What are 'things,' Barbara?"

"Things like I don't want to picture my husband when I'm holding you. Things like you don't need to drink when you wake up in the morning."

"You're not a lightweight on the bottle, yourself."

"Yes, but I'm not. . ." She shook her head and stood up. "I have to go now. You can let yourself out when you're ready. I'll see you later."

The front door closing made a sharp, ugly metal sound like a bullet ripping through a can of Crisco. I couldn't process being sad yet because my headache wouldn't let me feel anything else.

I had dared to imagine that for once I wouldn't be alone during the terrible period between Chinese New Year and Valentine's Day. Those are the two weeks when the streets are filled with happy couples and happy families looking for fun fun fucking fun.

I poured myself some red wine in last night's glass and threw it back. This apartment, which had seemed so endearing in its unfamiliarity only a week ago, now looked like a way station in someone else's busy life. I was getting an unwelcome vibe.

I had to get my clothes on, go out the door, and nearly run down the stairs to get away from it.

—

On my way home, I stopped at a small store and went to the back to get some beer. The glass in the cooler was cracked and held together with frayed pieces of duct tape. The tape made it hard to see what was inside. I tried to slide it open but the tape stopped that, too.

"How you supposed to get anything out of this?" I called out to the front.

"Go fuck yourself!" was the reply. I stomped over to the cashier, but I soon discovered that the comment wasn't for me.

The owner, about 50, medium frame, five six, was yelling at Yip.

"You killed your wife! I don't want a murderer in my store! You should be in jail, you dirty bastard!" shouted the owner.

"Excuse me," I told the owner. "A man is innocent until proven guilty."

"Innocent — bullshit!" He was obviously new in the community. He didn't seem to know who I was.

Yip's face was sad and calm.

"It's best that I leave, Officer Chow," he said.

When he heard "officer," the owner suddenly pointed at Yip and looked at me.

"You're a policeman? Arrest that guy before he kills someone else."

"We're leaving," I said.

We went onto the wet streets.

"I can't go anywhere anymore," said Yip, rubbing his eyes. "Something like this always happens. There's no sympathy. Only blame."

"People at your work like you, right?"

"They let me go," he said. "They said I was hurting business."

"If you know you're right, that's all you need," I said.

"You know this is true, Officer Chow. You ought to know that Chinatown hates the police as much as the criminals. We have to stick together, you know?"

"You want to play the cop, tomorrow, Yip? I'll give you a dollar to switch."

"Ha ha! No, I couldn't be you."

I saw another small grocery ahead.

"I'll see you later, Yip. I have to go get some steak sauce."

—

I woke up tangled in the sheets, ready to resume my string of lonely days and weeks. I was more tired than usual so I got two iced coffees from Lonnie.

"Two today?" she asked. "You have another date or something?"

"Both for me," I said. "I'm greedy."

"Not greedy — selfish," Dori muttered from the other end of the counter. "Don't worry, Lonnie, I'll bet that girl he was with is long gone."

"I'm just feeling sleepy," I told Lonnie. "Trying to stay awake."

"You're the hardest-working man I know," said Lonnie. Dori creased the top of a paper bag with a vicious scrape of her thumbnail.

I was about to leave when Lonnie stopped me.

"Hey, don't you want some hot-dog pastries?"

"Not today, Lonnie." I hadn't been finishing them, anyway. My appetite was slipping.

It was February 4. The opening ceremonies of the Winter

Olympics were going to be on later that night. China was boycotting the games because Taiwan was competing as the "Republic of China." I didn't know if I was going to be able to stay up to watch Taiwan in the opening parade, the only event in which they wouldn't come in last.

—

I was on the first lap of my footpost when I remembered my dream.

I was walking through waist-high elephant grass. Just ahead of me was an old woman. Sometimes she would turn around and gesture for me to follow her. No matter how fast I walked, I couldn't catch up to the woman, despite her leisurely pace.

We walked through an empty village. It was getting darker. There were clouds coming in. The woman broke into a run. I chased after her. Then rain started to fall. I stopped and looked at my arms. They were covered in white paint.

I struggled to remember more, but nothing else came. The first iced coffee was bottoming out, so I took the straw and stabbed it into the second cup.

"Officer!" said a loud, shrill voice. I looked across the street.

"Lily!" I said, recognizing Wah's supervisor.

She looked the wrong way for oncoming traffic on the one-way street and crossed over to my side. She had on a red coat that was made for someone shorter. When she got close, I could see that her eyes were twinkling.

"Officer, Yip told me you don't have a girlfriend."

"That's by choice," I said. "I could have one if I wanted to. Truth is, a lot of women love a man in a uniform."

"Don't talk to me like I'm a fool. I know a very pretty girl who wants to find a nice Chinese man."

"Where do you know this girl from?"

"From my business contacts. This girl's family had a five-story mansion in Shanghai and dozens of servants before the communists took over. They tore down the mansion and used the bricks to build houses for the servants."

"She must be very pretty and eligible."

"The family escaped to Hong Kong. They bribed some British sailors to take them over. The British took the gold but let them keep all the jade, which was far more expensive. Stupid white people!"

"They just didn't know."

"Of course they didn't know! That family bought a textiles factory. Now they have six. This girl was born in Hong Kong, went to school in Switzerland. She speaks four languages. Mandarin, Cantonese, French, and English."

"Why would she want a cop for a boyfriend?"

"She doesn't want just a boyfriend. She's very marriage-minded. She'd be proud to have a policeman for a husband."

"Oh, I get it. She wants an American citizenship."

"Of course she wants it. But she also wants a good man. The family would be very happy to make a large wedding gift. Do you want to visit her? The family would love to fly you to Hong Kong to meet her."

I imagined myself back in Asia. Walking through elephant grass and villages, shooting people.

"You know I'm a Vietnam vet, don't you?"

"Girls love soldiers, they're so brave!"

"Did you make a statement at the precinct about Wah?"

Lily acted like I had stepped on her big toe.

"Oh, Officer Chow! When you bring that name up, I feel physical pain!"

"Why don't you go in and make a report?"

"Me make a report? You're the policeman! It's your job to do that!"

"Don't tell me what my job is, Lily! Get in there and do it!" I barked.

She gathered her coat at the collar and the fingers of her leather gloves squeaked.

"Officer, I don't know anything," Lily said, walking away like we were on Park Avenue and I was begging for change.

—

The next day on my footpost, I made it around the corner and saw that spiky-haired punk kid who would hang out sometimes in Martha's with his buddies. He was trying hard to be a five-foot Fonz with his imitation-leather jacket.

He was smoking a cigarette but dropped it down the gutter when he saw me.

"Hey, Officer Ronald McDonald," he said. "You're a fucking clown. Tell me something. You ever actually arrest someone, or do you just go to banquets and store openings?" The other guys smirked, but they drew back as I approached. By the time the imitation-leather punk and I were face to face, his friends were across the street.

"How come you're not in school?" I asked him quietly.

"How come you're not a real policeman?"

"You want to shut up about that?"

"God, your breath stinks. Is that the only weapon they let you have? What kind of cop are you?"

"I'm gonna show you what kinda cop I am," I said, grabbing him by the armpit seams of his jacket. They tore so I dug my hands in further and shook him by the straps of his tank-top t-shirt. I pushed him into an overflowing city garbage can and I didn't let go.

"You want to talk shit with me, I'll smear you face-down a few blocks! People will think someone dragged a dead dog through here when they see the blood in the street!" I didn't realize how loud I was yelling until I felt my throat hurt.

His body felt thin through his clothes. I could have ripped him open like a bag of potato chips. I was aware of silent faces at open windows looking down at us.

"You hear me? Next time I see you, I'm gonna kick your face in! You're gonna see out the back of your head!"

Someone came up and put their hand on my shoulder.

"Chow," Vandyne said as if he were talking to a growling dog. "Let the boy go. C'mon. Just let him go." Hearing that voice opened up a steam valve in my system. I relaxed my eyebrows. Then I slowly let go of the kid.

My hands were sticky with soda and tea from cans and cups that had tumbled out of the trash. And with blood. I blinked and looked at the kid. Both of his nostrils were bleeding and his face looked bruised. He was crying.

"I didn't hit him!" I yelled. "I didn't hit him once!" I wiped my hands off on my slacks and looked around. All the punk kid's friends were gone.

"Have you lost your mind?" asked Vandyne, stepping

between me and the kid.

"He was making fun of me," I said, feeling extremely stupid as soon as I'd said it.

"He was making fun of you? Oh, I'm sorry, big man, that this boy over here hurt your feelings. I'll enroll him in the late-afternoon session of our etiquette class."

"I just put him through etiquette class," I said. The kid was leaning against a lamppost, pinching his nose and keeping his head down. He looked as vulnerable as a giraffe taking a drink, but I still wanted to hurt him.

"You okay, there, chief?" Vandyne asked the kid.

"Yeah, yeah, I'm fine," the kid said. Funny how the most brazen delinquents sounded helpless and meek when they spoke English.

"What did you say to Officer Chow?" Vandyne asked.

"Nothing. I didn't say anything," he said. I wanted to step on his throat.

"Do you want to see a doctor?"

"No, no. Everything's okay," said the kid, scuttling away. He hadn't looked at me once. Vandyne turned to me.

"What were you yelling about?" Vandyne asked me as we watched the punk slip into a crowd of unkempt black hair.

"Learn some Chinese, already, okay?"

"I don't want to tell you what to do, Chow, but you're getting seriously out of hand, taking it out on your own people."

"That kid is not one of 'my people,' okay? My people had respect for elders. My people studied hard. My people did the right thing."

"Okay, so maybe the kid is a little punk. Did you have to

make him bleed?"

"He's bleeding because he doesn't eat right. I just shook him a little bit."

"And that helped, I'm sure."

"Helped me."

"You watch it," Vandyne said, holding up a warning finger. "It's not funny. You know, you're lucky Chinese people don't file civilian complaints." He kicked away a soda can on the sidewalk.

"Say, Vandyne, how often do you find kids like that shot to death?"

"Once every two or three months."

"What's better, that punk ends up getting shot or I shake him up a little?"

"You're not that kid's father, you know. Leave the belting to daddy — he knows best."

We instinctively took inventory of the people around us.

"Vandyne," I said, "you're in the neighborhood early."

"Had to see English."

"What's going on?"

"One of our new strategies."

"Want to talk about it?"

"I don't have all the details, yet."

We left it at that. I drank some iced chrysanthemum tea, shook my head out, and continued on the footpost.

Outside the pharmacy on Elizabeth, a little girl sat in a battered ride machine that was a hybrid of copyright and trademark violations. It had the head of Mickey Mouse, the body of a tugboat that narrated a children's television show, and a Daffy Duck tail. The girl was straddling the tugboat and her hands were grabbing Mickey's ears where the paint was worn off. She rocked back and forth making train sounds even though the machine was off.

Her mother was inside the pharmacy looking at bottles of shampoo. She had on a long black skirt and a gray blouse. Her hair was up in barrettes. She was tired.

"Choo choo choo!" yelled the girl.

"Okay, kid," I said. Here was a chance to prove I could do something nice. I plugged a quarter into the coin slot of the Mickey tugboat.

Nothing happened.

I checked the change slot, but found only a flattened bottle cap. I shifted my weight back and kicked the coin box.

"Choo choo choo!" yelled the girl.

I grabbed the coin box and rattled it. It sounded like my quarter was in there somewhere. I went inside the pharmacy, walked past the girl's mother, and stepped up to the counter.

Mr. Chew was showing off his good standing posture in a crisp, white short-sleeved shirt. A cheap ballpoint pen jutted from behind his ear. Dark brown speckles danced on his cheeks as he talked to another customer, an old Chinese man in a flannel shirt and a Mets cap.

"I have a problem," I said to Mr. Chew. He turned to me and frowned.

"What's wrong?" he asked, leaning on the counter and looking up at me. He took a sniff. "Need some hangover remedies?"

"I lost a quarter in your ride outside."

"I guess you didn't see the sign that said 'Play at your own risk.' No refunds."

"I think your machine's broken and that's why you should give me my quarter back."

"No refunds," said Mr. Chew. Then the girl's mother came up to us.

"I told him I lost a quarter in the machine, too. He wouldn't give me anything. This man is cheap."

"I can't do anything, anyway. I just work here. If I give money back to people, the owner is going to be upset."

"Mr. Chew," I said, "Don't even pretend you're not the owner. Maybe if this place wasn't called 'Chew's Pharmacy,' you'd get away with it." Mr. Chew scowled.

"He's got you there, old Chew!" said the elderly Mets fan, laughing. "I told you, you should have named this store after a garden!"

"The problem with you two is that you have no respect," Mr. Chew said to the girl's mother and me. He pulled two quarters from his pocket and dropped them on the counter.

"I don't have to respect a liar," I said. "You should put an 'Out of order' sign on your machine."

"And you should use some mouthwash," said Mr. Chew. I was out of Tic Tacs but I wasn't going to buy them from him. Chew on that, Chew.

When we got outside, the mother thanked me and picked up her little girl.

"I don't like Mr. Chew," she said. "I only shop there because everything's so cheap."

"That's because he sells old stuff." I said. "That shampoo you got there, they don't even make it anymore. That company went out of business."

"But it still works, doesn't it?"

"Sure, if your hair doesn't fall out."

The little girl got off the mouseboat quietly and stood by her mother. She was a good girl.

"Choo choo choo!" I said to her. She looked at me like I was crazy.

—

I ran into Vandyne outside the Five. We agreed to grab a bite. I was already out of my uniform.

"You look happier when you're not in the bag," said Vandyne.

"The world looks happier to me when I'm in plainclothes."

"That's 'cause they don't know you're a pig," said Vandyne.

We went down Elizabeth Street and slipped into a below-street-level joint on Bayard.

"The chewy noodles that are wrinkly," said Vandyne. "That's the kind I want."

I knew that when Vandyne ate by himself, he'd get fried rice, but with me, he would venture into noodles, some greens. I'd tell him all the time that today's fried rice was yesterday's leftover white rice, but he was stubborn. He grew up eating fried rice in Philadelphia.

"I know which noodles you want," I told Vandyne. They weren't really noodles, they were tofu skins, but I wasn't going to bother to tell him that. "We can get that with pork and then get some mustard greens on the side," I said. I called the waitress over and ordered. She brought Vandyne a fork.

"He didn't ask for any fork," I said sharply.

"Sorry, sorry," she said, and took it away with nervous fingers. It fell to the floor with a clatter. She picked it up and scurried into the kitchen. Vandyne smiled and closed his eyes, rubbed his eyebrows.

"What did you say to her?"

"I told her we needed more Calgon."

"You're going to get us blacklisted at every restaurant in Chinatown."

"What do you mean? We already are."

"We've got to stop eating in Chinese places. Maybe we should go to Little Italy."

"Little Italy's doomed. It's all going to be Chinatown soon. They'll celebrate San Gennaro with lion dances."

"Let's just go to McDonald's next time," said Vandyne.

"Naw, let's go to Sambo's." We both laughed hard.

"Oh, no! Don't even joke about that shit!" said Vandyne, almost crying. The restaurant chain, based on the racist story of "Little Black Sambo," was facing nationwide boycotts by prominent blacks. Vandyne's wife was one of the main people on that campaign.

"How's the job treating you?" I asked Vandyne.

"It's all right, all right." He sipped his Coke. "Kinda dead, not too much going on. I'm kind of a superstar here. Little Chinese kids touch my legs to see if I'm made out of chocolate. So Chow, who's this girl you been seeing?"

"Aw..." I said, feeling my appetite slide down into my shoes. The midget must have seen me with Barbara and told Vandyne. "It came to nothing."

"Can't find a Chinese girl good enough for you?" asked Vandyne. "You're still young, you could. . ."

"I'm not young anymore. I'm 25. The game's over. Anyway, my mother always said the whole convention of dating and marriage is the government's way of keeping you too distracted by your personal life to see how they're ripping you off."

"They are ripping you off, all right. Only they're gonna rip you off if you're distracted or not. So it might as well be a pretty distraction."

Both dishes came in at the same time. Vandyne took the serving spoon and scooped a steaming, greasy heap of beef and noodles onto my plate.

"Serving the other person first. Very Chinese of you," I said.

"Naw, I just want to see you eat this stuff, see if you keel over." Suddenly, his eyes bugged out. "What the hell are those?" he asked pointing at the plate.

"Just some soy beans."

"Are those motherfuckers?"

"No, they're not lima beans."

"While I was in the Nam and I got ham-and-motherfuckers rations, I'd eat them all and wouldn't complain. But only because I swore to God that when I got back to the world, I would never eat motherfuckers again. No way!"

"They're not bad."

"Then how come you're not eating them?"

"Are you timing me? Just give me more than a minute to eat."

"If they ain't motherfuckers, they're cousins of motherfuckers." He was in genuine distress.

"Look, the only thing you need to be worried about is finding a piece of a plate in your food, especially if your serving plate doesn't have any chips in it."

"How come?"

"Because it means they dropped your original plate back in the kitchen. Then they scooped everything up and put it on a new plate. Only they missed picking out a fragment or two."

Vandyne turned purple.

"That's why he gave me that dish for free," he said in a far-away voice.

"This food right here seems to be okay, right now."

We ate for a while.

"So, yeah, I was seeing this girl for a little bit," I said.

"Who was this girl?"

"It's unbelievable in a way. She was the first girl I ever kissed."

"Your mom?"

"Hey, we said no mothers!"

"C'mon, now. I'm kidding. What's her name?"

"Her name was Barbara. Well, it still is Barbara. But she kinda broke it off with me."

"What was the reason?"

I shrugged and pulled my lips tight.

Vandyne took a mouthful of food. He chewed and exhaled at the same time for a minute.

"Didn't see her long?"

"Just a few days. That's all."

"So you don't seem too hurt."

"It just seems that, I don't know. It was just so fast."

Vandyne chuckled.

"Better too fast than too long, partner. Anyway, lots of Chinese girls in the sea."

"Who says I want a Chinese girl?" I asked as I served Vandyne some more beef, keeping the soy beans at bay. "Maybe I don't care what color she is. Maybe I want a black girl."

"Please," grunted Vandyne. "The real problem is you can't care about anyone else until you care about yourself."

"I care about you, man."

"Yeah, I got enough people caring about me. Don't you worry about me." Vandyne twirled his chopsticks around clumsily. "I still remember how hard it was not having anyone to come home to."

"I can't argue with a married man."

"I used to be a lone predator like you. Okay, a *lonely* predator. Thought I was too hardcore or whatever to settle down. Then I met that special girl."

"Great."

"Hey, what about that girl at the bakery? She likes you a lot."

"Who?"

"That girl Ronnie, Bonnie, Connie."

"Lonnie."

"Yeah, Lonnie. She's real nice and sweet."

"Her? I'm like five years older than her."

"Couple of years is nothing."

"Vandyne, let's talk about something else. Do you know anything about the old Chinese woman who was poisoned?"

He shook his head and wiped his mouth.

"It's my case, but I'm not holding out on you when I say there's not much to tell. I went over to Jade Palace with an interpreter. Nobody's talking. Nobody knows anything. People don't even remember Wah, even though she'd been there what, 30 years."

"How far do you think you can take the case?"

"Not too far. In fact, I think they kinda stuck me with it because there's no pressure or reason to find a resolution. Probably a natural cause, anyway."

"Probably doesn't mean for certain. Don't you think you need a Chinese guy on the case, too?"

"Well, English says that experience solves crimes not race."

"Nobody has more experience in Chinatown than me."

"Yeah, I know that and you know that, but that's not gonna fly in the detective squad. Anyway, people aren't gonna be more open to you because you're Chinese. In fact, they'll probably be even more closed."

"There's that 'probably' again."

"You don't have any investigative experience."

"Well, how the hell am I going to get any if they don't let me do the job?"

Vandyne suddenly jumped as a wad of noodles slipped down the front of his shirt, leaving a slime trail. I put my hand up and waved at the waitress.

"We're going to need that fork, after all," I said.

—

The next day was sunny and in the 50s, warm enough for old men to bring their birds out to the park. Some brought out canaries or parakeets, but the most popular bird had black feathers that looked like oily hair. In the sun, their bodies reflected back green, blue, and purple, like street pigeons, only better.

Birds are always kept one to a cage because the pretty ones are male and there's nothing male birds like more than tearing up other males. Put two males in one cage and you'll end up with one on the floor with its feet sticking up and the other one mortally wounded.

I slowed down as I walked by the bamboo cages set up in the grass. They were partially covered by burlap sacks to provide shade and keep the breezes away. All the birds faced north in their individual cages and chirped together, though none of them could see each other. The owners sat on benches, their backs to the cages, their hands flapping wildly as they told each other bird stories.

Yip came up out of nowhere and asked me, "You know how to make birds sing the sweetest song?"

I looked at the loaded wire laundry cart he was dragging at his side. It only had three wheels.

"How do you get birds to sing the sweetest song, Yip?"

"You take a slice of dried chili pepper and stick it down the bird's throat," he chuckled. "The bird will sing like an angel."

"You did that to your birds?" I asked, picking up my walking pace.

Yip had memorized my footpost and he waited for me along the route like a puppy that wants to play all the time. A slow-walking puppy that talked too much and reminded me of all the disappointments I was having on the job.

His never-ending presence brought so many things to the surface, I almost couldn't see straight. There was my visit to my mother's, getting dumped by Barbara, the dinner with Vandyne where he basically shrugged off on helping me get onto the detective track.

Of course I couldn't forget that Yip himself had told his pal Lily that she could do some matchmaking for me. I couldn't stand being around Yip anymore, but I did the Chinese thing by frowning at him a lot without telling him what was bothering me.

"You bet I fed my birds chili pepper!" said Yip, stepping quicker to keep up with me. A grating sound came from the laundry cart as another wheel threatened to break off.

"Maybe you should get a new laundry cart," I said.

"This one's good enough."

I waved to the midget as we walked past the northern boundary of the park. He nodded and popped something in his mouth.

"That's kind of mean, treating your birds like that," I said.

"I never killed any of my birds. It's like a little kid eating hot food for the first time. Some of them even started to like it."

"I never had birds."

"Maybe you should get one! Birds are the best pets. They sound beautiful and they're nice decorations, too. You don't need to walk them, and they're so easy to feed."

"Where are you going?" I suddenly asked Yip.

"To Bayard. That way." He pointed down the street.

"Do you need a hand?"

"No, no, no! I'm fine!" He set the cart down and his eyes went teary. "These are Wah's clothes. I'm going to donate them to charity. I can't have them in the apartment anymore."

I looked at the laundry cart. Everything had been stuffed in a dirty plastic garbage bag. If that was Wah's entire wardrobe, it couldn't have filled three dresser drawers. I had more clothes than her when I was a kid.

"Where are you going to donate them?"

"I was hoping you could tell me."

I took a deep breath. "How about taking them down to the church?" I asked.

"That's a good idea! Which one?"

"Any church," I said.

He had a lost look on his face.

"I've never been to a church. I don't know which one to go to," he said, biting his lips.

I felt a little bad for being so sharp with him. I looked at his little noodle arms. "How about the Lutheran church at the end of the park? I'm sure they have some sort of needy program."

"The one with the tiny windows?"

"By the bend in the street."

"I know that one! I walk by it every day!" He walked by it every day because I walked by it every day.

"Okay, Yip, I have to keep walking here."

"Okay, Officer Chow! I'll see you later!" He picked up the handle to his laundry cart again.

"Yeah, see you later, Yip." I watched the cart slip out of his hands, smash against the curb and fall over. I turned and walked away before he could ask me for help.

If I didn't watch myself, I'd end up taking those clothes down to the church myself. After that, I'd be carrying Yip up and down the stairs.

Chapter 8

On February 7, the communist-biased newspaper boasted that Beijing had named Hua Kuo Feng to succeed Chou En Lai as acting premier. Judging from the photo, Hua had the official look down pat — strong nose bridge, thick eyebrows, and big forehead.

I spent the end of my 1600-0000 footpost walking past closed storefronts and avoiding puddles.

I got back home and landed on my couch. It was about 0100, a time when all the good American shows were already over. I dragged out a few Japanese beers from the fridge and flipped over to the Chinese channels.

The Taiwan news program talked about how rising crime in America was due to violent shows like "S.W.A.T." and "Barretta." They didn't know these shows were about fighting crime, and that the bad guys always got caught.

The communist channel was broadcasting a concert put on by steelworkers' kids. Boys and girls dressed in scratchy gray suits hacked away with their bows. They were so stupidly serious in the close-ups that it looked funny. If they could have seen themselves, they would have fallen over laughing, but their eyes were fixed hard on the music sheets, as if the notes would change if they blinked.

The wide-angle shots were a hoot, too. Seeing that much black hair bobbing in time made me think of industrious worker ants storing up food for the winter.

I guess that made me the lazy grasshopper.

I laughed hard at that and pulled my feet up on the couch and stretched out.

There was a rude knock at my door. I shook my head and stood up, surprised at how stiff I felt.

I pulled the door open and a man came tumbling on top of me. It was Vandyne.

"What the hell's wrong with you!" he shouted at me. I stood there in a stupor, not knowing what I had done. I felt like I'd been caught not cleaning my room.

"Were you leaning on my door?"

"I was trying to listen in! How many knocks does it take for you to answer the door!" Vandyne shouted again.

"Cripes, what are you yelling about?" I asked. My mouth had gone dry and my voice was breaking. "Here, I want to show you something funny on the television." I tripped over to the couch, but the television was tuned to a show in German.

All the Asian channels switched over to European languages at 0500. That meant that it must be morning. I'd fallen asleep and the night was over. It made me smile.

"What's so funny? All I see is some fool sitting on his couch drinking all night. That's not funny. That's sad. You drink all this last night?" Vandyne thundered, kicking away an empty bottle.

"No," I lied, "it's from this week."

"You've got six, seven bottles sitting around. Nice life you got yourself here."

"You know that you're cramping my style?" I lay back down on the couch and leaned my head back to a comfortable angle. "Why are you barging in here at this sensitive time in my life?"

"Sensitive! Your problem is that you're anything but

sensitive!" Vandyne was sputtering. "This couple came into the Five, saying you assaulted them during the Chinese New Year parade. They also said you used inappropriate language and your breath smelled of alcohol."

I sat upright and cracked my neck bones.

"Fucking bullshit!" I said. "They were interfering with a police officer in the line of duty!"

"They're schoolteachers from Connecticut. They were there with their students. And they had a TV camera, Chow!"

"They touched me! You put your hands on someone, you better be able to back that up. I don't care if they're teachers or Muhammad Ali!"

"We're not talking about a scrap. You took on two liberals! They're going to the Civilian Complaint Review Board."

The CCRB sounded impressive, but it actually had no teeth. Maybe I'd get an order to do push-ups. I laughed at the thought of it.

"The CCRB! What a joke! That's not going to be a problem, Vandyne."

"You need help for your drinking," Vandyne said, softening up. "That's the honest truth, brother." He didn't know what to do or say, and that made me feel like I'd let him down.

"Vandyne, everything's going to be all right, man. It's okay," I said.

"One thing a good relationship will do for you is give you a source of strength. You need a good woman."

"You know what the divorce rates are like?"

"You take care of each other, you don't have to worry about it. Look at how my wonderful marriage works."

"Then how come you don't have kids?"

Vandyne made a face like he needed some dental floss. Then he relaxed a little and changed the subject.

"Anyway, Chow, that invitation to come to our home for dinner is still open. You should come soon. Rose hasn't seen you in a while, and you'll have another shot at making a good impression on her."

"Later this month. I promise. Tell me what to bring."

"Bring the good Robert Chow."

The last time I had seen Rose was at the minority policemen's picnic in Central Park. I'd known that alcohol wouldn't be served, so I'd juiced up before going.

I remembered laughing with people and having a good time. A few days later, they told me that I'd puked in a cooler.

A wave of exhaustion came over me and I thought about getting into bed.

"I'll come over for dinner soon, but right now I'm just gonna hit the sheets," I told Vandyne. The television suddenly seemed to grow in volume. I pointed to the set and said, "Vandyne, can't you turn that thing down?"

—

I was coming around Doyers Street later that week when the barber Law called out to me. He was leaning against the open door of the barber shop, smoking.

"Robert," he said, "when are you going to let me finish your haircut? It's still lopsided. You look like a crazy person."

"My hair looks fine," I said. "Everything's grown out. Anyway, I've got my cap on."

"I can tell there's something wrong! It's bad publicity for my shop!" Law stuck his cigarette into one side of his mouth and reached out with both his hands. "Look at this!" he said, pulling off my cap and brushing my hair. "Awful!"

Seriously, it had been looking all right to me. Barbara, too, I thought. But maybe it had been one more thing that had turned her off.

"I don't have time for this right now," I told Law.

Law looked my cap over. "What's this?" He pointed at the playing card stuck into the clear plastic pocket inside the crown.

I grabbed my hat back and stuck it back on top of my head.

"What was that, the eight of hearts?" asked Law.

"Yeah, the eight of hearts."

"What's it doing there?"

"It's for good luck. A lot of cops have pictures of Jesus or Mary stuck in there so they don't get shot. All I need is the eight of hearts."

"With your hair like that, you already look like you don't have a full deck up there, okay? Hey, come inside. Let me finish. Hey, free! I'll do it free!"

"Law, I don't have time right now."

"If you didn't have that uniform, everyone would think you were a delinquent!" he muttered, slipping inside the barbershop. He sucked on the cigarette like it was holding something back on him.

"I have a shield and a gun!" I said after him. "That's how people know I'm good!"

After the shift was over I went back to Martha's to go see

Lonnie. The place was a madhouse in the morning, but in the early evening, it was nearly empty. An old couple sitting near the door shared a cup of coffee and a Taiwan newspaper. A small piece of wax paper with some crumbs on it sat on the table between them.

The punk kids who usually slummed around the bakery weren't around. I hadn't seen them since I'd shaken up their leader.

Lonnie was sweeping the floor. Dori was probably in the bathroom, running an emery board over her fangs.

"Officer Chow," Lonnie said with surprise, her face reddening slightly.

"Hi Lonnie. I just came back here to ask you something," I said.

"Yes. What is it?" she asked.

"Well, you put something in my bag this morning, with the hot dog buns and coffee." I pulled out the crumpled flyer from my back pocket. "I'm sorry, but the coffee spilled on it. There's some kind of church dance or something this Saturday?"

Lonnie was very red now. "Yes, my church is having a spring dance. It's to celebrate the new year even though it's on Valentine's Day. It's not really a big thing. Not too many people go. It's not important."

"Are you asking me to go?" I asked.

"I didn't know if you like dancing," she said.

"Are you going?"

"I'm on the dance committee, so I have to be there. I'm in charge, actually. It's to raise money for the youth programs."

"Is this something I need a date for?"

"Do you have a girlfriend?"

"No."

"Well, you can just come by yourself if you want."

"Something tells me that I'm going to be the only one there who's old enough to drink."

"We don't allow alcohol at any church functions. It's just a social kind of thing. I don't have a boyfriend, so you know, I'll dance with anyone who wants to."

"I don't know how to dance."

"You don't have to dance. There'll good music to listen to there."

"I really don't think I'm going to go, Lonnie. There's a big game on that night. Rangers and Islanders."

"You'd rather stay at home and watch a baseball game?"

"Hockey."

"Well, maybe the next dance, you won't have anything to watch."

"Yeah, next time," I said.

"I have to go get the mop," Lonnie said, backing away. "I'll see you tomorrow morning, officer."

"I'll see you tomorrow," I said. Lonnie dragged her broom into the back and I walked to the door.

"Hey!" the old woman said to me. "You!"

"Me?" I asked.

"You're that policeman, right?" she asked. The old man grunted and rustled the newspaper he was hiding behind.

"Which one?" I asked.

"The one in the newspapers."

"Yeah, that's me."

"You don't know anything about women, do you? No wonder you're always by yourself."

"I'm alone but I'm not lonely."

"Shut up!" she said. "Didn't you know that pretty girl was asking you to go to the dance with her?"

"I was waiting for her to ask me."

"She was asking you to ask her!" insisted the old woman.

The old man grunted again. "Why are you like this?" he asked the woman in a smoky voice. "When you muddy up the water, no one can drink."

"You mind your own business!" the woman said to the man before turning back to me. "You're not going to be young forever," she said, taking a rationed sip of coffee.

You sure didn't stay young, lady, I thought.

I looked at Lonnie stagger around with the mop. I stuck my hands in my pockets and shifted my feet. I looked into my heart and found something there.

—

Lonnie's church was Transfiguration, which was on the inner elbow of Mott Street. The dance was being held to raise funds and to celebrate the Chinese New Year. They couldn't have had it on the actual day, since most of the young people had to be with their families.

The huge church with the stone-and-iron fence out front was an imposing sight in Chinatown mostly because it was bigger and more solid than the surrounding crappy brick tenements. The church looked like a stone battleship run aground on a Hong Kong block.

Transfiguration ran after-school and weekend Bible and pre-college study programs for kids. The details and hours were posted in a glass case mounted on the outdoor fence. Another glass case had a list of last year's high-school grads who had also attended the church's programs. Next to their names were the colleges they had gotten into in English. The non-Ivy League colleges had phonetic Chinese characters next to them so people would know how to say them.

I put my back against the case and checked my watch again. Lonnie was 15 minutes late already. I heard muffled beats from the church's basement. I reached up and batted a red balloon tied to the iron fence. I felt stupid. I was an old man, I didn't go to church, I didn't go to college, and now I was being stood up for a teeny-bopper dance.

I looked down at my wing-tipped Florsheims. I'd wasted a quarter on a polish and shine from the shoe guy by Columbus Park. I licked my thumb where I had burned it slightly on the iron. I'd forgotten you were only supposed to touch the handle.

A group of five boys in black suede jackets walked by. Two of them had their hair brushed into the Bruce Lee/flattened cotton swab look.

I watched them as they went up Mott and one of them looked back at me. I crossed my arms and lifted my chin. He smiled and pointed to my right.

I turned and saw Lonnie. Her hair was done in curls. She wore dark blue eye shadow with wet red lipstick that made her lips glisten wickedly. Two obviously fake diamond earrings shook nervously under her jaw, but you couldn't be unhappy about them on a girl like her.

She had on a black wool coat that was a little short. I stared at her legs. The long uniform skirt of Martha's didn't have a slit, and I'd never gotten a good enough look at them. The sight of those legs could derail a train.

"Robert, look at you, wearing a jacket and a shirt! I can't believe you got so dressed up!" When she touched my arm, it bothered me because it made me think of her in a sexual manner. I had always found her attractive, otherwise I wouldn't have talked to her so much at Martha's, but I never had the thoughts I was having now. And to be walking into a church at this point, even for a non-believer, felt horribly wrong.

"Are you okay, Robert? Why are you making that face?"

"What kind of face?"

"Like you're scared."

"I'm okay." I patted my pocket to check my wallet and I was dimly aware that my left arm was slightly restrained by Lonnie's right hand. I guess I could have slipped her hand into mine very easily, and maybe she was waiting for me to. I wasn't sure what to do, and I was still thinking about it when we got to the door. Lonnie broke off and pulled the door open.

"Officers first," she said.

"Thank you, miss." We walked in past the closed doors of the administrative offices. Upbeat music floated up from below. It sounded familiar and got louder as we went down the stairs.

Streamers were taped to the exposed pipes running along the ceiling of the church's basement, making the room seem a little less sad. The dance floor was exposed and empty, save for an older Chinese couple shuffling slowly. The high-school-aged disc jockey leaned against a pole, one hand on his hip.

He jumped to attention when we walked in.

About 20 kids, varying in age from early- to mid-teens, were sprawled around three round banquet tables against the far wall. Apart from the dancing couple, I was the oldest person in the joint. I stared at them, shocked at the sight of older Chinese people being affectionate in public.

"That's Mr. Jen and his wife," said Lonnie. "He's been the janitor here for as long as I can remember."

"Who's the disc jockey?"

"Oh, that guy. He's one of my brother's friends. He asked me to go to the dance with him."

"You didn't like him?"

"I told him I was coming with you. Actually, I told him I was coming with you before I even told you about the dance." She took off her coat and put it on a hanger. "Anyway, he's just a kid."

Lonnie had on a thin red blouse. There was no doubt in my mind that the Martha's uniform was designed to flatten every curve in the female body.

"You want to hang up your jacket?" she asked.

"No, I'll just undo the buttons a little." After thinking a bit, I said, "Lonnie, how come nobody's dancing?"

"Well, the kids really wanted disco, but the church said no." That explained why the DJ was playing bland Chinese pop music from a generation ago. "This music's really terrible, isn't it?"

"It's not bad, it's just old. When I was a kid, we used to dance to the Beatles and Rolling Stones. Kids don't dance anymore. They'd rather just be home playing with their CB radios, right?"

"Do you want to dance, Robert?"

"No, this music makes me want to watch Mr. Jen." We watched the couple dance. When the song was over, he bowed and she curtsied. Watching that made me wish I'd seen my parents dance. The DJ shuffled over to the record player. He threw on another record and put the tone arm down. That sulk of his could be contagious.

"Is everyone having fun?" Lonnie asked the tables of kids.

"No," the collective chorus said.

"Lonnie, this music stinks."

"I thought there was going to be dinner here."

"Well, we have punch and cookies," said Lonnie. "If you're hungry, you can have some."

"Those almond cookies are stale."

"Come on now, they taste fine."

I found a wall to lean against. I felt like I was at a surly 11-year-old's birthday party. Where were the toy whistles?

"I'm sorry you're not having fun, Robert," said Lonnie, running up to me. "I really thought some of the older people were going to show up."

"I'm here, doesn't that count?"

"Are you making fun of me?"

"No, Lonnie. I'm just a little irritable because these shoes are kinda tight."

"You want to sit down?"

"I'll sit down right here." I picked a dented metal folding chair that was far away from the kids. Lonnie hastily pulled out a chair and sat down next to me. She looked tired, too.

"I really tried to put something together that would be fun, but now I feel like I ruined everything. You just can't make everybody happy. The older people didn't bother to come and the younger kids hate this."

"Lonnie, it's not your fault. People never appreciate things."

"Maybe."

"What do you do here at the church?"

"I'm kind of a chaperone. I take the kids to museums or the zoo. I show them there's a whole world outside of Chinatown."

"I used to think there was. I thought that being in the Army would do that for me."

"It didn't work?"

"Only showed me that no matter where I was, I was a Chinaman, and I could never be anyone else."

"Did you wish you hadn't joined the army?"

"Join? I was drafted. I didn't have a choice."

"Oh. I've been with the church for more than 10 years. That's by choice."

"Me, myself, I never saw much use to the church. I mean, church is nice for people who believe in it, but it doesn't seem to do anything real. All they do is collect money, right?"

Lonnie shifted her mouth a little.

"Well, I come to this church because it was one of the sponsors for us to come to the U.S. So it's more personal obligation and my gratitude than a religious thing for me."

"I'm sorry if I made it sound like church was stupid."

"Don't worry about it, Robert. I don't care. I haven't even

finished the Bible."

"Look, how about we get out of here and go have dinner? I mean a nice one. We're all dressed up already."

"I was supposed to stay and clean up after the party."

"Don't worry about it. I'll talk to Mr. Jen. He'll shut the place down."

We got a table at Garden of Peking on Mulberry, a place I have walked by many times. They used tablecloths and didn't serve rice because at high-class Chinese meals, you're supposed to fill up on meat to show how much money you have.

"We don't often have dignitaries here, officer," the waiter said. He was staring down Lonnie's blouse. "You want me to roll for you two?"

"We got it, big boy," I said. We took the flour pancakes and threw on duck meat and skin, green scallion stalks, and a spoonful of plum sauce. I wrapped one up for Lonnie, who seemed to be struggling a little.

"Thank you, Robert! I'm so clumsy. My hands are tired from the bakery." After a bite, she said, "It's good. I can't remember the last time I've had this."

I thought about the last time I had eaten Peking duck. It was right after my father's funeral.

"Yeah, I can't remember the last time, either," I said.

"It's so fatty."

"That means it was a happy duck."

"I'm sure it wasn't happy when they killed it."

"This duck was happy to give its life up to feed hungry

people."

"Would you give your life up for someone else?"

"Lonnie, I'm a policeman. That's what my job's all about. I'm dying a little every day and nobody cares."

"Who was that girl you came into Martha's with a few weeks ago?"

"She was an old friend."

"Is she your Valentine?"

"No. Absolutely not."

"She's very pretty."

"That's not the most important thing."

"What do you look for in a girl?"

"I guess someone who has the capacity to like me."

"You mean, you want to find someone who will love you, right?"

"That's it. Hey, Lonnie. Does my hair look okay?"

"It looks really good."

"Are you sure?"

"Yes! It's really you."

"I like your hair, too."

I was a little uncomfortable and ate more out of nervousness than hunger.

When dinner was done, we headed for Bayard in the old part of Chinatown, where Lonnie lived with her dad and stepmom.

"What are you going to do now?" Lonnie asked.

"I'm just going to go home." And drink a little, I thought.

"It's still early."

"It's almost 10. What do you want to do?"

"Can I see your apartment?"

I was shocked by how forward she was.

"Maybe we can listen to records, Robert. I want to hear the kind of music that you like."

"Oh, Lonnie, I think I'm just going to sleep." I slouched some.

"You didn't seem that tired before."

"I feel it now, though."

I walked her to her door, which had sheet metal bolted in the front.

"I'll see you real soon, okay?" I said. Lonnie tried to smile then let go of me. I had almost forgotten we were walking arm in arm.

When I was alone, I put both my hands in my pockets. It was good I hadn't taken her home. I was five years older than her. That wasn't right. Five years. That's how long college is.

What was she thinking we'd do back at my apartment, anyway? Maybe she just wanted to neck. That would have been okay. Or maybe she wanted more? She lived with her parents, went to school part-time, worked full-time, and helped out ungrateful kids at church. That's tough for anyone to do and still feel like a woman. How much did I really like her? I wasn't sure, but I did know that if that DJ had come over and bugged her at the dance, I would have felt like playing piñata with his head.

The liquor store was two rights and a left from Lonnie's

apartment. It was below street level, so you had to go down a narrow, rusty stairwell and walk over a concrete slab that had a green streak where rain would trickle down and collect.

I hadn't been there in a month, since I didn't like to splurge much on the hard stuff when there wasn't anything to celebrate. Today there was a banner hanging over the door that read "New Management — 25% Off." I had to buy a bottle of something to celebrate that.

I ducked under the door frame and admired the Linda Lin Dai poster hanging behind the counter.

Wang the fortune-teller was wrapping a white ceramic bottle of rice wine with old issues of American newspapers. He called out my name as if I would be on sale for the next five minutes only.

"Policeman Chow! Policeman Chow!"

"Wang, looks like you've got a new line of work here."

"It's only part-time," he said. "They needed help figuring out the metric system, now that it's the law." I looked around and saw a sign that said one quart was now a liter, and half a gallon was now 1.75 liters.

Didn't two quarts make a half-gallon? And 1.75 liters sure sounded a lot smaller than two liters. Someone was getting ripped off here. The only other customer in the store was the midget.

"Big celebration?" I asked him.

"When you're as small as me, everything's a big celebration!" he said. "I'm going to get a little drunk and write some poetry tonight. Nothing exciting. Now what's the story with you being dressed up?"

"I went to a dance tonight."

"You smell like plum sauce."

"That's from the duck."

"Did you go to dinner or a dance?"

"I went to both."

"So, it was a date, huh?"

"You know, if you'd just put your probing mind into something constructive, you'd be a millionaire."

"I'm already as rich as I want to be," said the midget. "How much money do I need? I already get to play games all day. What else would I want to do?"

"Well, you could start a game store."

"Then games wouldn't be fun anymore. Anyway, Moy's hard-hearted dad would drive me out of business."

"Are you saying that your business would get beat?"

"You need to be ruthless to play games and run businesses. But at least there are rules in games; you don't get to move more than once per turn just because you have more money than the other guy."

Wang slipped the wrapped wine bottle into a doubled-up red plastic bag. "If the midget started a business, we'd all end up working for him, I'm sure," he said.

"I'd like having a Chinese boss for a change," I replied. "It'd make work a lot better."

The midget reached for his wallet and shook his head. "Think of the sweatshops. They all have Chinese bosses." The midget handed over a five to Wang. Wang reached his hands under the counter, shrugged a few times, and pulled out three bills for change.

"Come by and see me when you're free and feel like losing," the midget said to me. He swung the bag over his shoulder.

"Don't drink so much you can't play anymore," I told him.

The midget smiled. "I'll be dead before I can't play," he said on the way out. I watched his little legs waddle up the steps.

"Policeman Chow," Wang said slowly, "I understand that you're one of this store's best customers."

"Used to be. I've switched to beer for the most part. I was starting to have blackouts from this stuff."

"Beer kills brain cells. I'm not kidding, that cheap alcohol will ruin you. Oh, I have to tell you something. The midget told me not to sell you any alcohol."

"And why not!"

"He told me that you're an alcoholic."

"That's ridiculous. If I'm an alcoholic, how could I walk around with a gun?"

"What I think is that you're drinking the wrong alcohol. Beer is low-class. The best liquor puts you in a more profound state of mind. All the best Chinese dynasties were run by drunks."

"I don't know about profound. I would wake up and not remember what day it was after a night with the hard stuff."

"A lot of people don't know what day it is," Wang said, dismissively. "Try this," he said, holding up a plain-looking brown bottle. "You like coffee, right? This is the sweetest coffee you'll ever have." He punched the price into a calculator on the counter and turned it to face me. My eyebrows twisted involuntarily and he knocked off a buck.

"Okay," I said.

"I hope to see you here again," said Wang. "But don't tell the midget I sold you this. You want me to wrap the bottle?"

"Just put it in a bag. I don't need the newspaper."

"You don't read much, do you?"

"I don't trust the *New York Post*," I said, pointing to his pile of newspapers. "Don't you know there's a liberal bias in the American media?"

—

Back in my apartment, I put the bottle down on the coffee table. I took a glass out of the sink and washed it. I turned the TV on. The communist station was showing a reenactment of the Long March. It was a tearjerker.

The Taiwan station had a news magazine on. Scientists thought another earthquake would hit Taipei, followed by a tidal wave. Nobody could agree on when, though. The show ran through some stock footage from earlier earthquakes.

I reached for the bottle and twisted the cap. The metal tabs snapped like knuckles that had been waiting to crack all day.

I poured from the bottle into the glass into my mouth. I licked my lips and licked the cap. It was good and sweet and the lingering smell of it calmed a primitive part of my brain.

Some knocks came at the door. I doused my throat with another glass, hoping it was for my neighbor, but the knocks only grew louder.

I really hate to put a cap back on a bottle unless it's finished, but I screwed it back on and went to the door. Maybe it was Vandyne again to chew me out for drinking.

It was Lonnie. She was glaring at me with bared teeth. I saw why she didn't smile much. Her front two teeth were slightly turned in to each other like an inverted V. It didn't make much of a difference when you saw the rest of her, but I'm sure Lonnie was painfully self-conscious of it. At least in public.

"What are you doing here?" I asked.

"I came in the front door behind an old woman."

"I hope you didn't wait long. You know the lock's broken anyway."

"I thought you might be a little drunk by now," she said. "Maybe a little lonely, too."

"How did you know where I live?" I asked, backing away from the door.

"Everyone knows where you live." She came in and closed the door behind her.

"Lonnie, I was just sitting down for some Taiwan TV. Can I make some tea for you?"

"Why don't you give me some of that?" she asked, pointing to the bottle of coffee liquor.

"You ought to lay off that stuff, and stay away from any other alcohol, too. It'll stunt your growth."

"I'm not some little kid, you know," growled Lonnie. She grabbed the bottle, took the cap off, and hoisted it before I could do anything. Working at the bakery counter sure gave her fast hands. I grabbed her arm and twisted the bottle out of her grip.

"What's the matter with you? You know I could be charged with endangering the welfare of a minor?" I asked.

"I can drink! I'm over 18!"

"Yeah, but I'm older than you, and I say you can't in my house!"

I wanted to close the bottle but the cap was gone, so I took a swig and then another.

"You think I'm ugly, don't you?" she asked as her whole body heaved. She coughed and her eyes watered.

"You're not ugly, you're a very pretty girl."

"Then what's wrong?" She was crying full on now. "Why don't you like me?"

"I do like you. A whole lot." I could feel an all-nighter coming on.

"You don't think I'm sexy?" asked Lonnie. She swaggered to the couch and dropped.

"You're fine," I said. "Just fine." I took a few more swigs from the bottle.

"I liked you the first time I saw you. I could tell you were a great guy," said Lonnie, crossing her arms. "It's because I go to community college, right? You think I'm stupid."

"I don't think you're stupid! The movie review you wrote was really good. I couldn't write like that."

"You want to give me more of that drink?" she asked.

"No, you don't get any of this," I said. I finished the bottle to make sure.

Lonnie sighed. "I never cared what Dori said about you because I knew you were good."

"What did she say about me?"

"She said the only reason you got your job was because you were born here and knew English, otherwise you'd be waiting tables."

"I'd rather wait tables than work her dumb job."

Lonnie reared up and snarled. "Dumb job! You think my job is dumb! You don't think I'm good enough for you!"

I couldn't think fast enough to recover, so I tried the honest approach.

"Lonnie, don't worry, you're not going to be there forever. You're going to finish school," I said. I couldn't think of the next thing to say. I was feeling warmer and it was getting hard for me to focus. My ears were feeling tickly.

"Are you okay, Policeman Chow?" asked Lonnie, looking worried.

I sat down next to her and put the bottle between my feet.

"That liquor was strong stuff," I said. It occurred to me that I never bothered to check the proof. I bent down to pick up the bottle, but came up with Lonnie's hand instead.

I moved in and kissed her mouth hard. She turned her head and bit her V-shaped teeth into my neck. I shucked her coat off down to her arms. She let go of me to get the sleeves off and wrapped her legs around my waist. That was how I carried her into the bedroom.

—

The sound of cars honking woke me up. I was lying in bed, completely naked except for one dress sock. My arm was stretched over my nightstand and my alarm clock was on the floor. My throat and head ached. My lips and fingers were sore. I couldn't remember too much. I went out to the living room and saw an empty bottle on the coffee table. That was explanation enough.

I went by the window and I could tell by the way the cars

were double-parked that it was a weekend. I went to the fridge and got a beer. Everything was going to be okay.

I went to the bathroom and found a note from Lonnie on the closed toilet lid.

"Thank you for everything, Robert. I hope I didn't talk too much and bother you." Her phone number was at the bottom.

Can't be bothered when you can't remember. I decided not to call her because I didn't want to ruin whatever lie she'd told her dad and stepmom about last night. Even if Lonnie was the one who picked up, you can hear a phone conversation from every room in a Chinatown apartment.

I folded the note up, put it in the wastebasket, and lifted the toilet seat.

—

When I came into Martha's on Monday, Lonnie wasn't there. Dori was impatiently showing a new girl what to do. It was unseasonably warm that day and Dori seemed hotter under the collar than usual.

"Don't put the tongs on the counter, otherwise the customers might steal them. Put them on the shelf behind you," Dori said. The girl nodded and didn't say anything.

"Is Lonnie okay?" I asked Dori.

"Ha! She never came in this weekend. She had to be replaced."

"She never showed up? What happened?"

"You're the policeman, you tell me. Ask your missing persons department. If Lonnie's not working here, you don't have a reason to come back, right?" She was gloating.

"Aren't you worried about her? You've been working

together for years."

"I could always tell she wasn't going to make it," said Dori with a smile. "She was very clumsy and she wasn't too smart." Then to the trainee, Dori said, "This is the policeman who was in love with the old girl. If you don't look out, he's going to start liking you, too."

"I'll have one hot-dog pastry and an iced coffee," I said to the trainee, absently. Where was Lonnie?

The trainee picked up the tongs and looked uncertainly from tray to tray.

"Here, here, I got it," grunted Dori as she threw aside a sliding window and spanked a pastry into a cellophane bag. "Go make the officer an iced coffee," she said to the trainee.

When the new girl returned with my drink, Dori snatched it from her and held it up, looking at the color of the coffee through the transparent-plastic cup.

"You didn't shake it enough," Dori snapped. She gave it a shake and the lid flew off. Coffee poured all over her shoes and ice cubes skittered across the counter. "You stupid, stupid little girl!" Dori screamed. "You didn't seal the lid properly!"

The trainee gave Dori the finger and came around the counter. I tried not to laugh, but I couldn't help it when everyone in line behind me applauded the girl on her way out the door.

"You don't deserve to work here!" Dori screamed. That was so true. I thought about her spending the rest of the day in soggy socks. Some people deserve that.

She took a towel and wiped off the counter and her legs. Then she went to pour me a new iced coffee. She dropped it into a brown paper bag and tossed in my hot-dog pastry. Her face was red enough to stop traffic.

I paid Dori and stepped aside. I couldn't imagine being behind that counter by myself and handling all those Monday morning customers. She was in for it.

On my way out, I saw Moy cramped in the corner seat by the window. He looked unusually well-dressed in a button-down knit and wool trousers.

"Moy, shouldn't you be dusting off some G.I. Joe dolls?"

"Oh, no! I'm waiting for someone." He smiled a little.

"A woman? Are you on a date? Little early for that, isn't it?" It was five to seven.

"No, not a date. She's my girlfriend. We've been together for almost two weeks now. We got together over New Year's and we're going out."

"You've got a girlfriend and you never told me! I can't believe it! After all the years I've known you! Congratulations!"

"I wanted to keep things private. I haven't even told my father."

"That's amazing. Where is she?"

"It's Dori," he said. I was dimly aware of dropping my bag.

"Moy, are you crazy?"

"I know you two don't get along. She's a tough woman. You didn't have to laugh at her just now, when that girl quit."

"I'm sorry about that. But Moy, you know Dori hates me."

"She said you gave her cousin a parking ticket a few years ago."

"I probably did. It's my job."

"But it was her cousin. Do you understand?"

"I'd give a ticket to my own mother if she broke the law."

"What's wrong with you?"

"Moy, what happened to Lonnie?"

"She quit, I guess. I don't know where she went."

—

I was on the footpost, coming up to Jade Palace and the hunger strikers. This time Willie Gee's hired gorilla was standing in the street. He would say something into his shirt from time to time. To the left of the entrance, the stool-pigeon waiters held waist-level signs reading "Jade Palace Is Fair Employer" in English, and "Go Bury Your Parents" in Chinese, directed at the protestors.

To the right, three hunger strikers lay on cots surrounded by protesters with signs that read "Stop Stealing Money" in English and "Stop Killing Us" in Chinese.

It was about 1000 — too early for anyone to show much enthusiasm. People on both sides, apart from the hunger strikers, were drinking coffee and reading newspapers. I looked at the hunger strikers and saw a girl with her arms crossed and her eyes closed. She had a thin blanket wrapped around her. It was Lonnie.

I went up to her and shook her awake.

"Lonnie, what are you doing out here?" I asked.

"Robert!" she said, smiling weakly. "I haven't eaten anything for two days."

"You've got to get out of here. This is hurting your body."

"I want to thank you for listening to me the other night. You told me how hard it was for you to be a policeman, but it was something you really wanted to do. You told me to find something I believed in, and this protest is it."

"Yeah, but I didn't tell you to join the hunger strike."

"Yes, you did."

"Well, I didn't mean it. I was drunk, you shouldn't listen to me when I'm like that."

"I feel so much better, I'm working for justice here."

"You're not helping anyone by not eating," I said.

"My mind's made up. I'm staying here."

"No, you're not," I said. I reached in and pulled her up. "We're going to get something to eat." She came up easily, but then something pulled her away from me.

"What the hell are you doing, you fucking pig!" said a young man who looked like a campus liberal.

"She's leaving here right now!" I said. He put his hand on me and I pushed him against the wall of Jade Palace. I put my elbow into his gut. "You take her place on the hunger strike. I'm feeling a lot of fat here that you could lose." He was running out of air and the rest of the protesters were jumping around as if someone had turned a hotplate on under their feet.

"Stop that cop!"

"Get that pig!"

"He's working for Jade Palace!"

I grabbed Lonnie's arm and led her away to a chorus of boos. I turned back and saw Willie Gee's King Kong character smiling. He waved at me daintily with his fingers and made kissy lips.

—

I got Lonnie into an over-rice place and ordered pork, chicken, and preserved greens for her.

The cook was in the back of the tiny dining room straightening out a small altar for Guan Gong, an old Chinese general who was now worshipped as a god.

He flicked his lighter and lit up the incense sticks and a cigarette. The cook grunted when the waitress tapped his shoulder. He took a long drag on his cigarette before dropping it to the tile floor and mushing it with his filthy sneaker. He pushed into the kitchen's swinging doors and disappeared.

Lonnie poured us two cups of tea.

"I don't understand you, Robert. Why did you pull me out?" She sipped her hot tea and shivered. "I know it's warm out but I feel so cold. It's almost 60 degrees in February can you believe it?"

"Lonnie, a woman your age still has to develop. Not getting the proper nutrition now could lead to birth defects."

"Who said I wanted to have children?"

"Lonnie, you don't even know these people. They could be brainwashing you, like what happened to Patty Hearst. You could be doing this against your will."

"Nobody made me do anything. I believe in the cause. Anyway, I cheated a little on the hunger strike. I drank some soy milk this morning."

"Soy milk. I'm sure that made a big difference."

We were quiet for a bit.

Lonnie said, "This is the second time we've sat together in a restaurant."

"Sure it is. You're the only one who's going to be eating, though."

"Is this our second date?" she asked, smiling.

"No. This is my feed-the-children program."

"Are you surprised I wasn't a virgin?"

"I'm not surprised by anything, Lonnie. I'm trained to expect the unexpected."

The food came in and Lonnie went to work at it.

"I'm so hungry, I have to eat slowly or I'm going to choke."

"Take your time, Lonnie. I stopped by Martha's and Dori had a new trainee in your place."

"I feel sorry for her — the trainee."

"Actually, she quit. I'm sure Martha's would take you back in a second."

"Maybe. I was a really good worker." She ate quietly for a while, then asked, "Do you remember what else we talked about that night?"

"I don't. I barely remember you coming over."

"You said you would help my younger brother out."

"What's wrong with your brother?"

"Our stepmother keeps beating him and throwing him out of the apartment. He has a girlfriend and she doesn't want him to start dating until he's in college."

"That doesn't sound too bad. She should learn to live with it."

"She's evil. She doesn't want me to move out until I get married, even though I probably have enough to get a place with some roommates. If I did, I'd give it to my brother so he could live somewhere else. He's really smart and talented. He really deserves a chance to get out of here." Lonnie twisted her mouth like she was trying to stop herself from crying.

"Does she ever hit you?" I asked her.

"No, as a matter of fact, she thinks she's my best friend. She always wants to share makeup."

I took a deep breath and then I asked, "Has your family been to counseling? Or maybe you want to consider family court?"

"Counseling? That's only for sick, crazy people! And family court just breaks up families. We already have one divorce, we don't need another."

"Yeah, you're right," I said, crossing my ankles.

"I'll tell you what. Your brother can stay with me, but he has to get a job and pay part of the rent. How about that?"

"That's what you said that night!" she said. "Do you really mean it, now that you're not drunk?"

"Sure, I do. Any brother of yours is a brother of mine. Of course, he also has to do some work around the apartment."

She nodded and chewed.

"Lonnie, I've got to go make my rounds. It doesn't look good for a policeman to be sitting around." I stood up.

"Thank you so much for helping my brother. I'm going to tell him to stop by your place."

"No problem. I'll tell you what, this food's on me, too."

Lonnie's mouth was full, so she smiled and chewed.

I went up to the counter and paid the tab. I pointed to Lonnie and warned the cashier: "Don't let her go until she's done eating everything. I don't care how long it takes."

Chapter 9

February 20th was a warm but cloudy day in Chinatown. For the first time, the covers on the Taiwan and the communist newspapers were the same: ex-President Nixon and his wife were visiting the mainland for a week-long tour. Maybe the Chinese wanted tips on bugging offices.

I shivered. Cold sweat stuck my undershirt to my chest. It was about 1400. The park was devoid of cheer but had plenty of gray people and gray pigeons.

I saw the midget sipping a cold soybean drink, his arm propped up on the back of the bench he was sitting on. Opposite him, an Asian man in his mid-40s, about five-four, was twisting his lips with his left hand. He was in a spot. The midget waved to me.

"Officer Chow, how are you?"

"Good! And you?" I asked.

"Hey, stop talking! You're trying to disrupt my thinking!" growled the midget's opponent.

"It's too late to think your way out of this one," I said.

"Maybe you could use ESP to flip the board. That's the only

way your brain could help you now," said the midget. His opponent laughed quickly, then his face returned to being grim. He tightened his left hand into a fist and propped his chin on it.

"Officer Chow, can you suggest a move?" he asked with exasperation. His name was Chi and he ran a small restaurant over on Market Street under the Manhattan Bridge overpass.

"Maybe one of the cannons..." I started, but the midget tapped one of his own pieces. "My mistake. Missed that. Maybe you should just come back and lose again tomorrow."

"You better believe it's hopeless if Officer Chow is telling you to quit. He's the law," said the midget.

"It's just as well," Chi said, getting up. As he stood, I saw a horrifically bloodied apron wrapped around his waist. Most restaurants bought cut-up pig and chicken meat to roast, but Chi bought carcasses and chopped up his own meat. The apron looked like something a flesh-eating zombie would wear.

"I've got to go back to work now," said Chi. "Officer Chow, you come by some time after closing and have some spare ribs with me and the rest of the kitchen. I always save the best for the staff."

"Thank you, I will," I said.

"One quick game," the midget said to me. And it was quick. It took longer to set up than to play. Then I went home and had a nightmare about the apron.

—

Vandyne and his wife lived in a big ugly brick house in Elmhurst, Queens. The grouting was stained. Two bony evergreen bushes crouched on either side of the door. I came up the three steps to the porch and pressed the plastic doorbell.

Someone inside came over and shook off chains before opening the door.

"Robert, I'm so glad you could finally come over," Rose said. Vandyne's wife was wearing a flower-print dress with a Winnie-the-Pooh apron over it. Her braids had been tied back and her forehead was glistening with sweat. She was light-skinned and had metallic flakes of green in her brown eyes that sparkled when you looked right into them.

"I hope you're in for some heavy lifting. I've made six of my favorite dishes."

"Rose, I didn't know you were going to go through this much trouble. We're slobs — we're not worth it," I said.

"It's no trouble!" she said.

"As long as you've got rice and chopsticks, everything's cool." I came in and wiped off my shoes.

"I've got some yellow rice with the chicken. . ." she said in a searching and apologetic tone while shutting the door behind me.

"Rose, that's a joke, about the rice and all. Anything you've made will be wonderful."

Vandyne got up from the reclining chair and clapped my back.

"Glad you came out all this way," he said.

"I'm pleased and honored to be here."

"Would you guys like beers?" asked Rose. Vandyne shot her a look and Rose stuttered, "Or some Coke or juice or water?"

"Yeah, tonight's not a drinking night," I said. "I'll have a Coke."

"Have a seat, Chow." I dropped onto the plastic-covered couch next to Vandyne's chair.

"What's the idea with this?" I asked, drawing my hand up and down my chest.

"This?" asked Vandyne, flopping his tie up. "We don't have company over often, so I wanted to air out this tie while I had the chance." It had a loud orange paisley pattern on it. Vandyne flopped the tie again. "Christmas present."

"From who? Santa Pimp?" We had a good laugh about that. Rose dropped off two Cokes and Vandyne and I turned to the television. It was a show about snow leopards.

I looked under the television stand and saw a dusty plastic box.

"What's that?" I asked.

"That's a video-tennis game down there. I haven't played it in months. I just keep it hooked up because I get better reception with it plugged in."

"With the money Rose brings in, you should look into getting WHT."

"I'm not going to order pay television. That's the dumbest thing I ever heard of. Paying for something you already get free."

On the coffee table was a program for the funeral of Paul Robeson, who had died back in January.

"You went to Robeson's funeral?"

"Yeah, we did."

"How did you feel about it?"

"Felt sad, then mad, then glad."

"You think he was a communist?"

"No way! C'mon now, he was an emperor. Emperor Jones!"

"Whoa, that's a good one!"

I pointed to an acoustic guitar that was slumped behind his La-Z-Boy. "That's the guitar your mother forced you to play?"

"That's the one."

"Play something for me, man."

"Oh, I don't feel like it. I picked it up from the house after my mother passed, but I haven't had the heart to play it."

"Just for me, Vandyne, can't you? You said you were good."

"I'm sure I could still play pretty, but you know, all sorts of memories are tied to that thing. We lived in a tough area of Philly. We could have cracked the Liberty Bell if it weren't already. Understand?"

"Yeah."

"Well, my mother got me that guitar when I was five. Imagine me, this little kid, holding that big thing?"

"You were telling me she forced you to play Fats Domino and Elvis."

"She'd go to work and give me a 45, and if I didn't have one of those songs done perfect by the end of each week, I'd catch hell. My childhood helped define the term 'child abuse.' But she did it because she loved me. If I wasn't trying to pick out chords sitting on the floor in front of that phonograph, I might have been out on the streets on dope."

"But the experience scarred you. You can't have fun playing guitar when you had to learn like that. You can't even play a song for your best friend in the world."

"Yeah," said Vandyne in a neutral voice. "Music should be uplifting. Motivating. Something to give you a reason to keep going on."

"Are you ever going to play again?"

"It would have to be some special occasion. Something really happy."

"You'd have to pick it up to practice, though, right?"

"I am what I play. I don't have to practice how to be me."

"You know, my mother used to force me to read the Chinese newspapers. If she hadn't, I wouldn't know how to read Chinese. I would have been just another American-born Chinese who doesn't know how to read characters."

"Is it hard to learn to read Chinese? Harder than learning to speak it?"

"It's easy to lean, but just as easy to forget. If I don't read the newspaper every day, I start to slip."

"Maybe you just have a bad memory."

"Oh, I got more than one bad memory!"

We were laughing, but were interrupted by Rose calling from the kitchen.

"Can I have a hand in here, John?"

"Coming!" said Vandyne. I got up but he said, "Keep your seat, you're the guest."

"Let me help out. There's nothing on TV anyway."

—

Rose scraped another heap of sweet potatoes onto my plate.

"If I put that in my mouth, they're gonna have to take me away in a hearse. And I don't have clean underwear on," I said.

Rose wasn't fazed.

"Show me how much you love my cooking," she said.

"I'm surprised you don't weigh a million pounds," I said to Vandyne as I stuck my fork into the side of the potatoes and left it there. "Or a million kilograms, or whatever that comes out to."

"John hates the metric system," said Rose. Vandyne nodded his head and chewed.

"Who likes it? Some bureaucrat just wants us to act French," said Vandyne.

"Well, 'bureaucrat' is a French word," I said.

"John thinks Congress is pushing it to dupe consumers. Gas will be priced by the liter, not gallon. The deli will weigh meat in grams, not pounds. Since the public will be confused by the conversion, they won't realize that their dollars are buying less."

"That actually sounds pretty believable. Your man gets to the bottom of everything."

"I want you to get to the bottom of your plate! What am I going to do with the rest of this food?" said Rose.

"Rose knows I'll eat until I bust, so she controls my intake accordingly," said Vandyne. "You have to make up the difference, partner."

I shoved a forkful of potatoes into my mouth. I couldn't taste it, and chewing on it made my head and throat ache. I swallowed and put my fork down.

"No more. Thanks so much, Rose," I said.

"Now if you gents wouldn't mind doing the dishes, I'm going to leave you two alone," said Rose, unwrapping her apron and hanging it on the oven handle. "I've got to do two cost-analysis reports tonight. Or maybe I'm going to meet some Illuminati."

"They're around," muttered Vandyne.

"You can't argue with a General Electric executive," I said.

"I'm just an accountant there, silly Robert. Honey, make some coffee," she said as she left the kitchen.

Vandyne shuffled over to the freezer door and opened it.

"We got Blue Mountain View, vanilla bean, and some instant General Foods International," he said. "Watcha want?"

"What's the most expensive?"

"Blue Mountain View."

"I'll have that."

"Just as well. Keep in mind that it's not 100% Jamaican Blue Mountain — it's a blend. But we're still scared to drink it because we paid so much for it." Vandyne held the bag of coffee beans like a punching bag and took a few shots at it before pouring it into the coffee machine.

"Don't you need to grind them first?" I asked.

"Got a grinder built in. Saves time. It helps when you're groggy in the morning, too."

"I wish I could live it up like you rich people. You got it all figured out."

"I've been thinking," Vandyne said as he put the coffee beans away. "You know about the '20 and out' thing. After we do our 20 years and start collecting pensions, we should already have our own businesses going."

"What did you have in mind?"

"I got a cousin in Hawaii. Been there since the service dropped him off. Anyway, he came up with the idea of selling Hawaiian coffee in little shops here in the city. They grow it in volcanic soil. It's incredibly rich."

I shook my head.

"You know," I said, "I think Chock Full O' Nuts has you beat on that front."

"But it would be better stuff. Gourmet coffee. We could charge 75 cents a cup!"

"Nobody's gonna pay that!"

"Well, maybe you're right. But I'm still working on a plan to have some kinda business."

"You and all of Chinatown."

"Yeah," said Vandyne, drumming his fingers with his eyes to the floor. The last time I'd seen him like that was when we were in the sector car, talking about how our fathers had died.

"There's something I gotta tell you, Chow," Vandyne said. He came over and sat back down at the table.

"What have you got?"

"They're giving me a gold shield. I'm going to be third-grade." My stomach hurt but I smiled. Vandyne was now officially a detective — the lowest grade, but still a detective.

"That's great! That's wonderful!" I said, slapping his shoulder. "When does this happen?"

"On Monday. I just wanted to tell you first, so that you heard it from me and not from an announcement."

"I'm happy for you, Vandyne. You deserve it. I mean, it's what you want, right? You wanted to be a detective, right?"

"Yeah, that's right. And I know you do, too. But they don't

give you the investigative jobs and there's no other way to get the gold shield."

I wasn't understanding what Vandyne was saying. The coffee machine gurgled.

"Did they say something about me?" I asked.

"Hold on a sec." Vandyne got up and poured two cups.

"Cream?" he asked.

"You know how I like it."

"Bittersweet." He came back to the table with the coffees.

"They say anything about me, partner?"

"Well, they haven't said anything about you in terms of making it to the detective track."

"What did they say about me?"

"They said you were interviewing people for that poison case."

"I never actively looked up those people. They came to me and spilled everything they had. I was in a coffee shop the other day. . ."

"Having coffee with the husband, Yip."

"Yeah."

"Pardon me, but why the hell were you having coffee with him? A potential suspect?"

"He asked me to go." I didn't want to mention that Yip had been following me around like a pull toy.

"You gave him your phone number?"

I sighed and took a sip of coffee.

Vandyne started again. "Your problem is that you're getting too close to the case, not to mention that it isn't your case to begin with."

"My problem is that when Chinese people have problems they want to see another Chinese person, not someone who's going to need a translator. Believe me, it's not like I love these people or anything," I said.

Vandyne frowned.

"So who else is on the case?" I asked.

"Just me."

"Just you?"

"Yeah, contrary to popular belief. I went to talk to Yip and he clammed up, saying he'd told everything to you. I also saw Lily, who was Wah's immediate supervisor, and she pulled the same thing," said Vandyne, playing his spoon against the lip of his cup.

I shrugged.

"I told them to go to the station and make statements," I said. "It's not my fault if they don't come. I can't tie a rope around their necks and drag them in."

"No, but we can tie a fence around the case and tell you to stay the hell out," said Vandyne, his eyes flashing. He took a sip of coffee and cleared his throat. "There are people higher up than me who are ready to bust you down to janitor if you don't watch your step."

"Your longtime association with me doesn't help you out, either, does it?" I asked.

Vandyne drank some coffee and didn't say anything.

"This coffee's too sweet," I said.

—

I took the F train out of Queens back to Chinatown. It was an express train, but the ride was long, and the only seats available were next to other people, so I stood and held on to a pole. A little Korean boy came up to me.

"Are you a policeman?" he asked.

"How'd you know?"

"I can tell by your feet." I looked down and saw my feet spread and squared with my shoulders.

"Smart kid," I said.

"I'm in the fourth grade," he said. "I'm going to have my own company."

"That's nice," I said. I looked around for his parents, and found a woman in the corner, slumped over her propped-up arm.

"Have you been to the Statue of Liberty? I want to go there," the boy babbled.

"Yeah, I've been there." The train slowed to a stop. I groaned when I saw the station sign. We weren't even close to Manhattan yet and this kid was driving me nuts already.

"My daddy has a shoe store. He sells shoes to policemen."

"Why do policemen buy shoes from your daddy?"

"Because he gives them a special price."

"You know he's not supposed to do that. Those policemen are supposed to pay the full price. It's against the law."

"Are you going to arrest my daddy?" he asked, suddenly scared.

"I'm going to arrest your daddy if you don't sit next to your mommy right now and stay quiet. If you don't, I might have to arrest your mommy, too." He scrambled to the seat next to the sleeping woman, his eyes and mouth wide open.

About 15 minutes later, the mother woke up. When you

commute regularly, your body remembers how many stops the train makes to get to your station, even if you fall asleep. She finished stretching out and stood up just a few seconds before the door opened at their stop. She said something to her boy, who was still staring at me, and they got out.

I took their old seat and rubbed my eyes. Damn, Vandyne had made detective. I pushed my hands into my pockets and waited for the doors to shut and the train to get moving again.

—

My favorite story about the origin of the dragon in Chinese mythology claimed that during one of China's many periods of disunity, each rival kingdom took a different animal for its symbol. These included snakes, deer, horses, tigers, and everything else. The snake people carried banners of snakes when they went to war, and everyone else rallied behind their respective animals as well.

When the snake and deer kingdoms merged, their new emblem incorporated parts of both animals. A snake with deer antlers. As more states combined, more animal elements were added.

When the entire country was united, the final banner displayed an animal with a snake body, deer antlers, horse mane, tiger claws, rabbit eyes, fish scales, and lizard dorsal fins. A period of stability followed, and the war-weary people became enchanted with the power of the new symbol. They began to see it in lightning strikes in the sky and reflected in lakes. Dragons became gods that controlled the rain and fishing harvests.

Something had gone wrong when Chinese people had

come to America, though. They had split back into their snake, deer, horse, tiger, rabbit, fish, and lizard groups. Every block in Chinatown was crowded with association headquarters. Formerly known as tongs, these associations had been formed by people who had the same family name, came from the same town, or had the same trade.

Some associations owned four-story buildings that provided daycare services. Some were below street level, their signs spelled out in pieces of bitten-off duct tape. Some associations had been founded to destroy others.

One of the most powerful was the Golden Peace Association. It occupied a five-story building in the heart of Chinatown, where Mott and Bayard intersect. "Gold," "Peace," and "Association" gleamed in metal characters near the top of the Mott-facing facade.

The third floor on the outside was a replica terrace from Chinese antiquity, complete with a row of eight huge eight-sided hanging lanterns. A lot of tourists liked to get their picture taken with the terrace in the background. They didn't know that the Golden Peace members were Cantonese merchants who ran some of the biggest businesses in Chinatown, including Jade Palace. My old pal Willie Gee just so happened to be the president of Golden Peace.

—

I was going by the Golden Peace building when I noticed Willie's bodyguard ape hanging out with some kids across the street. He kept his hands in his pockets, but looked in their eyes dead serious as he talked, like a football coach on the team's last timeout of the season.

Only most of the team was smoking. King Kong smiled, hoisted one hand out of his pocket, and waved delicately to me. The kids laughed, cigarettes clamped in the corners of their mouths. The setting sun bathed them in a soft orange glow.

The temperature was in the high 60s even though it was February 29th. The kids were wearing tank tops that displayed their bony shoulders.

"Hey, Officer Chow, ya find any bank robbers, yet?" the big ape called out. He spoke in a clipped Cantonese accent that comes from years of hard street living. The kids smirked and looked away.

I stood my ground and stared back, not saying a word. I didn't give him anything to push against.

"Let's go eat," King Kong said. He and his barrel of monkeys slunk off to Jade Palace. I continued on my footpost.

—

When I got to Mott and Grand, I noticed water streaming out of an apartment building entrance. As is usually the case, the front door lock was busted, and I pushed my way inside no problem. I got to the stairwell, where water was cascading down. It looked like the source was on the third floor. Water was pouring in under apartment doors and people were shouting about it.

When I got up to the third floor, I saw a Chinese man with a crew cut in his mid-40s, 160, and wearing a grey winter coat over a vest and a thin t-shirt. He was leaning on the handle of a rusted sledgehammer next to a woman in her late 60s, 90 pounds, crooked black wig, wearing a blue sweater that was torn at the elbows. She had socks and slippers on. The two were yelling at each other and a little boy of about three was hiding behind the old woman. A sheet of water ran out from an open apartment door.

"What's the problem? Is there a busted pipe?" I asked.

"Officer, arrest this man!" pleaded the woman as she fidgeted with her wig. "He came into our apartment and broke the toilet!"

"Officer Chow, I'm the landlord! I own this apartment. These people haven't paid the rent in two months! You know me! I met you at the landlord association dinner." The man took one hand off his sledgehammer. I watched him slip it into his pants pocket and ball it into a fist. "I told them, 'If you don't pay, I'm going to come over there and break the toilet!' And look, now I did! They forced me to!"

"There are other ways to handle this," I said. "You should have gone through the proper procedures, because now I have to arrest you for destruction of property and maybe assault."

"It's my toilet, officer! I can break it if I want to!"

"Not when other people are living there. Not when you're creating a potential hazard with the water."

"She owes me money! I'm the damaged party, not her!"

"Let go of that sledgehammer," I said.

He took off for the next floor. You stupid asshole, I thought. I ran up after him, but lost traction on the fourth step. I slipped and fell, almost falling on my face. I heard the old woman scream. I rolled over into a sitting position and shook my head.

"Don't worry about me, I'm fine," I told her. Then I saw why she had screamed. The man was coming at me slowly down the stairs, pointing the handle end of the sledgehammer at my left eye.

"Stay out of this," he warned, "it's not your business."

"If you don't put that down, I'm going to shoot you," I said. He paused for a second, which was exactly what I was looking for. I grabbed the sledgehammer handle and pulled him down. He did a funny dance routine as he tumbled down the stairs trying to stay on his feet.

The man fell on the landing on his side. I was tempted to swing the sledgehammer down on his knee. Instead, I chucked it aside, flipped the man onto his stomach, and cuffed his hands behind him. Then I got up and kicked him in the ass like I was Pelé on a penalty kick. He groaned.

"That's enough," I said out loud to myself. I got on the radio for a car to come over.

"Hey," groaned the man, "can you take these handcuffs off? They're too tight."

"You want another kick in the ass?"

"How can you do this to me? I worked so hard all my life, officer. I'm just trying to get my money."

"Stay there," I said to the man. I got up and noticed the old woman and the little boy again. "Everything's going to be okay," I told them.

"Thank you so much, officer," said the woman.

"You just have to come down with me and make a statement, press charges."

"Oh, no! I couldn't! No, I have to work. Early in the morning! Just lock him up."

"It would really be easier if you came," I said. "But first let me get that water shut off."

The old woman's eyes grew wide with fear as she backed cautiously into the apartment, blocking my way.

"Come on," I said, "water's getting everywhere!"

We walked down the warped hallway floor, making splashing sounds. I got a minor flashback to Nam and put my arms out to touch the walls on either side. The bathroom was at the end of the hall, but before we got to it, we passed two tiny bedrooms on the left side. Each had a nightstand with several bottles of lotion and a woman in a slip sitting on the edge of a bed. I'd say the women were about 25, one had curly hair while the other's was straight. The men sitting next to them were easily twice their age.

"How about you guys put on your clothes and get the fuck out," I said quietly.

I took a peep into the small kitchen that was opposite the second bedroom and saw a cot, which must've been where the old woman slept.

I heard some splashing sounds behind me. I turned to see the little boy run into one of the bedrooms. I followed him.

"Mommy," he said to the woman with straight hair. She looked at me hard, defiant. The man in her room had put on his shoes first and was having trouble slipping his pants on over them.

I went into the bathroom. The toilet looked like a shell after someone had eaten out the soft-boiled egg. I got on my knees and turned off the valve behind the base of the toilet.

Peepshow got there shortly thereafter with a sector car and I put the handcuffed landlord in the back seat.

"Assault and attempted battery of an officer," I said.

"Looks like this guy's all wet," said Peepshow.

"That's not bad. That's actually funny," I said.

"I'm very rich!" said the man from the backseat. He started kicking around a little.

"You keep that up," I said, "and we're going to have to stop and start short a few times, knock your head around. You get me?"

I slammed the back door and sat up front. We headed back to the Five. I thought about calling the vice squad about the pross house, but they probably knew about it already.

Chapter 10

I was waiting at Chatham Square, which is actually shaped
more like a triangle squeezed in by Bowery, East Broadway,
and Catherine Street.

The bank on the northern tip of the triangle used to be a
movie theater with haunted bathrooms on the basement
level. Before the building had even been a movie theater, it
had been a brothel, and both bathrooms were supposedly
haunted by Chinese girls who had hung themselves. When
we were kids, Moy had told me that he'd once been washing
his hands and had seen the ghost of a woman with no face
in he bathroom mirror.

I felt a chill and walked away from the bank to the western
part of the triangle that was overshadowed by a stone
memorial arch for Lt. Benjamin Ralph Kimlau, a Chinese
American who had fought in World War II. The arch didn't
say anything about what had happened, but I had heard
a tour guide say that Kimlau had been piloting a bomber
in the Philippines when the plane took a hit. Kimlau had
ordered all his men to bail out. Kimlau had stayed on to steer
away from civilian homes and had crashed into a river.

Everybody knew that sitting at one of the benches carved
into the memorial would bring bad luck. Only tourists and
foreign Chinese sat there.

The midget came by and slapped my elbow.

"Policeman Chow, you're looking pretty nervous."

"I'm just here to meet a friend."

"Are you working undercover right now? Are you trying to
get a drug dealer?"

"No, no. Nothing like that. We're going to the Latin American Chinese Benevolent Association."

"For dominoes, right?"

"Yes," I said. I was waiting for Yip. After hearing Vandyne complain about me interfering with the case, I'd decided that I couldn't hang out with Yip anymore. I'd tell him not to follow me around, too. He could wave if he saw me from across the street.

It sucked that I had to meet him in order to tell him I wouldn't be hanging out with him anymore.

But a night out in the fancy association building was a big thing for Yip. I personally never liked gambling, even for fun and not money. I felt like I was reinforcing the stereotype of Chinamen who live to press their luck.

"There's nothing good about gambling," said the midget, pulling off his backpack and stretching his arms back.

"You never made any money playing games?" I asked, raising my eyebrows.

"I made some money, but I stopped. It didn't mean anything to me anymore. If you're a good player, you don't need a bet to intimidate your opponent."

"Money's not important to me, either. It's just gambling for kicks in there, not for money."

"Anyway, I know you're going just for the girls in short-shorts!"

"They have girls in short-shorts?" I asked, my voice going up an octave. It had been a while since I'd been to the association.

He pulled his bookbag back on. "Maybe you oughta measure those shorts-shorts, make sure they're legal! Good luck!"

After the midget left, I paced around the triangle and checked my watch. Yip was 20 minutes late. What was the holdup? I untied my shoes and tied them again. I watched pigeons strutting into each other as they took turns holding a piece of bread in their beaks. A tiny sparrow hopped in and flew away with it. But the pigeons didn't chase him. Instead, they rubbed against each other, saying, "Koo, koo, koo."

A few minutes later, Yip stepped onto the triangle.

"Officer Chow! I'm so sorry!" He was panting. "I meant to get here earlier, but I couldn't find my good luck charm."

"Don't worry about it," I said. We walked down to Oliver Street.

"How many times have you been to the Latin American association?" Yip asked.

"Twice," I said. "But I haven't been there since they converted to a club."

Chinese who had come over by way of Cuba, the Dominican Republic, and Mexico had founded the association. Ever since they'd formally converted into a nightclub and bar, they'd been throwing parties like no other association. There were tables of dominoes in the back for older men, but no betting was allowed.

"You any good at dominoes?" asked Yip.

"I only know how to set them up and knock them down."

"Too bad."

"How did you learn?"

"I used to mop floors with Spanish and black guys. We would play on breaks."

"You win most of the time, or is it about half and half?"

"It's never half and half," said Yip, giggling. I could see that he really enjoyed hanging out with me, and it made me sick. "You're either winning or losing most of the time. Maybe you can't tell?"

"I don't gamble enough to tell," I said.

"Every day's a gamble. Everything you do is a gamble. Sometimes you don't know if you won or lost until years later."

What the hell's that supposed to mean, I thought. "What's your good-luck charm?" I asked.

"It's this," he said. Yip pulled out a little charm of a clay pig tied around his neck with a tattered red string.

I was about to ask him if it came from Wah, but I caught myself. The last thing in the world we should have been talking about was his dead wife, especially since we were having a fun night out, our first and last.

"You win when you wear that?" I asked instead.

"I always win when I wear this. Sometimes I have to lose, go home, and then come back to win, but I'm always a winner in the end with this on," Yip said.

"Did you know about the girls who wear short-shorts?"

"Very nice scenery there," he said, giggling some more.

Did he really care that his wife was dead? Do men his age really get any pleasure at watching girls in short-shorts? At least he was happy to have found me, someone in the community who didn't shun him for having a dead wife and being interviewed by the cops about it. It was too bad I had to tell him I couldn't hang out with him anymore.

When we strolled into the association, it was like a new day was beginning. Christmas lights flashed and random neon signs hummed. Reflections sparkled in the glasses and smiling teeth of old men. Everyone was a winner.

I was about to take a seat when Yip pulled me to the dominoes games.

"Maybe you can learn if you watch enough," he said.

The back room was a sea of smoke and dyed black hair. Brown hands with dirty fingernails clawed drinks, table edges, and the backs of chairs. The seat rental fee was $8 to play until you lost, but it included free drinks the whole time.

"There's a seat at the first table," said Yip. "You want to go first?"

"You go ahead. I'm going to wait a little."

A bar was set up in the corner with a little kitchenette to cook noodles and dumplings. Three girls hanging onto their 20s wove around the room in tank tops and sequined short-shorts — one white, one red, one blue.

I stopped the blue girl and asked for a Seven and Seven.

"I'm sorry, I can't..." she started.

So I tried English.

"Where are you sitting?" she asked.

"I'll be standing right here," I said.

"I can't serve you complimentary drinks unless you're at a table."

"I'll take the drink without the compliments," I said.

"Okay, but you have to play soon."

"Tell me why this association hires staff who don't speak Chinese."

"For the record, I am fluent in Mandarin and I know some Cantonese, but it helps to pretend to only speak English. Especially in a room full of old, drunk Chinese men. Cuts down on the lewdness factor."

She went away and I looked over at Yip's dominoes. Looked like Braille to me. The man to his right was wearing a black satin jacket that had a blotchy rabbit head and "PALYBOY" misspelled on it. Must be his lucky jacket. He kept both his hands in his pockets and rocked back and forth.

After a bit, Yip won. He looked around and I waved at him. He lifted both his fists in the air, but he looked sad and weak.

The girl came back with my drink.

"I would have been back sooner, but that guy over there pinched my ass and I spilled my tray."

"You tell your boss?"

"He doesn't care."

I took my drink and threw it down my throat.

"I'm a cop, you know?"

"Sure you are."

"Which guy?"

"The one wearing the suede jacket. Please don't make any trouble."

"This is no trouble at all, sister," I said.

He was at the last table and gave me a sideways glance before winking at the girl. He looked like an extra from an early Golden Harvest movie, the older brother whose death early on had to be avenged.

I went over to him and leaned into his ear.

"You touch that girl?" I asked.

"I touch a lot of girls," he said.

"How about you touch me?"

"I didn't come here to fondle men," he said. "Maybe you did, but I sure didn't."

"I want you to go over there and apologize to her."

"Go do some yo-yo tricks in traffic!"

I reached in and grabbed some of his dominoes.

"You little bastard!" he said, jumping to his feet. He was a little taller. "Give 'em back!"

"Go over and apologize," I said. I looked over, but the girl was gone. Something bounced off my chest. It was the suede-jacket guy's fist, and it was pathetic. Old women who get parking tickets hit harder.

I swung my hip and checked him into the table. He crashed into it and the edge caught him in the gut. From nowhere, two big men in suits surrounded me and grabbed my arms. They pulled me through the association quickly and quietly. They gave me a nice seat on the curb.

Yip came out a few minutes later, his face twisted like he'd had a lemon-pickle drink.

"What happened with you! You ruined my game!" His voice sounded like ice skates sliding on a tin roof.

"Look, I'm sorry, I can pay you back."

"You hurt my luck! You can't pay that back," he said. "Next time, you're paying for all my games."

I stuck my hands in my pockets.

"There isn't going to be a next time, not for a while," I said.

"That's good!" he said. Eight wasted dollars can buy years of resentment in the Chinese community.

"Here's how it stands, Yip. I was going to tell you tonight. I'm a policeman, and you're the subject of an investigation. We can't be friends."

Yip sighed and fingered his little pig. "I see, I see. I was hoping that if I had a Chinese policeman for a friend, everything would go smoother."

"What do you mean?"

"All the other policemen are on the side of the tourists. You're the only one here for us. You're supposed to be on my side."

"That's not true. All the police are on the side of the law."

"The law isn't on my side," said Yip. "I didn't do anything wrong and I get investigated, and now I lose a young friend."

"I'm sorry about this."

"You could change so many things. You could be speaking up for the Chinese people at your police station, explaining what we want."

"What do Chinese people want?"

"They want something more than one policeman who's just a lantern to hang at parties."

"Are you calling me a ..."

Yip interrupted. "Right now the police are wasting time and energy investigating me. An old man whose wife..." He couldn't finish. "I was hoping you could do something for me."

"Yip, I can't talk to you anymore."

He nodded.

—

The Brow had me in his office and motioned for me to close the door. This meeting was going to be about those two teachers in the Chinese New Year parade.

"Are you undisciplined, Mr. Chow?"

"No, sir, I'm not."

"What does discipline mean to you, Mr. Chow?"

"It means doing what I'm told, sir."

"A very good answer, but not quite correct. You're supposed to do what you're told and what you're understood to do. Are we eminently clear on this?"

"Not really, sir."

The Brow stomped his foot and pointed a finger at me that went through my throat.

"You understand that this matter was going to be brought before the Civilian Complaint Review Board before I intervened."

"I stand by my report, sir."

"Now, son, I don't doubt for a moment that those two hippy schoolteachers were troublemakers. No doubt in my mind. But you handled it the wrong way, and unfortunately they were part of a school project for public television. The entire event was recorded on film. But it's not just an oriental police officer that they have on film — it's the entire NYPD. It reflects badly upon all of us."

"I'm sorry about this, sir," I said, feeling like I'd put a baseball through his porch window.

"Well, today's your lucky day. I've got the matter settled. It won't go before the CCRB and there's nothing on your record."

"Thank you, sir."

The Brow chewed on a part of his cheek a bit. "Chow," he said in a tone I'd never heard him use before. "Do you know about our upstate, uh, campus?"

"The Farm, sir?" I asked. The farm was a counseling program where they sent cops for a week or two to dry out, usually after incidents involving drunk, off-duty cops and the destruction of private property.

"Yes, the Farm. I think you should consider a brief evaluation period. You'd still be on salary and, again, there'd be nothing on your record about it."

"I'm okay, sir. I really am."

"On the other hand, I can't make you go. It's strictly voluntary. If I could, I'd put you into alcohol counseling for at least two months. Everyone can use some counseling — you don't have to be a common drunkard. Even I see a counselor every week. I hope, Mr. Chow, that in the future, your personal life doesn't interfere with your duties. Our biggest battle isn't out there. It's in here." He tapped his chest. "Consider yourself dismissed, Mr. Chow."

I nodded and got out. The Brow thought that I had been drunk, and that drinking was why I'd gotten pushy with the tourists. He didn't know that drinking was why I got out of bed.

—

I was standing in front of the locker room's bulletin board when English Sanchez nudged me.

"So I heard you got pretty good legs," he said, wearing a taunting smile. English had maybe 20 pounds on me, tops.

"Yeah, that was some time ago, though," I said. We both looked at the sign detailing the benefit hockey game between the police and the firemen. It was next week and our side was still short on men.

"You skate?" I asked English.

"Yeah."

"They're probably having a tough time signing up guys looking for freelance injuries. Last year, they let high-school kids from the Police Athletic League substitute on the roster."

"That's how you came up, isn't it?" asked English. "Weren't you in PAL when you were a kid?"

"Who told you that?" I asked.

English smiled, which deepened the pockmarks in his face. "I hear things about you, these little interesting things. Like how you were a real bastard on skates."

"I always remembered to give the right amount of change," I said. "I went to the PAL for a few years because there's not much to do in Chinatown but work, study, or get in trouble. PAL was fun, like an extended gym class rather than hanging out with cops."

"Mike Donovan told me you used to sock the other team's goalie when he made a save. And that was in practice."

"He's a captain now, right? I remember Mike. He showed me how to skate backwards."

"He was a captain in the Bronx. He quit to play the stock market."

"How about that," I said.

English kept smiling. It gave me a queer feeling.

"Enough about hockey," I told him. "How about you give me some investigative assignments?"

"C'mon, Chow. Everyone knows you. No one in Chinatown is more conspicuous than you."

"But a bunch of white guys and one black guy in plainclothes is a lot more discreet? None of them speak the language, I might add."

"You might add that, but it doesn't make a difference. Those men are hard-working and they get the job done."

"If you'd just give me a shot, I could really do something for the bureau."

English shifted his stance and tilted his head. "I want you to know, Chow, that when they were laying guys off, we lost a lot of good young men. You know what I mean? They didn't have a record in the military to count towards seniority like you did. And honestly, you're not the most likely to succeed in this house. In fact, I'd be more willing to give investigative assignments to guys with even less experience than you."

I didn't say anything.

"Anyway, you've got a good gig going. Why would you want to give it up? Every day's a party for you! Show up, shake some hands, pose for some pictures, then sit back, hook your thumbs into your belt. You're using the system. Easy, right?"

"Yeah," I said. I turned to go but English put a hand on my shoulder.

"So what did they call you back then?" he asked me. "Donovan said the other kids in the PAL would call you something and you'd go berserk."

"I don't remember."

"Come on, man, tell me. What'd they call you? Something racial?" He stuck his elbow lightly into my ribs.

I didn't say anything. I kept my eyes on the flyer. Practice was tonight at Wollman Rink. I figured I'd go; it would be two free hours of skating.

English was still at it.

"Come on, Chow! What'd they say?" He drilled a fist into my shoulder.

I turned to him slowly. "You don't touch me like that," I said. "Ever."

—

I was a little tired on the subway ride up to the rink, but the smell of sweat on ice got my legs moving again. I skated a lap backwards, which got the boys cheering.

I knew two guys from the academy, but everyone else was on the older and heavier side, and I hadn't seen them before. The coach was Lieutenant George Teeter from the Seven precinct.

"That's real pretty, very pretty, detective. Good speed," he said.

"I'm not a detective," I said.

"You're on track, though, right?"

I felt my stomach quiver like a bagpipe under someone's squeezing armpit. "Wish I was," I said, looking at Teeter and giving a corner smile like a guy trying to cover up bad teeth.

"Well, anyway, excellent job, officer. I'm thinking you're a prime candidate for a right wing. Chow, from the Five precinct, right?"

I looked around at the other blues.

"I don't anyone else who could pass for a Chow, do you?"

Teeter laughed awkwardly.

"I just don't want to presume or assume things. Who knows, you could have been adopted or something."

"I'm going to be doing the adopting. Those firemen are gonna be calling me 'Daddy,'" I said.

"That's the spirit. Good attitude. I like that."

We started with laps around the rink, then shot some pucks

into the empty net. I was getting a decent lift on the puck, but I couldn't pull it as high as I wanted to.

Some of the guys paired off in two's and three's to practice passing. I stepped off the ice to tape my stick again. It was already obvious I could skate figure eights around and between pretty much everyone there.

I stood the stick straight up and held the handle between my feet. I cut the tape off the blade of the stick and peeled off a new roll. I wound it tight like it was a kid's broken leg. Then my hand slipped. The stick slid and clattered a few feet away.

It landed at Teeter's skates. He picked up the stick and walked it over.

"Looks like you need more tape on the handle, too, Chow."

"Yeah, I'm just taking it one step at a time."

Teeter cleared his throat and said, "I understand that your participation in the game may not be ideal in light of a little incident you had over Chinese New Year."

"What?" I said. "That's supposed to be confidential!"

"To the public. Not within the department."

"What does this have to do with playing hockey?"

"Well, naturally, there's nothing wrong with you participating on the surface of it. But families are going to be there, with kids. What would happen if word got out that we had a potentially unstable person playing in the rink?"

"I can't skate in a dipsy-doodle game of hockey, but it's okay for me to walk around with a shield and a gun?"

"You're getting the wrong idea. Think of the PR angle. This is the 10th year we've been playing the firemen. You know who's dropping the puck? Miss New York. It would be a shame if this game were marred by…" He waved his right hand as if trying to shake off a mitten.

I gave the tape a vicious tug and it screamed as it rolled around my stick.

"I'm fine," I said, "and I'm going to score a hat trick, how does that sound?"

He took in a deep breath. It was the sound of better judgment whistling down the elevator shaft.

"Chow, I'm going to level with you. I got a call from someone at the Five who told me I shouldn't let you play. He said you had a history of not being able to control your temper."

"I'm managing to stay pretty calm right now."

"Okay, but anytime you're not feeling good, I want you to let me know. I'm telling you, if I see that things are amiss, I can't in good conscience let you play."

"Who called you from the Five?"

"That's undisclosed. Don't worry about it. I'm giving you a green light. I think you're okay. You're just the guy we needed."

"Thanks, coach," I said.

Teeter smiled. I tossed the tape away and hit the ice again. English must have called Teeter. Motherfucker. I imagined my skates running over his fingers. I scored goals, but held the stick too tightly. There were blisters on my hands at the end of the night. I bit into my skin and drained them.

———

I took Lonnie to a double feature at the Music Palace. The old man must've been away and left his kinds in charge of the theater. They were giving a Steve McQueen double feature: "The Blob" and "Papillon."

We walked by the Graceful Heaven Buddhist Temple on
Bowery on the way up. Not too many people were inside.
I've always held the view that most Chinese don't go to
Buddha unless they're unhealthy or know someone close
who's unhealthy. The solution was always the same: donate
some money.

"Ever go to a Buddhist temple?" I asked Lonnie. Her hand
was around my arm.

"Only once in a while to bow."

"The last time I was in a temple was back in Nam."

"Why did you go?"

"I had a friend who was hurt by a bouncing Betty mine.
He got shrapnel in his legs. I carried him back to a chopper
and they took him away. When I found a temple in Saigon, I
prayed for him."

"What happened to him?"

"I don't know. I never saw him again. His name was Roy.
He said he was going to be a poet when he got back to
the world."

"The world?"

"We called America 'the world' because Vietnam felt
like hell."

"I'm glad you came back."

"Are you crying, Lonnie?"

"I know you're still having a hard time fitting back into
society. I read a story about veterans becoming alcoholics
and drug addicts and criminals!"

"It's all right, you don't have to cry."

We were waiting to cross the street now to the theater.

"Are you sure you want to see these movies?" I asked.

"I do. I've been so busy. We haven't been able to see each other and do things together."

"You're in school. You have to study."

"I can't even go to see your hockey game. I just don't have the time. But maybe that can be another outlet for you."

We got into the theater and got some dried mango strips and popcorn at the concession stand. I walked Lonnie down the aisle as far away from the smoking balcony as possible.

We had some good laughs through "The Blob," but Lonnie had to nudge me awake a few times during "Papillon." Seeing a guy struggling to endure just wasn't that interesting to me.

Chapter 11

I took the subway to Atlantic Avenue in Brooklyn to catch the LIRR line out to Long Island. The game was going to be held at an arena where the Ice Capades practiced. I'd heard that the firemen were in better shape than us, and I wasn't surprised. They cooked their own meals every day while we were basically forced to eat fast food.

But I'd be damned if I was going to get beat by a bunch of hoseboys.

I walked into the locker room with my bag over my shoulder and my stick in my right hand. A bunch of the firemen were changing with us in our locker room.

"What are you guys doing here?" I asked the first guy I didn't know.

"The other room is locked and they can't find the key," said a white guy with curly brown hair and a bushy mustache. He was about six-two, 220. "We just figured we'd share with you guys. If you don't mind."

"Oh, I don't mind," I said, "but we don't have a place for you to plug in your curling iron." The firemen and cops all went, "Whoa!"

"I'm gonna plug you, pal," curly head muttered, pulling on his socks.

"C'mon, I'm only joking. I like men who play with fire."

"What's really not funny is that we save more lives than you guys do," he said, smiling. "You guys are only good for shooting unarmed suspects and taking drug money." The firemen laughed uncomfortably, but none of the cops were smiling.

"Don't you guys have some liquor heirs to kidnap?" I asked.
Last August a fireman had gotten busted for kidnapping
the kid who was going to inherit the Seagram liquor fortune.

Teeter walked in before any of the firemen could respond,
but I could tell from their cold stares that I was a marked
man. Teeter clasped his hands together and addressed
the room.

"I hope all you guys are getting acquainted with each other.
My name's Teeter and I'm the coach for the NYPD. We're not
expecting any rough stuff out there, but there's gonna be
two referees on the ice and that's me and Art Block from the
firefighters. Stand up so the guys can see you, Art."

Who stands up but big and curly? My head felt like I was
in an elevator that was running express down to the
basement. Teeter went on.

"So I want you all to know you're doing a great thing for the
kids, and a lot of them are out there watching. We also got a
few people from *Newsday* who might do a story and a photo,
so look pretty out there. It doesn't matter who scores more
goals. It's the kids who win. Let's have a good game, guys."

Before Teeter dropped the puck, the mayor of the town
made a little speech at center ice about how pleased he was
to host the benefit for the Police Athletic League and some
stupid firefighters organization. Spotty Spot, a Dalmatian
that was the fire-safety mascot, ran around the stands. I'm
sure the kids learned a lot from that.

Then they played "The Star-Spangled Banner." During the
song, I kept an eye on Block. He had his right hand over his
heart. With his left he drew a line through his neck and
then pointed at me.

"Let's go," I mouthed to him.

Miss New York came out and dropped the puck in a

ceremonial face-off. She was wearing an Islanders jersey and sweatpants. The centers half-heartedly dueled for the puck. We won. Then Teeter dropped the puck for the real face-off and the firemen's captain pinned our guy's stick and kicked the puck back to his men with his skate.

The first period went badly for both teams. Some of the mediocre skaters slipped and fell on their own. But once they got their legs going, the firemen were pretty quick. In the interests of not killing ourselves, we were playing three 10-minute periods instead of the standard 20 minutes. Near the end of the first, there was still no score. Then I saw a lane open up for me up the right side.

I jabbed my stick between the legs of a fireman defender to trip him up and ran up the ice with the puck. Nobody could touch me. I drew back and slapped the biscuit home. One-nothing at the end of the first.

When I scored again at the start of the second, the going got tougher for me. I got a few stick butts in the gut and a nice rap on the back of my leg, where there was no padding.

"Hey ref, you saw that!" I yelled at Block.

"I didn't see nothing," he said. Teeter was at the other end of the ice. I bit my lip and kept going. But whenever I saw any firemen coming at me, I put up my elbows up at nose-level.

The crowd came alive. The kids were screaming and even the parents hooted. Now this was hockey. I could feel wind in my face as I went up and down the ice. Having the option to give in to violent impulses at any time freed a primitive instinct in me.

I shoved one guy's face into the glass wall and when he dropped, who was sitting in the stand right there but that punk kid whom I'd given a bloody nose. Only he was cheering for me and pumping his arms. I nodded to him and Teeter came over.

"That's it, Chow. Two minutes in the penalty box for roughing." I couldn't argue. The fireman was clinging to the wall, trying to stand up. As I shuffled off to the penalty box, one of the cops swooped by and yelled, "Should've sent you after Serpico!" I raised one hand in triumph. I stepped off the ice and into the penalty box at the edge of the rink. I picked up a bottle and squirted cold water over my face that made my skin scream.

A few firemen skated by and shouted stuff. I saluted them. Then Block came by, took his fingers and chinked his eyes at me. I looked for Teeter, but of course he was down at the other end again. I swatted my stick at the door to the penalty box. Then I dropped my gloves. I didn't want them to get in the way when I got out of the box.

When my two minutes were up, I skated the length of the ice to get at Block. I grabbed him by the collar and hauled him down, face-first. I threw punches into his back. After a few seconds, the firemen dropped their sticks and slid over. The cops held them back and Teeter pulled me off Block, who looked like he was having a good dream.

"What the hell's wrong with you! This is a benefit game! We've got goddamned kids here!" he screamed.

"He was making faces at me!" I yelled.

"Head for the showers, you're out of the game, Chow!" Teeter said. Skating off the ice, I raised two bare fists as the audience roared. I was a fan favorite.

I sat down in the locker room, my entire body dripping with sweat and melted ice. I was by myself and that was fine by me. I threw off my helmet and screamed. Then I dug into our cooler and started drinking. I was on the fourth beer when the other guys started coming in.

The score was two-nothing when I left and we ended up winning two-one. I got a pat on the back from two police.

A fireman sat down and stuck his face at me. He was a white male with black hair, five-nine, 180.

"You got a serious problem," he told me.

"Yeah, something ugly next to me wants a few punches in the face."

"My son and daughter are out there. What am I going to tell them after the game? How am I going to explain why some crazy cop out there was pummeling the ref?"

"You tell them that the Chinese people have stood up," I said.

Block was waiting for me to leave before coming into the locker room. I saw him in the hallway on my way out and blew him a kiss.

Teeter came over to me. "I'm not against having a physical presence," he said, sounding like he was on sedatives, "But you were just out of line. I couldn't let that go."

"But we won because of me," I said.

"There are more important things than winning."

"What kind of sports fan are you?"

Teeter shook his head and rubbed his stomach. "God, I hope those fights looked staged."

"Fights?"

"After I took you out, a fireman took a shot at me."

"Did you throw him out, too?" Teeter nodded.

"He went straight to his car — he didn't want to be in the same locker room as you."

"Those hoseboys are all cowards when it comes down to

it. They'd rather face a fire than another man because fires don't hit back."

"Hell of a game," said Teeter, shaking his head. "Hey, you came on the train, right? You want a ride back to Manhattan? We still got room in the bus. I think the PAL kids would get a thrill out of riding with you."

"Yeah, that would be great."

We walked over to the bus, which was a half-sized job, the kind for disabled kids.

Only one seat was left. I tossed in my bag and my stick and dropped next to the punk kid.

"Since when have you been with the Police Athletic League?"

"For about two years," he said. "Nobody else I knew had bats and mitts for softball."

"Hey, speak English! This is America," joked Teeter, but we ignored him.

"I saw what that guy did," said the kid.

"Which guy?"

"The guy who did the thing with his eyes."

"Yeah."

"I'm glad you hit him."

"Me, too. Sometimes it's right to hit people."

"It wasn't right for you to hit me."

"I never hit you! I just shook you."

"Maybe you hit me by accident, but you still hit me."

"Okay, I'm sorry if I hit you. But I didn't, so..." I looked out the window. Long Island was a blur of highway lights and roadside garbage. "When I look at you, I see someone who's throwing away their life."

"I'm not throwing anything away."

"Listen to me. I was hanging out with the wrong crowd when I was your age." Then dropping my voice I asked, "You ever hear of the Continentals?"

"No."

"Yeah? Well, we were the biggest gang in Chinatown."

"I've never heard of it."

"Anyway, we were a bunch of tough guys just like you and your friends. Back in those days we had to fight Spanish and Italian kids."

"Then you should know it's easier to be in a gang than not to be in one. If you're going to get beat up anyway, you might as well have some people on your side."

"That just means you're going to be doing even more fighting. They'll get two more guys and you'll get three more. Someone gets popped. Then what?"

He shrugged.

"Listen," I said. "You keep loitering around, the best thing that can happen is you ruin your posture. Just go home and stay there."

"I'm hanging out in the street because I don't get along with my parents."

"What's going on?" I asked, rubbing my calves and thinking I really should work out regularly. I was going to be hurting tomorrow.

"They throw me out of the house."

"For what?"

"Don't know. They think they're still in Hong Kong."

"What's that supposed to mean?"

"They think that if I'm not studying 24 hours a day, that I'm not studying at all. I tell them school is easy for me, but they just yell at me and lock me out of the apartment."

"You must have done something to them. They wouldn't kick you out for nothing."

"Look at this," he said. He pulled down his shirt collar and showed me slashes on his shoulder. "That's from a belt."

"I'm sorry it's like this," I told him. "You should see a counselor at school."

"I did. They told me I had to learn to communicate with my parents."

"That's it?"

"Yeah, you know, they only deal with more serious problems, like sex abuse or drugs."

Someone tapped me on the shoulder. I turned and saw a little boy with dark blond hair.

"What are you speaking?" he asked.

"It's Chinese."

"Are you from China?"

"No."

There was an awkward moment before the kid spoke again.

"Oh. I just wanted to say that you were really great tonight. You were my favorite player."

"Thanks, kid."

"Where did you learn to skate?"

"I first learned right here through the PAL and then I skated at Wollman Rink when I was in the academy.

"You smell like beer," the little boy said.

"You get to drink beer when you're a winner," I said. Then I turned back to the punk kid.

"I'm sorry, I never got your name."

"Paul."

"My name's Robert."

"Yeah, I know."

"You have to look at it this way, Paul. The way you dress and the people you hang out with, everyone thinks you're trying to be a hood. What kind of life are you going to have?"

"I look like this because I'm tough and angry and I want everyone to know."

"If you were really tough and angry, you wouldn't try so hard to look like it. No wonder you keep getting thrown out of the house. You know, if you ever came by my apartment, I'd frisk you before I'd let you in."

"I don't carry weapons. My mind is my weapon."

"Bruce Lee tell you that? Because your mind didn't help you when I gave you that bloody nose."

"You know my parents yelled at me when they saw me bloodied up? They thought that I'd done something wrong. My parents will never understand me."

"Well, that's true, but it's something you have to learn to live with."

"Do you talk to your parents?"

"I don't talk to my father because he's dead," I said. We

slowed to get off an exit ramp and I slid slightly into Paul as we made the turn. "My mother, I talk to sometimes."

"That's too bad about your dad."

"It is. But a man's gotta do what a man's gotta do."

"What do you mean?"

"You'll find out soon enough." I sat back in my seat and settled into my sore body.

—

I lifted the smoked-plastic lid to my turntable and put on Marvin Gaye's *What's Going On*. I played it at least once a week. Every time I listened to that record, and I've had it for years, I would hear some lyrics I hadn't known were there.

Suddenly, the record skipped during "Mercy, Mercy Me."

I put a dime on the needle. Then I tried a penny, a nickel, a quarter, and then two quarters. The record still skipped. One little skip ruins an entire album in my book.

I tried a hair dryer and a dry toothbrush. I even ran the sharp end of a thumbtack over it. Nothing worked. I played that groove over and over, just to see if I could get used to it, but hearing that skip physically hurt me.

I turned off the stereo. Then I got a beer and sat on the couch. Then I got another. And another.

I heard a door slam in the apartment building. Then nothing.

I picked up the PBA newsletter and looked at the pictures. I folded it into a plane, then crumpled it up and threw it into the trash.

I tried the record again and it skipped.

I grabbed the basketball and rolled it around the coffee table with my feet.

I opened up the freezer and looked at the ice-cream bar.

I drank a glass of water.

I tapped my fingers on the coffee table and scratched my face.

I stretched my back and legs.

I tried the record again. No dice.

I turned the TV on and off.

I went back to the freezer, got the ice-cream bar, and ate it.

Then the buzzer rang.

I stuck my head out the window and looked down. There was no one down there.

"Hey!" I yelled. Someone backed out from the apartment doorway and looked up. It was Paul. "What are you doing here?"

"You have to let me in," he yelled up.

"Kid, it's late. Shouldn't you be out somewhere, smoking and drinking?"

"Let me in!"

"I'll let you in, but I'm going to frisk you."

"I'm not carrying anything! Buzz me in!"

"The buzzer's broken, just push it open!" I suddenly realized that that was the wrong thing to be shouting into the street after midnight.

Soon there was a knock at my door.

I looked through the keyhole and opened the door.

"You got up those stairs pretty quick," I said. "Must have strong legs. Now spread 'em."

"I don't have anything," he said, but complied.

"If I knew you were coming," I said, patting him down, "I would have told you to bring some beer."

"You've been drinking enough," said Paul, brushing my dirty fingerprints off his jeans.

"Now you wanna tell me what the hell you're doing here?"

"They threw me out of the house again."

"Surprise, surprise."

"At least I took the old man's cigs."

"And what else?" He hooked both hands into his front pockets.

"Nothing."

"How much did you take?"

Paul rolled his eyes. "Twenty," he said. "But it was my money! I won the winter science fair and they took it from me."

"What are you gonna do with 20 dollars, anyway?"

He shrugged. "I don't know. Keep my pockets warm."

"What's this?" I asked, dangling a note with a sticker on it. Paul turned red and his eyes bulged. "Those jeans of yours leave a lot of room for pickpockets."

I read the note. It was from a girl named Lei. She said she liked him. Paul wasn't talking. He was barely breathing.

"Lose your tongue?" I asked.

"Give it back!" he said.

"Who's Lei?" I asked, handing the note back to him.

"She's a girl."

"She's not one of the girls running with you and your friends?"

"I don't have any friends anymore. Ever since they saw you beat me up, they don't talk to me anymore."

"I didn't beat you up."

"My nose was bleeding."

"That's because you were too excited."

"I could sue you."

"For what?"

"Assault and battery."

"You'd be a real credible witness, Paul."

"That doesn't mean I don't have civil rights."

"I'm gonna give you the right to remain silent and also the right to get the hell out of my apartment."

"I don't have anywhere else to go."

"I'm sure there's some nice park out in Brooklyn that ain't too crowded. . ."

"My sister Lonnie said I could stay with you."

"What! You're Lonnie's brother?"

"She said you said I could stay here."

"I said you could stay here," I said to myself. I suddenly felt tired. I went over to the apartment door and slid the door chain into place. I waved my hand at the couch. "You can sleep over there, Paul."

"Thank you. You're not going to regret this."

"But I already do. Where's your stuff?"

"I'll go get it when they're gone in the daytime. I only need two dresser drawers." I became a little suspicious of him.

"Paul, what was that science project you did?"

"It was about plasmids." He looked into my unblinking face. "Do you know what a plasmid is?"

"Sure, it's when a star turns into a black hole."

Paul gave a short, smug chuckle.

"Well," I said, "good night. Get some rest." I went down the hallway.

"Um, do I have to go through the bedroom to get to

the bathroom?"

"Yeah."

Paul pushed past me. "Excuse me," he said, "I have to brush my teeth."

—

The next morning, I felt good when I saw Lonnie back at the counter at Martha's.

"They give you a hard time about coming back?" I asked her as she gathered up my two iced coffees. I didn't eat in the mornings anymore. Two beers at home would fill me up.

Lonnie smiled.

"They gave me a raise. Paul is staying with you, right?"

"Your brother."

"He's actually my stepbrother. Did you know that after my mother went to San Francisco, other girls stopped playing with me because my parents had split?"

"But it wasn't too bad for your father."

"Is it ever bad for the father? He got married again and they had Paul."

"Your father beats Paul."

Lonnie shook her head. "It's my stepmother who beats Paul. But you beat Paul, too. You gave him a bloody nose."

"I didn't touch his damned nose. That kid's got bad capillaries."

Lonnie sighed. "I guess everything's okay, now. You know, he's never had a strong male figure who really cared about him."

"So you figured he could just move in with me?"

"You said he should!"

I propped my arms up onto the counter. "Can you explain to me why he just got thrown out of the house?"

"I told you already. He's got a girlfriend. But my stepmother doesn't want him to have a girlfriend until he goes to college."

"That kid's bound for stripes, not college."

"He gets straight A's in school."

"Are you kidding me?"

"He's really smart. Everything comes really easy to him."

"Then why is he hanging out with those delinquents?"

"They're not delinquents! They're all really smart kids. I let them hang out here to keep them off the streets and away from the bad kids."

"Those kids are in a gang."

"You were in a gang."

"It was different back then. It was more like a club that didn't have a tree house. Kids are getting killed these days."

"Paul and his friends are just trying to look tough so they don't get picked on. You know kids."

"I know I don't like them."

"Lonnie," growled Dori, "when you keep talking to the customers, you leave more work for me."

"I'm not just a customer, I'm a regular," I said.

"A regular cradle robber," said Dori.

"Shut up, Dori! You can't have kids so you won't have to worry about cradle robbers!" yelled Lonnie. It was the first time Lonnie had ever snapped back, and the sharpness of it tore across the filthy and busted foam tiles of the ceiling all the way to the front door, where an old man was standing, uncertain if he should come in or run for it.

Dori screwed her mouth up and pounded the counter once.

"No respect!" she cried. Then she went into the back, kicked aside an empty plastic bucket, and went into the bathroom.

Lonnie wiped her forehead and said, "Hey, come on! Who's next?"

—

When my shift was over and I got back into street clothes, I went down to the park to see the midget. Some fool tourist was playing him at a board game I didn't know.

"Why are your hands all black?" the midget asked me.

"I had to replace the ribbon in my typewriter. Stupid thing tried to eat my hand. What game is that?" I asked him.

"The game's called Sorry!" said the midget. "It was released by Parker Brothers in 1934, a year before they acquired the rights to Monopoly."

"I heard of Monopoly, but not Sorry!" I said. "How do you know so much about this game?"

"I read it off the side of the box. Basically, you have to get these pieces around the board and into the space marked 'Home.'"

"Hey, no outside help!" said the tourist. He was a white male in his mid-30s, five-seven, 180, brown eyes and hair.

"Calm down, he's just explaining how to play to me. I haven't seen this game before," I said.

"I'm a lifelong Sorry! player," the tourist said. "I heard there was a little guy in the Chinatown park who'd never lost at any game, so I came down all the way from Boston to check him out."

"You ever lose at this game?" I asked the tourist.

"A few times, but honestly, it's hard just finding people to play with."

"You must've been a lonely kid," I said. He gave me a dirty look. The midget fiddled with the pieces on the board.

"Hey," the tourist told the midget, "you're supposed to say 'Sorry' when you do that!"

"I'm not sorry," mumbled the midget.

"I'm reading these rules," I said, "and it doesn't say anywhere where that you have to say 'Sorry.'"

"Well, even if it isn't a rule, it's a common courtesy."

"This guy's getting in a bad mood because he's losing," the midget said to me.

"Hey, while we play I want to impose an English-only policy, okay?" said the tourist. "Just so you don't cheat this white devil."

Okay, my friend, the midget said in English, I'm sorry. Then all of us laughed. Then the midget won, and went on to beat the guy two more times. Each game was shorter than the previous one.

After we were alone, I asked the midget if he'd known that Paul was Lonnie's brother.

"Oh yeah, I knew."

"Why didn't you tell me?"

"I thought you knew, too."

"How could I know?"

"How could everyone else know?"

"You heard I had a run-in with Paul, right?"

"Yeah, but I guess you guys patched it up. You're living together now, right?"

"I didn't know the details of my life were public information."

"It's not public," said the midget. "Very few people know about it."

Chapter 12

Willie Gee came up to me and flashed a wicked smile.

"Thanks for taking care of that hunger striker the other day," he said. "Maybe you can just pull out one protestor every day. That's a good strategy. I really underestimated you. You're the kind who likes to work with discretion."

We were standing on a corner around the block from the restaurant, out of view of the protest.

"I didn't pull her out of the strike for you or for Jade Palace," I said in a way that cleared my throat at the same time. "I knew the girl and was concerned about her health. I didn't think the hunger strike was good for her."

"That's how I feel, too," said Willie, trying to wrinkle his face into something that resembled concern. "I'm worried about the well-being of those hunger strikers. I want to invite them inside to have a good hot meal. No hard feelings. Can you tell them that? If they end this silliness right now, they can come inside for a full banquet. Free! We're all Chinese here. Chinese people don't let other Chinese people starve."

"Willie, the State Attorney is filing charges against your restaurant. A freebie meal for the protesters isn't going to change that."

"Officer Robert, can you please tell me what the fuss is all about? We don't force anyone to work here. If some of the waitstaff and busboys don't like it, there are hundreds of other restaurants they can go to. If they don't like the wages we pay, let them find better jobs somewhere else. We don't pay minimum wage, because the tips make up the difference. That's perfectly legal, you know that."

"If you're abiding by the law, you've got nothing to worry

about. The truth will come out in court. But right now, I have some people to see and you're in my way." I side-stepped him and went on.

"Let me tell you something, officer," said Willie as he grabbed for my elbow and missed. He tried to follow me. The sidewalk was so choked with tourists it would be nearly impossible for him to stay on my tail.

"Willie, get back to your office and stop bothering me," I said over my shoulder. I doubled back and headed to the restaurant, hoping he'd follow me and I could ditch him there.

"That lawsuit is without merit and when the charges are dropped, I'm going to stand up..." Willie was cut off by a group of Germans, but he managed to make up lost ground by walking in the street and coming around a parked Firebird. "I'm going to stand up at the next community board meeting and demand to know why our police force stood by while our business was harassed."

"You don't like the job I'm doing, go file a complaint against me."

"You got a lot of nerve. I was a part of the group that lobbied to get a Chinese policeman on the force years ago. You owe your job to me."

"I've got news for you, Willie. You're not getting a cut of my tips." I was amazed at his ability to stay within talking distance of me. Must've been a talent developed from walking through a crowded dining area.

"I don't take money from anyone. I only provide for other people. God is on my side."

I didn't say anything. I walked straight, looking for an oncoming a baby stroller that I could wedge between me and Willie. As we got closer to the restaurant, I noticed a minor ruckus going on at the entrance.

Three protesters were trying to pull customers away from Jade Palace's doors. The hired muscleman stood before them, his two fists at his hips. His bulging muscles pulled his suit so tight it looked shiny.

"Can I hit 'em? Can I hit 'em?" he asked when he saw me.

I held up my hand and walked up to the protestors.

"Lay off, all right?" I said to the protestors. "You can't touch anyone who wants to go in. Respect their rights like you want respect for your right to free speech." I freed the diners and they scurried up the steps into the restaurant.

"This officer is here to arrest you for disturbing the peace," said Willie, who walked up and stood in front of me, one index finger raised as if he could pick someone for me to cuff.

"I'm here to enforce the law," I said. "Now get out of the picket area or I'll help you get out," I said to Willie.

Less than a dozen protesters were left, including the two hunger strikers. The protest had lost momentum after the State Attorney's charges against the restaurant had been announced; most people figured that the court would sort things out. The remaining protestors wanted to hurt Jade Palace's revenue for as long as possible.

The big man came down the steps and stood on the sidewalk, his arms crossed.

"Hey stupid, get out of there!" Willie yelled at him. "You want to scare off all the customers? Get back inside!" He shrugged and trudged back up. Willie turned to me and said, "Remember, officer, I tried to be nice."

"And you failed," I said.

—

Lonnie had some books to read and papers to write so I stopped by the Hong Kong supermarket for some beer and Japanese rice crackers.

"Rangers are playing tonight, huh?" the girl at the counter said to me.

"Oh, yeah," I said, handing her a ten. She held the bill up to the light and rubbed her fingers hard against the paper to see if it felt greasy. "Can't trust a cop?" I asked her.

"I don't trust anyone who drinks like you," she said.

I thought about that on the way home. It actually hurt.

Back at the apartment, Paul was cooking something.

"I didn't know you could turn on more than one burner at a time," I said.

"This was probably the cleanest stovetop I've ever seen."

"I'm a clean person."

"With a filthy bathroom."

"It doesn't look that bad." I popped open a beer.

"I've been cleaning it at least an hour every day! It's slow progress, too."

"No wonder it's been smelling like chemicals."

"You ought to smell what it's like when you're on your knees, scrubbing."

"You'd have a really hard time paying half the rent, Paul."

"OK, OK," he said. He took out some dry spaghetti and broke it in half before putting it into the boiling water. He was also browning some meat. "Do you want some spaghetti?"

"No, thanks. I'm not that hungry."

"You're just going to drink beer and eat rice crackers?"

"Who are you? Mr. Four Food Groups?"

"You're probably an alcoholic, Robert." He turned to look at me. "You don't even have milk or orange juice in your refrigerator."

"Paul, you're only an alcoholic if you have more than 21 drinks a week. I usually have less than 20 and I'm bigger than the average person."

"If you're trying to count drinks to figure out what you can get away with, you have a problem. You even drink in the morning. That's not normal."

"I have the hardest job in the world, okay? You don't even know what it's like to work for a living."

"You want me to get a job. Fine, I can get a job. But let's not change the subject. I learned about alcoholism in school last year. If you're an alcoholic, there's no such thing as a drink at the end of the day, or a casual drink. You have to stop drinking entirely."

"Maybe I should stop eating everything, too. Everything causes cancer, you know."

"They showed us this film about an alcoholic, and you're like the guy in it. He hid bottles in the pockets of coats in the closet and under the sink. He even thought about drinking his wife's shampoo because it had some beer in it. He counted his drinks, too, but he didn't count the ones he hid."

"Of course they don't count," I said. "They're like bonus drinks. You get extra points for finding them."

"I found them and I didn't get any extra points."

"Stay the fuck out of my stuff!" I yelled.

Paul turned back to the stove.

"I'm sorry I yelled at you," I said.

"That's okay," said Paul. "I have to live with it. It's better than home." After a while, he got his dinner together and sat as far away from me as possible on the couch.

"Don't forget," he said, "I need money if you want me to buy more groceries and cleaning supplies."

"Hey, Paul, I want to see those receipts."

"You don't trust me? You can just add up what's in the refrigerator."

"I'm bad at math. You might be sneaking Baby Ruths on the side."

"What about the charge for my labor? It's not easy lugging shopping bags back from the store. I cook for you sometimes, too."

"You know how much it would cost for you to live alone?"

"The midget told me that where he lives in Queens it's really cheap."

"Don't talk about the midget. He's smarter than both of us."

"I'm pretty smart," said Paul. "I'm the school valedictorian, so far."

"You still have two years to go."

"What were you?"

"I was in the top median."

"You were a C student. Don't forget that everything's a lot harder now than it was when you were in high school."

"What do you mean? We never had science films. It's easier to learn now. It's not as hard as it used to be."

"You talk like an old man. I can't believe my sister's in love with you."

I sat up and stretched out my back.

"She talks about me, huh?"

"All the time."

"What does she like about me?"

"She says you're hard-working and you always look tired in the morning."

"What else does she say about me?"

Paul twirled his fork and stuffed his mouth. He shook his head the entire time he chewed. When he was done, he said, "Women always love guys who need a lot of fixing."

"I'm in pretty good shape."

"What are you going to do with my sister?"

"What do you mean?"

"Are you going to marry her?"

Beer almost went up my nose.

"It doesn't make sense to rush into anything now," I said.

"I've been good about disappearing when you need the apartment some nights."

"Sure you have."

"You've been sleeping with Lonnie."

"Yeah, I have. We're both adults."

"She's not 21 yet."

"She's over the age of consent."

"Hey. You went to hookers in Vietnam didn't you?" Paul asked.

"I did."

"What were they like?"

"Young. Skinny."

"Younger than my sister?"

I didn't say anything.

"C'mon, tell me!"

"I don't want to fucking talk about this, Paul. You want to talk about girls, let's talk about movie actresses."

"Like who?"

"Like, I don't know, like that woman in the Bruce Lee movies, Nora Miao."

"She's ugly," he said, bringing his dishes to the sink.

"Have some of these rice crackers," I told him.

"No thanks. I'm going out."

"Don't stay out too late." When he was gone, I thought, Where the hell is he going? It's close to 2200. I snapped on the TV and the Rangers were down three-zip in the second period.

That called for a drink.

Later, the Rangers came back and tied it up in the third.

That called for another drink.

Then the goal posts got loose and held up play. That called for another drink. I got up to go to the bathroom and accidentally kicked a can under the couch. I'd have to take care of that later. I leaned against the wall for support and rubbed my head.

—

When I opened my eyes, I was back on the couch again. It was morning and time to hit the shower. I struggled up and got through the bedroom.

"I'm surprised you got up," said Paul. He was propped up in my bed, reading a book. "I was gonna wake you up in a few minutes."

"You slept on my bed?"

"You wouldn't get up off the couch. You kept saying something about a can under the couch."

"I have to get moving, Paul. Hey, aren't you supposed to be in school?"

"It's Flag Day."

"Flag Day?" But I didn't have time to argue. I showered and dressed quickly. Luckily there was still one beer in the fridge. I drank it on the first landing and left the can where someone had kicked out a baluster.

—

English Sanchez came by my desk.

"I'm sure you heard about Vandyne's promotion," he said.

"Yeah, I'm real happy for him," I said.

"I wanted to tell you that unlike you, he's not a head case."

"I'm a head case?"

"The problem is, you got to thinking that you deserve special privileges because you're a minority. Some of us around here don't care about color because we have serious work to do. And let's face it — you can't handle serious work. You might get hurt."

"I don't want anything special. I just want to be treated like everyone else," I said. "This is the main precinct of Chinatown, and you got no Chinese detectives."

"Your language skills would be an asset to the squad. But that's where the positives end. Don't think it's your race holding you back. The fact is that I made it and so did Vandyne. If anything you have the stereotype in your favor. Charlie Chan and his Chan Clan were pretty good oriental detectives."

"Don't give me that stereotypical crap!"

"See, you're too confrontational to work on a team. Anyway, there are no more open slots."

"When does one open?"

"It opens when it opens," said English brushing imaginary crumbs from his shirt. "Now about the murder case, the old Chinese woman, it's not a murder anymore. You can go pal around with that old Yippie, or whatever his name is."

"What happened?"

"I don't have time to explain. Ask Vandyne about it. He solved it."

—

I met Vandyne at a tea house before his shift began. His mouth was full of hot tea, so I asked, "Was it ruled suicide?" He made a painful face as he swallowed hard.

"Not even that. The poison in Wah's blood was traced to cans of preserved bamboo shoots from Hong Kong."

"When did they find this out?"

"I picked up a few food items from Yip's refrigerator. The

opened can was still wrapped with cellophane. There was lead in it. I might have saved Yip's life by taking it away."

"Lead! I can't believe that."

"I can. You see those cans of food in Chinatown? They don't have expiration dates on them. Hell, they don't even list ingredients or provide cooking directions. Who knows when and where they were made?"

"Don't even start with that. That's racist, you know?" I said, with a nagging feeling that those cans were probably tainted as hell.

"No, it's looking out for my health. That's what it is."

"That comes from the same people who think they have cut-up cat in the dumplings. Or rat sauce in the lo mein."

"It's based on fact. Are there lower standards of living in Asia? Yes. Is food from those countries — even in cans — less healthy to eat? Yes."

"Are most Americans overweight? Yes. Are most Americans leading unhealthy lives? Yes. Americans don't eat healthier than Asians, they just eat more. Let's stick to the facts."

"Okay. There was lead in the can of bamboo shoots. Wah ate them. She died. Those are the facts."

"That's what really happened?"

"It is," said Vandyne. "Got a congratulation from English for it."

"That man suffers from a case of anti-Asian hate. He's still sore about losing the Vietnam War."

"English isn't about hate at all. He's an appeaser. He's a schmoozer. Someday, he's going to be the C.O. of the Five."

"That'll be a sad, sad day."

"You know that day is coming," said Vandyne.

—

Yip was waiting for me on the sidewalk outside of the Five.

"Hello, officer, I was wondering if you were free now?" he asked.

"Yip, how's the leg?"

"No more cane anymore, much better."

"Well, I was going to stop by the supermarket. I'm running out of food." And beer.

"Let me take you out. It's my pleasure. I'm so happy to have my old friend back. The black man told me everything's okay again. You have to eat anyway and you can shop another night, too." His old hand gently dangled on my shoulder. "I'm so glad you did something about my case."

"I didn't do anything, Yip," I said. I didn't necessarily want to hang out with Yip again, now that I could. The old man took his hand off me and walked just ahead.

"I know you can't officially say you helped me, but I appreciate it all the same. Say, would you mind if we went to a little store first? I want to check in at this coin and stamp store."

"Coins and stamps? I didn't know you were a collector, Yip."

"I'm not really a collector, it's just a hobby for me. There used to be so many stores selling Chinese coins and American coins, but now there's just one left. Run by a Korean man. His Chinese is very good."

The store was about 10 feet wide and was little more than a single display case with a glass counter and an outside steel gate to roll down and lock.

The Korean nodded his head and said nothing when he saw Yip. Tarnished faces on the silver coins on the top shelf of the display case stared at the fluorescent light on the left side. A bin of post-marked stamps sat at the bottom of the case like a collection of colorful, dead butterflies.

The Korean was also selling regular bank notes that had a lot of eights in the serial numbers. Chinese believe that eight is a lucky number because it sounds like "luck" in Chinese. Chinese believe in a lot of stupid things, which is why the Korean could sell the "lucky" bills for twice their face value.

"Did your father get you interested in hobbies when you were young?" Yip asked.

"He showed me a racing form once and let me pick some horses."

"I think it's important to have a hobby. It makes you a more-rounded person. If you pursue an interest, it helps you to keep some perspective in life." Then to the Korean Yip asked, "Do you have that book?"

The Korean nodded and pulled out three thin cardboard sleeves. He put a staple through them. Then he took out some tweezers, picked some stamps from the display case, and stuffed them into a glassine envelope. He handed everything over to Yip. "Two dollars," he said in Cantonese.

Yip paid him and we left.

"This is for you, Officer Chow," he said. "It's a present."

I took the cardboard and stamps. I knew from years of accepting presents I didn't like or want that it was best to show outright gratitude and then dump them in the garbage later.

"Thanks so much, Yip."

"These are stamps from all over the world, not just China. You can look them up in a book at the library and find out all about them. There's a whole world you can hold here in your hand. Then you have the book to preserve them."

"Wow, that sounds great," I said. "Thank you, again."

I stuck the envelope into the cardboard book, which I turned over and over in my hands.

"Tell you what, Yip. You'll have to allow me to buy dinner."

"You're younger than me, I would have no shame if I allowed that to happen! Besides, I asked you out for dinner."

He was steering me to a popular Shanghai restaurant when we ran into Wang, the fortune-teller and liquor-store salesman.

"Wang, how are you doing? How's the liquor store?" I asked.

Wang shook his head. "Didn't pan out. Business slowed so they let me go." He looked at Yip and nodded his head.

"Hello, sir."

"Hello," said Yip, shifting uncomfortably.

"Wang, this is Yip, an old friend."

"Yes, we've met, right?" said Wang.

"I don't think so," said Yip.

"Well, we're about to go to dinner. Would you like to come?" I asked.

"I have to get back home," said Wang. "Some other time. I'll see you later." He nodded and left.

We walked on and Yip picked up the pace.

"You two seem to know each other," I said. "Did you guys

have some sort of argument?"

"It's just that, you know, I don't respect someone like him. I know him. He's never had a steady job and he's very irresponsible. I wouldn't be surprised to see him collecting cans and bottles. I don't want to associate with his kind. No self-respect."

I was getting fed up with Yip. Not only was he a drag to be around, but he was a jerk to other people, too. People I liked.

My mind raced as I put my hands in my pockets. There's got to be a way I can get out of having dinner with this guy, I thought. I could fake a stomachache or a headache. A migraine.

"You know, officer," Yip said slowly, "the black man said they cremated my wife's body. I complained to the translator that nobody had even told me. But the translator said that this way, I wouldn't have to pay for anything. Otherwise, it would have been a lot of money for a burial."

"That's terrible, Yip," I said. "Are you going to keep her ashes?"

"No. They're going to find a place for her ashes in one of the city plots. It's probably best that way."

I felt bad for this lonely old man and that made it too late to try to get away from him.

We went on to the restaurant and the food was great, but I couldn't help but grind my teeth all the way through it.

—

I was getting ready to go on the 0000-to-0800 shift, but Paul wasn't around to cook something for me. Where the hell could that punk be? I couldn't really get on his case, though. He had done my taxes way before the deadline and had gotten me a pretty big refund.

I jogged over to Market Street by the Manhattan Bridge
overpass. There's a restaurant there that I like with no
English name that's built into the southern trestle. Outside,
crumpled paper and soot collects around the doorframe.
Inside, the low rumble of traffic feels comforting, as if you
were in a hidden chamber behind a waterfall. The sun never
made it in, but at around 2000 the streetlamps would shine
into the windows and everything inside would turn yellow.
It was nice.

The three square tables in the tiny dining room had uneven
legs. You had to eat with your elbows on the table or slip a
folded newspaper down there to even things out.

Tourists weren't welcome or even tolerated. The only
English in the joint was the "Thank You" printed at the
bottom of your check. There weren't any menus, only a list
of a few dishes written in marker taped to the walls and the
front windows. They might also have some specials that
your waiter might tell you about if you didn't piss him off.

I climbed the three uneven concrete steps into the
restaurant and slouched into a chair by the doorway to the
kitchen. My watch said 2012. Chi, the cook whose apron had
given me nightmares, came out looking mad. Then he saw
me and smiled.

"Oh, it's you, Officer Chow! When I heard the door, I thought
those foreign Chinese had come back."

"What are you talking about?" I asked. He came over and
put a dented metal pot of hot tea in front of me. A few
seconds later, he slid a scratched ceramic cup by the pot.

"Hah, a group of foreign Chinese came in with their devil
friends, acting like they owned this place. They couldn't
even speak Chinese."

"What's so bad about not speaking Chinese? A lot of the kids don't learn Chinese these days."

"It's disrespectful to our people. When they look in the mirror, do they see an American or a Chinese? Who do they think they are? Also, they were making fun of me to their devil friends."

"What did they say?"

"I know when people are laughing at me." Chi crossed his arms.

"But you should take it as a compliment that they want to eat your food. At least they like genuine Chinese food."

"I made them go across the street, down to Long Life Noodles." That noodle place had become hot after it had been reviewed in the *New York Times*. It had been praised for being authentic while accommodating the Western palate. But the menu priced out anyone who actually lived or worked in Chinatown.

"They're making a lot of money over there," I said, pointing out the window. A line of tourists snaked out from the stone lion in front of Long Life Noodles — even though the dinner rush was long over.

"Their food, that's what those foreign Chinese deserve. They don't deserve to eat here. They can eat that garbage."

"It got reviewed in the *Times*. It must be pretty good." That made Chi mad.

"Those motherfuckers don't know what Chinese food is supposed to be like. Let me tell you something, officer. These recipes I use were developed by cooks on the battlefield who fed hundreds of thousands of soldiers. For most of those men, it was their last meal. You know how many millions of Chinese died over the centuries eating the same food? Do those foreign Chinese think they're better than those soldiers?"

I didn't say anything because this was obviously a burning issue for Chi, even though I didn't buy the storyline. I poured some tea and nodded my head.

He went on, "Some people don't have respect for all those men who died." He went over to the front window and lifted a piece of paper that had "snakehead fish" written on it to get a better view of Long Life Noodles. "Some people are whores, and their parents are whores," he muttered. "Their grandparents are whores, too. That stupid fake-Chinese restaurant even uses broccoli!" Then he crossed his arms and spat in the corner.

"Say, can I get the beef tendons and snow-pea sprouts?" I asked.

"Yeah, I got some of that," he said and moved reluctantly into the kitchen. From the back he yelled out, "Hey do you want some congealed pig blood? It's fresh and there's lots of iron in it. Good for you!"

"No, not today," I yelled back.

In a little bit, a bowl of rice came out with plates of translucent strips of flesh and sautéed sprouts.

He sat down at the table with me.

"You're not closing soon, are you?" I asked. He waved his hands.

"No just taking a break. When the late shift is over at the garment factories, more people are going to come in. How're the sprouts?"

"Pretty good, very fresh."

"Not too much sand is there? It's tough to wash out."

"It's good. Real good. Very clean."

"How come you never come in with the black man anymore?"

"We used to be partners, but we got split up. Actually, he just got promoted."

"I like him. He's always very respectful of Chinese culture. Very quiet. Much better than the foreign Chinese. I see him in the park playing chess with the midget, too."

"He's getting better, too. Someday, he might be the first person to beat the midget."

Chi laughed and then folded the bottom of his apron over.

"So officer," he said. "Tell me what you're working on now. What kind of cases are you investigating?"

"Nothing. No cases. I'm not a detective," I said. I pushed my elbows onto the table and leaned on them. "I'm just the face the police send around the neighborhood for public relations."

"Ha! I heard you were looking into the old woman who died. I heard it was food poisoning."

"It wasn't my case, and it's closed, anyway."

"What do you mean, not your case? Aren't you a policeman?"

"It's not my area."

"Chinese people aren't your area? Then why are you here?"

I didn't know if he meant in his restaurant, in Chinatown, or on the planet. I just kept eating.

Chapter 13

Thursday night I came in and found Paul sitting on the couch, his face in his hands.

"Come on, it can't be that bad, champ," I said. I was holding a paper bag with a Hungry Man dinner in it, and I was the hungry man — too hungry to risk coming home with nothing if Paul wasn't there to cook for me. I wanted to pop it into the oven right away, but I felt that I had to cheer up Paul first.

"Paul, I would've brought some ice cream if I knew you were having it tough. Girl let you down?"

Paul raised his head. He was squeezing his nose shut with his two hands. There was dried blood on his neck. One eye was swollen. He wiped his upper lip, checking for blood. There was a dark band on his forehead that looked like it had been made by a crowbar.

"Who the fuck did this?" I said.

"Couple of guys," he said. It didn't sound like any teeth were missing.

"Tell me who they were!"

"You don't know them."

"Why'd they do this?"

"Because of you."

"Because of me?"

"Some of my old friends jumped me because they thought I'd given them up to you. Cops were taking Polaroids of them while they were playing handball in the park. They said Vandyne was one of the cops."

"I've got nothing to do with that. That's the detective bureau. They're trying to keep track of juvenile delinquents." Problem was, all the bad apples looked like all the other kids. You couldn't tell by the way they dressed or how they acted.

"They didn't do anything wrong," he said.

"Look what they did to you! Nice friends there, Paul."

"This isn't too bad. Anyway, I think they'll leave me alone now."

"How do you know they won't come after you again?"

"They have other things to do."

"Lemme show you something," I said. I ripped a small piece of cardboard from an empty box of corn flakes I'd been meaning to throw out. I folded it into a tiny wad. "Put this between your teeth and your top lip and press down on it. It blocks the blood vessels to the nose."

"I'm not putting that thing in my mouth. They teach us in school to squeeze our nose shut."

"This works in combat conditions," I said. He took the cardboard and stuck it under his lip. "You get bloody noses in school a lot?"

"You gave me the last one," Paul said glumly.

"I'm sorry. That was before we were friends."

He shifted the other hand onto his nose. "We're friends?"

"Sure we are."

"Then let me tell you something. I hate being smart."

"What?"

"I hate being smart! I fucking hate it!"

"You're lucky, Paul! You know how many people are born stupid?"

"I wish I were stupid. And strong. Smart doesn't mean anything here."

"Paul, you can go to college and really make something of yourself."

"How am I going to pay the tuition? I'm going to end up at some stupid community college like Lonnie!"

"Don't call it stupid! A lot of really great people went through community college!"

"You didn't even go to college, right?"

"I was too stupid to go to college. I ended up getting drafted."

"How did you get stuck in Chinatown?"

"I'm not stuck in Chinatown!"

"If you had a choice, you wouldn't be here, would you? If you weren't a cop and you had money and a good job, you'd be living uptown. You'd only come in for dim sum on the weekends."

"Aw, bullshit, man!"

"Did you choose Chinatown, or were you assigned here?"

"I was assigned. You can't choose where you want to go."

"Out of all the precincts in the city, why were you assigned to the one with one of the lowest rates of crime? Because you're Chinese. The police are using you as a token yellow face."

The kid had taken potshots at me before, but now, saying it straight out without trying to give me grief, he had put it to me hard. It took me a little while to think of something to say.

"If I wasn't here, where would you be, Paul? Out on the street, that's where. Maybe even dead."

Paul took his hand away from his nose.

"I wish I were dead," he said. Paul tried breathing through his nose a little to see if the blood flow had stopped.

"You're talking stupid, you know that? You get straight A's in school and you wish were dead. You're young and smart. You know how many people would love to switch places with you?"

"So I should be happy I'm alive?"

"You're damn right."

"What's so good about living in Chinatown?"

"It's not the greatest place in the world, all right? But you're here for the short term, so make the best of it for now. Take a lesson from your elders. Old people are happy here because they don't have to go more than a few blocks for food, groceries, laundry, or the park."

"What if you're not old?"

"Well, then you got the library, you can do more reading. There's going to be another mural painting this summer. You can do that. You know that Bruce Lee mural by the N and R stop?"

"Yeah?"

"They did that a few years ago, isn't that cool?"

Paul sat back a little bit and crossed his arms. "You yourself ended up in a gang because there was nothing to do here," he said.

"It was different back then, Paul. Kids weren't popping each other."

"Nothing really matters if I can't get out, anyway," he muttered to the floor.

"You hungry, Paul?"

"Sorry, I couldn't cook anything. I couldn't get my nose to stop bleeding."

"That's all right, I wasn't counting on it. I already ate. I brought this Hungry Man dinner for you."

For the first time, his face brightened. "Really? I've never had a TV dinner before."

"It's the best one, the fried-chicken one. Lemme stick it in the oven for you."

"Wait for my nose to dry."

"I'm gonna do it now. It takes like 45 minutes to bake." I set the oven, ripped the entire foil top off the dinner, and put it in. "I'm going to take a shower now, you need the bathroom?"

"No, I'm okay."

I went into the bedroom, opened my sock drawer, and found two bottles of Bud near the back. I drank the warm beer as fast as I could and then I hid the empty bottles back in with my socks.

—

The next day, I saw Vandyne hanging out in the park, away from where the midget played games.

"Let me ask you something, Vandyne."

"Go ahead. I ain't stopping you."

"Paul tells me you were one of the guys taking pictures of kids on the handball court."

Vandyne rocked on his feet and took a deep breath.

"You know I don't like it, but there doesn't seem to be an alternative."

"Where does the bureau file those pictures?"

"We keep them in mug books for suspected Chinese gang youth. Only we're not allowed to call them 'mug books.'"

"I think I'd call them a civil-rights violation."

"It's necessary because of the system. When a lady in Chinatown gets her purse stolen, she doesn't know how to describe the suspect sufficiently."

"What do you mean?"

"She says it's a short Chinese youth with black hair and black eyes. They all look like that. We can't look for someone based on that. The police artists can't do anything with that, and besides, they only know how to draw blacks and Hispanics."

"So basically, it's okay to consider all the Chinese kids as suspects?"

"It's not okay, but it has to do."

"How would you feel if I was up in Harlem taking pictures of black kids?"

"That's been going on, partner. We're talking years."

I looked out across the park. Nothing was happening.

"Look, Chow. You think I don't know what the average Chinese person thinks about me and my people?"

"You know what the average black thinks about Chinese people?"

"Well, get this. I had a toothache — this was while you and I were partners. I didn't tell you about this, because I didn't want you to think I was accusing you indirectly. But anyway, I went into this Chinese pharmacy, thinking I could get some relief. I'm looking through the oral-care section, and what did I find? A tube of toothpaste called 'Darkie.'"

That was the one thing in Chinatown that I had hoped Vandyne would never find.

"You know that toothpaste, 'Darkie'? Got the black-faced minstrel with the white smile on it?"

"Yeah, I know it."

"My point is that. . ." Vandyne trailed off. "Hey, you know, I know there are four major ethnic Chinese groups in Chinatown: Cantonese, Toisanese, Hakka, and Fukienese. I don't know what they're saying, but I can tell the difference between the dialects. I can even play an okay game of Chinese chess. I went pretty far to learn about Chinese culture. But when they see me, I mean, I'm the first black person they've seen up close and personal. The only thing they know about blacks is, well, the negative media. Black guy did this. Black guy did that. But if I conduct myself in a professional and upstanding manner, as a policeman should, it will give them something positive to see. Just seeing a black man living amongst them changes how people think. You yourself told me you never had a black friend until the Nam."

"My company was about 60% black. Everybody treated each other black. The Asians, the Mexicans, the Hawaiians, and the whites. We all hugged each other, threw dice in a box, flew the black flag. We were an all-black company. We just didn't look it."

"So that makes you black, huh?"

"Look, who are you to be talking like this? You eat Chinese

food. You've developed a taste for Chinese cigarettes, which are going to kill you, by the way. You're standing here in Chinatown talking with a Chinese guy. What's that make you? I think your eyes are getting more slanty every day."

"You mean like this?" he asked, pushing up the ends of his eyebrows.

"No, push them higher."

"This far enough?"

"Yeah. Now you know how I look to black people."

"Hey, come on, now!" said Vandyne as he dropped his hands to his sides.

"I'm tellin' it like it is."

"Not all black people are like that."

"And not all Chinese people are racist. Just a minority."

"Minority racists? That's the situation exactly. Minorities who are racists."

"Why let the white people have all the fun, huh?"

"This is an ongoing discussion, Chow," said Vandyne, transitioning into a thoughtful mode.

Some older people came into the park and dumped out a bag of mahjong tiles on an empty table. All four of them reached in and stirred the tiles around noisily.

"I had a nightmare last night," I told Vandyne.

"Oh, yeah?"

"Yeah. I think it was because I didn't eat dinner. I dreamt that I was lying in my bed. The room looked normal, but I knew that everything was booby-trapped. I had to get down on the floor and start feeling around for tripwires in the rug.

I was crawling around, touching every corner on every leg of the dresser. Then I had to check out my shoelaces, because if you pulled on them too hard, your shoe would blow up and you'd have a stump where the ankle was."

Vandyne made a scoffing sound and shook his head.

"Then I got really scared that someone would call and the phone would blow up. So I crawled over on the floor and unplugged the phone line from the jack — real careful of course. I went ahead and unplugged the lamp, my alarm clock, I mean everything that had a cord. I'm thinking, what else could be booby-trapped? Naturally, the doorknob to the bedroom. As I was looking at it, it started to turn."

"And then, 'Boom!'?"

"No, it was Paul. He came in to use the bathroom and he found me crawling around on the floor."

"Paul? Oh, Lonnie's brother. Yeah, the midget told me he was staying with you. That's good because now you got someone to check on you on a regular basis. Anyway, you were really on the floor?"

"Yeah, I was."

"Maybe it wasn't a nightmare. Maybe you were having a flashback."

"What's the difference?"

"One is if you're sleeping. But the other is if you're getting delusional."

"I don't know which one it was, but it felt good on the floor. It felt safe. Safer than the bed."

"Hmm. You know, I never have the slow, paranoid, look-out-for-the-booby-trap dreams. What I experience are the fighting and shooting sequences. I have this recurring thing happening to me."

"What is it?" I asked.

"I have this nightmare that that little boy in that hollow tree comes after me. He's smiling and laughing, and he's holding this little knife. He finds me and cuts a slice in my leg. Then he sticks his hands into the wound and crawls into my body. He crawls up my leg and he's hacking away at my organs. He's hollowing me out the same way he did the tree. I can feel him inside and hear him laughing.

"When he crawls into my heart, he puts his arms in my arms and makes me pick up a machine gun. He makes me start shooting. He puts his head in my head and makes me laugh. I'm shooting up my wife, my whole neighborhood. I mean everything. I always wake up screaming from that one."

"Have this nightmare often?"

"About once a month. But I had it two days in a row this week." Vandyne sighed. "It's bad."

I blew into my hands and rubbed them.

—

I ran into Wang by the Manhattan Bridge overpass on East Broadway. He was selling cellophane-wrapped baked goods out of a shopping cart along with several other older women and men.

"Those are some nice rice cakes in there," I pointed out.

"Hello, officer, they're good today. The red-bean ones are very sweet, maybe too sweet for adults. Try the cakes with black-bean filling. Eight for a dollar."

"Hey, what's wrong with them?"

He laughed. "The only thing wrong is that nobody's eating them now."

I gave him a dollar. "They're not fattening, right?" I asked.

"No, there's no meat, how could it be fattening?" Wang shook open a crumpled plastic bag and dropped a package of rice cakes into it.

"Wang, did you know that man I was with the other day? The old man, Yip?"

"Yeah, I do. I was selling used appliances at this repair store run by a handyman from Hong Kong who would buy things from the Salvation Army and fix them up."

"Did Yip buy something from you?"

"We had things like radios, TVs and some 8-track players. He picked up this coffee grinder and thought it was a food processor. I showed him some of the food processors we had, but he still wanted the coffee grinder because it was cheaper. I told him it was a final sale, because there isn't much demand for them with Chinese people. Next day, that bastard brought it back! Screamed until I gave him his money back!"

"It wasn't working?"

Wang screwed up his face.

"It worked fine. He'd gotten all these pieces of eggshell in it, too. It was a mess."

"Eggshells?"

"Old people eat them for their bones."

"How long ago was this?"

"Just in December. Early December." That was a few weeks before Yip's wife had died.

"Thanks, Wang."

"No, thank you, officer. Would you like some crispy honey noodles, too? They're very good."

"I can't. I'm on a diet."

"A diet?" Wang howled. "Diet for what?"

—

I went to a pay phone and called Yip. He answered on the third ring and I asked if I could drop by. Fifteen minutes later, I was huffing up his stairs. He greeted me in a rumpled shirt and permanent-press slacks. A kettle was gurgling. Spots on the wall by the stove showed where paint had blistered and broken off.

A somber picture of Wah sat on the windowsill above the sink. A dish with a whole peeled orange sat in front of the picture and was reflected in the frame's glass.

I turned to the kitchen table.

"Those are very nice," I said, as Yip set two ornate cups on the table. Dragons and phoenixes leered at the drinker from around the handles.

"Special gift from Lily," he said. "She sent them from China."

"How did she manage to get in?" Because the U.S. didn't officially recognize the country, there were no direct flights. Nixon could visit China at will, but for a regular American it was impossible to get a visa to go to China. For an ethnic Chinese who had been corrupted by American capitalist ways, it was even tougher.

"Lily has the connections in Hong Kong to get her through."

"Good for her," I said. "Yip, I'm actually more in the mood for coffee."

"Are you sure? I have some very good black tea."

"Coffee would be best for me."

"I only have instant, I don't have ground. Is that okay?"

"Sure. Oh, I brought some rice cakes, too. Black bean."

"Perfect. My favorite," he said. "Sit down, sit down!"

I took a seat and lifted one of the teacups. "Heavy," I said.

"Best kind of ceramic," said Yip, "keeps the tea warm even without a lid." He brought over a jar of Pathmark instant coffee and put it on the table. "You take sugar or milk?"

"Black is fine."

Yip poured the hot water into each of our cups. He dropped into his cup a small handful of dried black leaves curled lengthwise that looked like tiny twigs. I twisted the lid off the glass coffee jar and shook some of it into my cup.

"How are you enjoying the book of stamps?" Yip asked.

"Oh, it's really nice. Thanks so much." I was using the book for a coaster, the last time I saw it.

"If you keep studying the stamps, they'll provide a lot of enjoyment in the long run. I still have stamps my father gave me when I was very young."

"I have to study them some more, I guess." I took a tentative sip from my cup. It was stale. "I didn't know you only drank instant coffee," I said.

"What do you mean?" he said, taking a full swig of his scalding hot tea and biting into a rice cake.

"Do you remember that man we ran into? The one you don't respect? He told me he sold you a coffee grinder."

"That coffee grinder," Yip spat. "That thing was broken! He

cheated me! That man's a thief!" What would Yip do if he knew where the rice cakes were from?

"Yip, you don't even have a coffee machine," I said, looking around the opened cabinets above the sink.

"I was buying it for a present," said Yip, finishing a rice cake.

I picked up a rice cake and popped the entire thing in my mouth.

"Is Wang a friend of yours?" asked Yip.

I mushed the glutinous snack around with my tongue, which was as close to chewing it as I could come. I couldn't talk, so I only nodded.

"I guess that as an officer, you have to associate with some criminal types."

I drank some coffee and felt it dissolve away some rice cake, freeing up my jaw.

"Everyone's a criminal. Everybody's guilty of something," I said. "You're guilty of trying to be my father."

Yip chuckled. "Maybe I am, but that's not a crime."

"Yes it is."

"Officer Chow, what are you guilty of?"

"Seeing things only in black and white."

I only stayed about 15 minutes, but before I left, I promised Yip I'd see him for dinner the following week.

I thought about his strange explanation for the coffee grinder. Chinese people don't give each other second-hand appliances for gifts. They give that traditional standby Chinese gift of Danish butter cookies in a blue tin, or liquor that the recipients put on the shelf and never touch.

In my house, the liquor never even made it to the shelf.

A bottle placed in my hands was as good as empty.

—

From now on, I thought as I leaned forward and practically willed myself up the stairs of my building, I should do less drinking in bars. I don't even like to talk to people when I drink, so why not stay home? Turning the key in my lock was more difficult than remembering my gym locker combination from sixth grade. The door suddenly swung open.

"Where have you been?" asked Paul.

"I was in the park. I had to collect some evidence," I said.

"I have to tell you something," he said cautiously.

I felt a flare of heat down my neck. "Shut up about me," I grunted. "You've got problems, too."

"It's not about your drinking," said Paul, raising both his hands. "This really big guy in a suit was here looking for you about two hours ago!"

"Was it that guy from Jade Palace?"

"I don't know."

"What did he want?"

"He said he wanted to talk to you."

"About what?"

"I'm not sure, but he was pretty worked up. He said he'd be back later."

"It's 2300 right now. Sorry, 11 o'clock for you, son. When was he planning on coming over?"

Paul shrugged. "Anytime he feels like it. He's a big man.

Anyway, I'm going out now. I wanted to tell you in person because you never read notes when I leave them for you."

"I don't like your handwriting," I said. "Hey, where are you going now?"

Paul slipped off for the bathroom. "Just hanging out."

"Hanging out? Where, and doing what at this time of night?"

"I don't know yet!"

"When are you going to get a job? You know, that's one of the conditions of you living here."

"I'm going out right now to type up my resumé."

I heard the bathroom sink go on. I put a pot of water on the stove. It was going to be an instant-ramen-noodle night.

"Hey, did you see the mouthwash anywhere?" Paul called to me from down the hallway.

"Naw, I didn't."

"It was right here in the. . .hey, here's the bottle in the garbage! What did you do, drink it or something?"

"Yeah, I might have drunk it," I said. I looked at the calm surface of the water in the pot and turned the heat higher.

"That's disgusting. You know, I got that mainly for you to use."

"What are you complaining about? I used it."

—

About half an hour after the kid left, someone knocked at my door. I picked up my hammer and held it over my head as I went to the door.

"Yeah?" I said.

"Officer Chow, hey open up, I wanna talk."

"Willie Gee send you?"

"He didn't send me nowhere! I'm coming over on my own. I want to tell you something about that old woman who was poisoned."

I stuck the hammer under a couch cushion and opened the door. The Jade Palace brute was wearing a denim jacket, jeans, and a baseball cap. A pair of shades completed his disguise.

"You're not fooling anyone," I said. "I could recognize you from the other side of Shea Stadium."

"I ain't trying to hide. This is how I wanna dress. You gotta minute?"

"You just want to talk? Why didn't you call?"

"I don't carry change for the public phones." He smiled. "I only got big bills."

After I let him in, I asked, "What did you want to tell me?"

"With me being at the front of Jade Palace all the time, sometimes I get propositions from people. They think that because I'm big and all, I can handle problems. For the most part I can. I got one rule, though; I don't physically harm nobody."

"Sure," I said.

"You know Willie Gee wanted me to crack some skulls of those protestors? You know that?"

"I can guess."

"Well, anyway, a couple months ago was a woman who came up to me asking if I could handle someone. She shows me a picture of this old woman, and I was like, 'You need me to take care of her? A boy scout with a sore throat could handle her.'

"She says, 'This woman's been making trouble upstairs in the restaurant.'

"'Look, lady,' I says, 'I don't do that kind of thing. You want me to deliver a warning, that's what I do.'

"'She's already been warned. We have to take the next step,' she says.

"'That's not me, lady,' I says. 'You're asking the footwear department about bedding.'

"Then she tries to play it off as a joke and scampers off. I didn't think nothing about it until I saw the picture again in the Taiwan paper. Said she was poisoned by a bum food can."

"Who was the woman you talked to?" I asked.

"I don't know her name, but she works at Jade Palace and I saw you with her and that old man at one of the coffee shops."

"You mean Lily?"

"I guess. You were having coffee in a booth."

"Where were you? I couldn't have missed you in a small place like that."

He smiled and adjusted the shades on his face. "Oh, I was way over in the back," he said.

"Why are you telling me about this now?"

"Jesus, I didn't know the lady was dead until I saw her picture in the paper. Were you were one of the detectives on the case?"

"No, I'm not. I wasn't. Anyway, the case is closed. It's over."

"I thought I'd just let you know what I knew. Before I left town."

"Why are you trying to help me?"

"I have a natural instinct for doing what's right. Call me a sucker. In any case, you won't see me for a while."

"Where are you going?" I asked.

"Up to Canada. I'm tired of working for that fucking prick."

"Good for you. Where in Canada you headed?"

"Aw, it's a big country, I'll find somewhere," he said. "I'm taking a train tonight." He shoved his hands in his front pockets. I could hear the seams in his pants scream.

"You used to be a cop, right?" I asked him.

"In a time and place far, far away," he said.

Chapter 14

"Still have time to meet with the little people?" I asked Vandyne as he settled into the booth. We were at my favorite Szechuan restaurant.

"Oh, yeah, always time for you. This is the place that has a section with Chairman Mao's favorite dishes, right?"

"You bet. Chicken and potatoes got your name on it."

"That's good. They don't have iced coffee here, do they?"

I shook my head.

The waiter came over and I ordered for us. I said to Vandyne, "So I understand you talked to Wang."

Vandyne nodded and bit his lip. "Talked to him. He's working at a hardware store now called 'Good Lock.'"

"He told you about the coffee grinder, right?"

"He did, but buying and returning a coffee grinder isn't a crime."

"Something's funny with it. I just don't know what."

"The key to solving a murder, if it is a murder, is to find the motive. That's the most direct path between the killer and the victim."

"I guess I'm not privy to the kind of training you get," I said.

Vandyne shifted in his seat. "Hey, come on, now. We're both on the same side. We solve crimes."

The chicken-and-potatoes dish swooped in and landed on our table. The scent of hot chili jabbed at the soft roofs of our mouths.

"You have to exercise better judgment," Vandyne said,

licking some sauce that had spilled onto his thumb.

"What are you getting at?"

"Well, look at Wang for instance. Maybe you know him well and all, but you also have to realize that any information he has is limited in its usefulness. He's a guy who drifts from job to job, probably doesn't pay taxes, and probably isn't a legal immigrant."

"Even if he isn't legal, that doesn't mean he can't testify."

"That's true, but from what I understood from the translator, Wang doesn't have any records of the sale. He can't prove he sold Yip anything. It's going to be his word against Yip's."

"Yip could be getting away with murder."

"What is with you, anyway? You were tight with him before and now that he's been cleared, you want to hang the guy. I think you might be displacing issues with your father onto Yip."

A vegetable dish came in and clinked plates with the chicken and potatoes. Two bowls of rice landed on the table with dull thumps.

"I'm not displacing anything. I think there's something funny about Yip, but apparently the NYPD doesn't care enough about this old woman Wah to make a more thorough investigation."

"Hold on, Chow. You're saying that I didn't care or that I didn't do a good job on it."

"Well, I understand you're doing a pretty good job of taking photos of youth who are suspected of being Chinese."

"You don't have a monopoly on race grievances, Chow. At

least Chinese kids don't get physically harassed by the cops, like our kids do." He took a bite and chewed while I didn't say anything. "Okay. It's all bad. But I still think you're wrong on Yip."

"What if I get him to come in and make an admission of guilt? How about that? Would that reopen the case?"

"If you can get that done, we'll throw the book at him and it would make English consider you for investigative assignments."

"You think?"

"That's what this is really about isn't it? It's about the detective track?"

"It's about getting the job done," I said.

"That sounds like a damned lie. Now, you asked me here to eat, and if you don't eat already, you really are a liar."

I tilted the entree dishes and scraped food onto my empty plate with my chopsticks.

"What are you working on now?" I asked.

"I thought I'd be shadowing gang bosses with this new Asian gang unit, but for now they just have me taking more Polaroids of kids in the playgrounds. English said some bigger things were going to happen real soon, but it hasn't come yet. The biggest challenge I have now is keeping those kids in focus when they move."

"You want more challenge? Try living with a troubled but gifted teenage boy."

"I'm glad you're showing some responsibility by taking Paul in. Interesting way to get in good with his sister. How's it going with Lonnie, by the way?"

"Smoothly."

"Well, all right. Paul isn't getting too much in your hair, now, is he?"

"I told him he had to get a job to stay in my apartment."

"Taking care of you and your place must be a job in itself. The midget told me Paul even cleaned your bathroom. He bought the cleansers and everything."

"My apartment isn't a dump."

"Your bathroom had to be in pretty bad shape if a teen-age boy felt the urge to clean it up. Must have been gunk all over."

I set my chopsticks aside. "Please, Vandyne," I said, "I'm eating."

"I'm sorry. Say, I need a favor from you, Chow."

"What is it?"

"I need to get a collector's stamp at the post office."

"What's the problem?"

"I didn't have time to go to the post office today and I'm not going to tomorrow, either. This is for a nephew on Rose's side. He's a little stamp collector."

"You want me to go for you tomorrow? It's a swing day for me."

"Aw, man, you're a life saver. Okay. It's the 13-cent Telephone Centennial Commemorative Stamp. It has something about Alexander Graham Bell on it. It should come on a souvenir page stamped for the first day of issue. Unless it's sold out."

"You owe me one, now."

"I sure do. Man, thanks. Hey, I'm eating everything. Don't like the food or something?"

"Naw, I've just been cutting back." We left it at that.

—

Chinatown has two post offices. One was in the district controlled by businessmen loyal to the KMT in Taiwan. The other was on East Broadway, in the part of town controlled by businessmen loyal to the communists.

The KMT had been established in Chinatown ever since Sun Yat Sen himself had set up an office on Mott to solicit money to topple China's Manchu rulers. KMT money went into a huge community center that ran Chinese school classes on Saturdays, set up lion dances, and generated anti-communist propaganda.

The center also provided translation services for letters, since all mail was required by law to be addressed in English in addition to the Chinese. The younger people could handle the English, but not the older people. Early in the mornings, elderly Chinese clutching onion-skin envelopes would be lined up at the center.

The post office in KMT Chinatown on Doyers usually became crowded as old people ambled in with their newly addressed mail. Sometimes you'd see a bent-over man leaning on someone younger for support. It was heartwarming.

The communist community center was younger than the KMT one, but it was so bogged down with immigration cases that there were no letter-translating services. The problem was that the KMT center refused to address mail ultimately destined for China although they would make an exception for Hong Kong, which was under British control.

The post office in communist Chinatown on East Broadway

was about twice as big as the one in KMT Chinatown, and luckily it had two large desks in the back. For a few hours a day, a man would sit there, writing out addresses in English. That man was Moy's dad, and he'd been at it for about 20 years.

—

When I got the East Broadway post office, people were lined up to see Moy's dad, who was sitting at a side table on a seat that folded out from a metal walking cane and formed a stool. He was addressing envelopes, filling out international mail forms, and sometimes even writing letters. People paid him five cents, no matter what services they needed. When they were done, they waited in another line for the clerk windows.

I stood in line for a clerk and waved to Moy's dad, but he was stooped over and intently writing.

"Old Moy," someone was asking him, "Have I gotten a letter from my mother?"

"I already checked my post-office box," Moy's dad said without even looking up. "Nothing for you."

"It's just that she's very old, I'm a little worried. It's been some time, now."

"There was nothing for you! Now please, there are other people here to see me." Moy's dad waved the man away. He caught sight of me and nodded his head once. Then he toyed with his glasses and put his head back down.

I looked down at the piece of scrap paper in my hand. "Souvenir page of the 13-cent Telephone Centennial Commemorative Stamp." I had written it down because I didn't want to get some other commemorative stamp by mistake.

When I got to a window, I looked at the stamp that was mounted on a presentation page. The main design was a line drawing that looked like bad abstract art.

"You're the first to ask for one of these in a while, mack," said the clerk.

"No wonder," I said. "They're so ugly."

Then I went to Martha's to see Lonnie. It was amazing how the dynamic had changed ever since Lonnie had stood up to Dori that day. Lonnie was behind the counter mixing up hot batches of Horlicks and Ovaltine — British drink mixes that a lot of Hong Kongers had grown up drinking and now were hooked on. The batches were going to be chilled overnight and served cold.

Dori was dejectedly pushing a mop around. Moy was in a seat by the garbage can, reading a newspaper.

"Hi, Lonnie," I said, putting my arms up on the counter.

"Robert, how are you?"

I looked over at Moy. He put his hand up and I nodded my head at him. We didn't do lunch on Mondays anymore. Funny how people change when they get girlfriends. Dori didn't bother to look at me.

"Robert, I'm worried that you've been losing a lot of weight."

"That would make most women happy, Lonnie."

"Weren't you the one forcing me to eat before?"

"That was a state of emergency. I'm doing fine."

"You never take the pastries with your coffee anymore."

"I don't need them. They keep my body from absorbing the coffee."

"OK, Robert."

"What do you mean, OK?"

"Hey, I have to study tonight, but let's go out after my exams next week."

"All right with me."

———

I wasn't hungry exactly, but I felt like I should eat to keep Lonnie happy. I didn't want to stop at any of the food carts or go into a restaurant, so I stopped at the Hong Kong market and picked up a frozen dinner that bragged about having "Half a Pound of Meat!" I picked up another one, too.

When I got back to the apartment, Paul was there, on the phone.

"Um hm," he'd say into the phone every few seconds.

I took a butter knife and cut the foil from around the potatoes. I popped both trays into the oven and set the heat to 400. I opened the fridge. Paul had been out grocery shopping. I reached around a bag of apples for a beer.

"Um hm, okay. Bye," Paul said into the phone. I put my beer down and slapped him lightly on the shoulder.

"Hey! What was that for?" he yowled, rubbing himself.

"That's for not saying you love her," I said. I waited a few seconds and then I smacked him again.

"Now what!"

"That's for not hitting me back." I went back to the beer.

"Keep punching me and I won't be able to carry the groceries up all those stairs. I don't think you've ever eaten fruit in your life, have you?"

"There's fruit in the TV dinner. Tomato sauce. Tomato's a fruit, not a vegetable. You know that?" I put the empty bottle behind the kitchen garbage can that Paul had bought.

"Wow!" Paul mocked. "Tomatoes are fruit? You must be a nutritionist!"

"Hey, Paul, don't get like that with me. I'm cooking tonight. Sit down and relax." I went over to the couch.

"Those TV dinners don't taste very good."

"You can eat whatever and whenever you want."

"You're lucky I don't drink your beer."

"No — you're lucky you don't drink my beer. Speaking of which, would you grab me another one?" He went to the fridge and passed it over. "Thanks."

"Your problem only gets worse the more you ignore it."

I checked my watch. "My only problem is that I gotta wait 45 minutes to eat."

"I'm going to boil some frozen dumplings, instead. They only take about 10 minutes. I can make some for you, too."

"Naw, I'm good," I said, popping the beer open. "Since you're forcing me to eat two TV dinners, the least you could do is tell me more about the girl."

"Nothing to say," said Paul, who was fishing a pot out from under the sink.

"This the girl you had the note from, right? Lei?"

"Yeah."

"Jesus, you really don't wanna talk about it."

"Nothing to say."

"How old is she?"

"Fourteen."

"What's she doing with you?"

"She likes me."

"When do you see her?"

He shrugged. "Sometimes."

"You bring her to the movies?"

"Don't have enough money."

"Get a damn job."

"I'm working on it, I told you."

"Then get me another beer."

"That was the last one." I pulled off my shoes.

"You don't want to do me another favor, do you?"

"I'm not going to buy you some beer. That's what you get for hitting me."

"C'mon, we're just being guys here. Like how friends slap each other around."

"I'm not going. I have to watch this pot." I went over to the window and looked down into the street. I was feeling hot and the window was closed. The one that was supposed to be left slightly open at all times.

"The problem with you, kid," I said, fiddling with the window latch, "is that you lack respect for your elders."

—

Paul went out to wherever he goes and I threw my foil trays into the garbage and the fork into the sink. At about 0100 I put my shoes on and went to a Spanish place to get a six-pack of Bud. You can't be too choosy at that time of night. All the places in Chinatown that sold beer were already closed.

I was going to head back to the apartment, but then I got worried Paul might walk back in and give me more shit about drinking. He should really just shut up. I decided to find someplace else to go.

I headed to Seward Park. Lotsa benches and trees to hide behind. City parks were supposed to close at dusk and drinking is never legal there at any time, but I could be alone.

I found a bench mostly hidden by the branches of an overgrown maple tree. It smelled like rotten leaves, but the seat was dry and I took it. I popped open a beer. I felt happy.

I poured the first one down and it felt so cold and honest, it was like God breathing life into me. The second one was even better. I became aware that I was making loud slurping noises. I could hear sounds from my drinking echoing back from the chipped wall of the handball court.

I got up and went to the park's men's room. The door was locked, so I kicked it in.

I was washing my hands when I heard something rustling in one of the stalls. I approached the stall door with caution and swung it open slowly. On the floor was a pigeon. He seemed dazed.

I picked him up and carried him outside. By the light of the park lamps, the filmy coat of grease on his feathers reflected every color of the rainbow, red and purple in particular. I put him down by a bush and he winked at me. I went back into the bathroom to wash my hands all over again. When I came out, he was gone.

I left the park and braced myself against a streetlight. I looked up and saw a sign that read, "Littering is filthy &

selfish so don't do it!"

I didn't want to be filthy.

I didn't want to be selfish.

I couldn't remember if I had thrown my empties into the garbage. I swung back into the park to check, but somehow I ended up on the path for home.

—

The next morning the Brow wanted to see me. I walked into his office, put my hands in my pockets, and coughed. He was sitting, with the back of his chair swiveled to me.

"Hello, sir. You wanted to see me?" I asked.

"Ah, yes. Mr. Chow. Have yourself a seat." He turned around slowly. A pipe wriggled in his mouth. "Do you smoke?"

"No, I don't, sir."

The Brow nodded. He struck a match on the sole of his shoe and lit the pipe. He blew out the match and dropped it into a wastebasket filled with paper.

"We've got a problem on our hands, Mr. Chow. There's this older Chinese gentleman who's been operating a bit of a business in the post office on East Broadway. It's something we can't have."

"Sir, I think I know who you're talking about. He just helps people address envelopes in English."

"There's no need for him to be there. There are already a number of community agencies that provide that service."

"But none of them will address mail destined for the People's Republic, sir. They only send mail to Hong Kong and Taiwan."

The Brow took a good hard puff and said out the side of his mouth, "Are you a postman, now, Mr. Chow? Or are you a policeman?"

"Sir, this man is providing a service to the community. He's not hurting anyone."

"This man is conducting business on federal property. He takes nickels."

"He's been there since the 1950s, sir, why do we have to remove him now?"

A grinding sound came from the Brow's clenched mouth. One eye clamped shut and the brow went up.

"Listen, mister, I don't care if he's been doing it for five minutes or a hundred years. We're putting an end to it now."

"Sir, this action is going to be bad for the community. It's going to alienate everyone aligned with the People's Republic."

The Brow stomped his foot and I heard everyone in the Five hold their breath.

"Don't tell me anything about community! I suppose you think the bars and the pross houses are providing community services, too!"

"Sir, this isn't about drinking or whoring. It's about sending mail."

"Now I understand what you're talking about. You don't want to arrest him because he's another Chinaman. I suppose if it were some mick in there selling potatoes or some wop bastard selling sausages, then you'd be fine about putting them in cuffs! Sending them to the guillotine, eh?"

"Sir, there's going to be an uproar, maybe a riot, if they see a white cop arresting this man."

That seemed to calm him down.

"That's where you come in, mister. You're going with Peepshow Geller. Take one of the sector cars. Make sure everyone sees you. Better yet, handcuff him yourself. Bring the Chinese gentleman back here and book him. He's not going to understand a simple warning."

"We should really reconsider, sir."

"*I've* already reconsidered."

—

I slouched in the passenger seat as Peepshow drove.

"Go down Mott," I said.

"What you want to do there? We hafta go get this guy, Chow."

"He might be at the toy store. I'm just going to tell him to not go to the post office anymore. End all the bullshit right here, Geller."

I went into the store, but Moy said his dad had already gone.

"I'm going to level with you, Moy. I'm taking him out of the post office."

"Why?"

"I've got orders. He's doing business on federal property."

"Can't he get a license for it?"

"You can't get a license for something like that."

"But he's been doing it for so long. Why are you stopping him now?"

"It's illegal. He shouldn't have been doing it in the first place."

"He doesn't do it for the money, you know? He just likes to help people," said Moy, his voice jumping an octave.

"He's been doing this since we've been kids, but that doesn't mean it's okay. It's a crime. My job is to stop crime."

"My father's helping people. That's your job, too!"

"Don't tell me what my job is, fatso!" I said, planting my feet. I didn't really expect anything from Moy, but getting ready for a problem was second nature.

"You were born here, so you think you're better than my dad and me!"

"I don't think I'm better than anyone! Your English is perfect."

"That's so condescending! Do I say, 'Hey, your Chinese is so good! Who could have known you're not a real Chinese?'"

"You're a real Chinese and I'm not?"

"That's right! You don't help the Chinese people. You're only looking out for yourself! My father let you work here at the toy store! All he ever did was help you! Did they promise you a promotion for this?"

I stepped away to the door. "I'm wasting my time here, Moy."

"This is the last time you come in this store. You understand? If I'm being held up, I'm going to ask for an American policeman!"

I got out of there and hopped back in the car with Peepshow.

"What happened?" he asked.

"He's not there. We've got to go to the post office on East Broadway."

"Oh, hey, I almost forgot. I saved one of these hot-dog

doodads for you from lunch." He held up a bag from Martha's. "I started eating these things because I saw you doing it. Good call!" I looked at him in the face.

"Hey, Geller, have you been taking that food on the arm?"

"No, I paid for it! Well, sort of. I try to pay. I give a five and they count out five singles and give it back every time."

"Who do you think has to pay for it when you take stuff on the arm? The girls at the counter!"

"Well, I goddamn tried, Chow! You want me to force them at gunpoint or something?"

"No, but you could just drop the money on the counter."

"Okay, okay, I'll do that! Don't take it out on me just because some people want to be nice."

I pulled my hat over my eyes when we pulled up to the communist post office and said, "Geller, listen, you go in there and get him, and I'll be right here."

"You're not coming in with me?"

"Can't handle an old man by yourself?"

"All right, all right. Jeepers creepers, you're lazy."

Peepshow got out, fixed his belt, and went in.

I put my head in my hands. I wanted to crumple my face up and throw it away. This man had taken me in and given me a job when I was back from Nam and had nothing going on. I rocked a little bit in my seat.

Peepshow came out of the post office, dragging Moy's dad by the arm. The old man could yell. It wasn't long before people were gathered there.

"Look what the police are doing to Old Moy!"

"He's hitting Old Moy!"

"Leave Old Moy alone!"

Peepshow wasn't hitting Moy's dad, but the old man was making a show of flailing his arms and legs. I watched the two of them do an awkward do-si-do on the sidewalk for a little bit. His folding stool fell to the sidewalk.

People from the fruit-stand groceries came running up. Some of them had baseball bats. When you have a sidewalk business, you've always got some weapons handy. Bats and 2 X 4s. And knives.

Now it was time for me to get out and help.

"Officer Chow!" said Chi, wiping his hands on his dirty apron. "You have to help Old Moy! He's being attacked by that white motherfucker!"

I stepped through the crowd.

Moy's dad broke Peepshow's grip and stood up.

"Robert!" he said with an air of indignity. "I'm going to sue the damn police department for harassment if you don't straighten this foreign bastard out." He brushed off his arms and let out a heavy sigh. "Robert, pick up my stool and come back inside with me. I still have a lot to do."

"I'm sorry, but you can't do this anymore," I said to him.

"What's wrong with you, don't you call me 'Uncle' anymore?" he asked, with a smile. "I was just kidding about suing the police. Please don't worry about it. Just tell this white boy to leave me alone."

"You have to leave. You can't transact business here anymore," I said.

"Business? This is no business," said Moy's dad, looking at

me like I was going out of focus. "I'm just helping people with their mail."

"They pay you for writing the addresses down. You're doing business on federal property."

"I've been helping write people's mail since you just a kid!"

"I don't personally have a problem with you doing this, but it's illegal. You shouldn't have been doing this from the beginning."

"I never wanted to charge money, but everyone gives me a nickel to show their appreciation. Their respect. Even you have to show me respect."

"I have respect for the law, and my job is enforcing it. Please, let's go."

"Okay, I don't care about the money. I'll just do it for free! That make you happy?"

"It doesn't matter. You have to leave."

"You can't tell me to go if I'm not doing anything!" he yelled, crossing his arms.

"If you're not using the postal services, you have to leave the premises, or I'll arrest you for loitering!" I said. My throat hurt as I went from talking loud to shouting.

"Look at all these people here!" Moy's dad hollered, swinging one arm in a crazy arc. More people had come and black hair was pressing in on us. Peepshow stayed close to me, invading my space. "If I wasn't here," Moy's dad continued, "who would help with their mail? How could they write to China?"

"They're in America now, so they have to learn English!" I said. It was the wrong thing to say.

"Not everybody here grew up with as much money as you, Officer Chow! Okay? They weren't as fortunate to be born here, go to school, and learn English like you! Okay? They work for a dime an hour, sleep 10 people to an apartment!

Okay? They can't be like you and drink themselves drunk every night! Okay?"

He made an indignant face and reached for his stool. I grabbed it before he could and folded it under my left arm. With my right I grabbed his arm and pulled him along. It was pretty easy handling the old man.

Moy's dad screamed. "You're hurting me! You're hurting me!"

"I'm not hurting you, and you know it!" I yelled.

"Officer Chow, Officer Chow, what are you doing!" Chi was shouting to me through the crowd. "That's Old Moy you have there!" I walked on, determined but not rushed. I pushed Moy's dad into the back of the car and slammed the door. I got in the passenger's seat and Peepshow hopped into the driver's seat.

"Let's get out of here! They're going to kill us!" said Peepshow, panting.

"Nothing's going to happen," I said. I looked back at the crowd as we pulled away. Most people were looking more disgusted then mad. Everything they had ever suspected about me was true. Chi was shaking his head at me.

I glanced back at Moy's dad. His eyes were tearing.

"Robert, don't you get it?" he asked in a soft voice. "They hate us here. We have to help each other. Even the black people have their own politicians. We don't have anybody. We're all so helpless. I can't even go home to be buried in the family graveyard because the U.S. doesn't recognize China. It's my last wish, but the Americans stole my body from me! My own body!"

"If you go back into that post office, and you don't have a letter to mail or a package to pick up or your own stamp to lick, I'm going to handcuff you," I said.

I stayed in the car and let Peepshow bring Moy's dad into the Five. They booked him and fined him $100. I let Peepshow put in his own name for the paperwork and the credit.

—

When the shift was over, I walked in a big spiral through Chinatown back to my apartment. I felt like a big traitor. I had rounded up another gook for interrogation. Some people I knew came up to me, but I looked away and kept going.

The worst thing was that maybe the Brow was right. If it were an Irish guy or Italian in place of Moy's dad, I would have had no problem yanking them out. But if I hadn't been there, Peepshow would probably be in intensive care right now.

Moy's dad had taken a lot of shit from the pro-KMT community for doing what he did. In the early days, Moy told me, people would leave death threats under the store door, calling him a "communist sympathizer." But Moy's dad was one of the few people who truly worked for the benefit of all Chinese people. He co-sponsored a float for the KMT Chinese New Year parade and also helped send mail to the People's Republic. He didn't let politics tell him he couldn't help someone. He was a brave man. I was a rat.

I slowed my walk down. I looked down a street that the Continentals used to own. Where were they all now? The world seemed so small back then. Central Park was as distant and vast as Canada in our minds.

I thought about people like Paul, Lonnie, Dori, and even Barbara who were trying to get by in Chinatown because they couldn't get out for whatever reason. I knew people like my mom who dreamed of owning a place far away from the tenements, and people like my dad who had lost all hope.

I looked up and saw an old Chinese man squatting outside a restaurant. He must have been one of the cooks on a break. An empty bowl lay at his feet and he was smoking. His arms were folded over his bent knees as if he'd been told that was all the space he was allowed to take up in America. How many years had he been here in the same shitty job? I tried to catch his eye, but he wouldn't look up.

Chapter 15

The next day, I walked the footpost, but avoided the toy store. I was scared I'd run into Moy in the street, but it didn't happen, and I went home as soon as I could.

Between beers, I caught the American evening news and saw that Kissinger wanted to normalize relations with Hanoi. It was March 26, but it felt like an April Fools joke.

"Why the fuck were we there!" I screamed at the TV because Paul wasn't there to hear me. I suddenly felt a rotton taste in my mouth that I had to get out. I went to the bathroom.

Paul had bought a tube of Chinese herbal toothpaste because we'd run out of Crest. I squeezed it onto my toothbrush and shoved it into my mouth. It tasted like they'd counted sugar as an herb. I looked at my face in the mirror and pulled one eyebrow up with my free hand.

"Are you a postman, now, Mr. Chow?" I asked out loud, spraying toothpaste foam around. I tilted my head and spat onto a plastic robot soaking in the sink.

I stuck my hand in and pulled it out. It was about a foot high and metallic gray. One hand was shaped like a hook and the other held a serrated sword. Wasn't Paul too old to play with toys like this?

The early evening was muggy. After I'd finished brushing, I stripped down to my briefs. I went into the living room and turned the TV back to the Chinese channels. The communist channel was following Chinese dignitaries on a tour of Japan. The Japanese already had full relations with China. America couldn't be too far behind, especially if we were already talking to Hanoi. The Taiwan channel featured a show on raising koi, but unfortunately, it was in Mandarin with no subtitled characters. I could pick out "fish" and "water." I settled for watching the huge fish wriggling through the water and working their mouths open and shut.

I wondered about how long I could go without having a drink. When Paul came in, he was carrying two plastic bags packed with boxes. When he saw me in my briefs he said, "God."

"It was a tough day at the office," I said. Then I pointed at his bags. "What did you buy? Cigarettes?"

"No. Old Moy's closing his toy store! Everything's 75% off, so I got a bunch of robot models. I had to borrow money from my sister to buy more."

"What's going on?"

"The old man's furious! He was saying he won't stand for police harassment."

"Why?"

"Pretend you don't know what happened, Robert."

I thought about Old Moy and Moy and how helpless they would be outside of Chinatown.

"Paul, you left a robot in the bathroom sink. I thought you

were too old to be playing with toys."

"These aren't toys. These are limited-edition Japanese models. These usually go for ten bucks. Sorry about the sink. You have to soak the plastic to clean it before you can paint them."

"When's that toy store gonna close?"

"Soon, I guess. It's a madhouse there. After I got through with it, all the good stuff was gone."

"I'm not going to buy stuff. I just want to talk to the guys."

"You sure you want to go there? A lot of people saw you beating up the old man. I think it's a really bad idea for you to go," Paul said.

"It's okay. I'm an old friend."

—

As I made my way over to the toy store, I thought about all the years I'd gone to Moy's family store to play wind-up toys, long before I ended up working there. Kids from all over the city would come to that one store because it had the best prices.

After hours, Moy's dad would open one of every robot or car for me and Moy to play with. He'd let us play as long as we wanted. When we were done, he'd bring the games in the back and reseal them in plastic.

When I turned the corner to the store, I saw the lights were turned out. The midget was leaning against a nearby fire hydrant.

"What happened?" I asked him.

He shrugged. "The old man collapsed and an ambulance

took him away."

"What!"

"I'll assume you've heard what I said but can't process it yet," said the midget. "Anyway, I feel bad for Old Moy. Not just because he's gone to the hospital. For a businessman he had no marketing sense. I used to buy board games from him. One time I told him to give me some games free and I'd challenge people to play there in the store, but he said no."

The midget turned and spat. Then he looked at me hard. "Hey, you okay?"

"I'm fine," I said. "Just that I knew the guy."

"I know. You were pushing that poor old man around."

"I didn't push him around!"

"You pulled him out of the post office. All he was doing was helping people with their mail. He wasn't selling drugs or girls."

"It's against the law."

"Helping people with English is against the law?"

"People should learn English and not depend on someone to do it for them all the time," I said.

The midget scratched his chin and said, "When people learn English, that's when they stop writing back to China."

"But anyway, you understand that what he was doing was illegal. He was taking money."

"I guess it was."

"It's federal property. There are laws."

"Sure there are. Of course."

"He shouldn't have been there, and he forced me to do what

I had to do."

"You're absolutely right, Officer Chow."

We didn't say anything for a few minutes and watched people slip into restaurants and dried-beef stores. I looked at the midget's open denim jacket and saw a tie that reached down past his belt.

"What's this?" I asked, opening the jacket some more. The midget was also wearing a dress shirt and slacks.

"Remember that tourist, the one who wanted to play Sorry! against me? He's a filmmaker and he wants to do a documentary about me. We're shooting in a studio tonight."

"You're going to be a movie star! People are going to ask for your autograph."

"He brought down Chinese chess players and American chess players from Boston. I'm going to play a dozen people in a row."

"You don't need to dress up for it. You might hurt your luck."

"Believing in luck is for people who don't believe in themselves! I only wanted to look better for the camera. I don't want to make the Chinese people look bad." The midget fidgeted with his tie. "So Paul really cleaned up, huh?"

"Yeah, he came back with two bags of toys."

"Those aren't toys, they're precision models."

"I can't believe Lonnie lent him all that money."

"It wasn't much, it was only $40."

"How do you know?" I asked.

"Lonnie wouldn't give him the money, so I did."

"Hey, I'm going to make that stupid kid pay you right back!"

"Don't worry about it! It's not much money to me. He'll pay me back."

"How's he going to pay you back? He doesn't have a job."

"I wanted to give him a break, just like you're giving him a break by letting him live with you. You know, nobody ever helped me, not that that stopped me from becoming who I am. I carved my own first chessboard pieces from dirty, dried-out sponges the cleaning lady threw away. I got sick a lot because there were germs and bacteria on all those pieces. My mother used to say that that was why my body didn't grow up right."

"That's not true. It's genetics."

"Yeah," said the midget. "Anyway, I wanted to loan the money to Paul to get him started."

"How is he going to make a career out of toys?"

"I've never made a bad investment in anything or anybody," said the midget.

Paul wasn't around when I came home, but he had placed all his robots in a small plastic washing tub in the corner of the living room. When I went to sleep that night, I had a nightmare that Paul's robots were lined up and shooting at me.

—

The next morning, I went to Martha's to find Lonnie.

"Paul didn't come home last night. Do you know where he is?"

"He wasn't at my parents' house. Did you hit him?"

"No, I didn't hit him! I didn't even yell at him. He's been hanging out late at night, but this is the first time he never came back."

"I'm sure he's okay. Robert, are you okay? Your eyes are all red."

"That happens when I get worried."

"Maybe you should ask the midget."

I went to the park. When I found the midget, I went up and said, "Paul didn't come home last night."

The midget looked at me.

"I'm sure Paul can take care of himself," he said.

"This is the first time he's been out all night. Maybe something happened to him."

The midget folded up his arms and crossed his legs.

"Paul said you were pushing him hard to get a job, so he got one serving drinks in a gambling hall. He works late."

"Where's this gambling hall?"

"I don't know."

"Why would he work in a gambling hall?"

"Hey, it beats waiting tables," said the midget.

—

I waited until about 0200 before going over to an unremarkable storefront on Chrystie Street. I went into an adjacent alley and found crude, uneven concrete steps leading down to a lower level.

I could hear upbeat Cantonese pop music and men's voices talking loudly and quickly. I held onto an unpainted metal handrail as I made my way down to the noise in the dim light.

I stood in front of a dull gray metal door and heard a peephole cover swing open and shut.

"I'm not real good at secret knocks or passwords," I said to the door, at about where someone's head would be on the other side. "But I've got on steel-toed shoes that can bust this door off the hinges."

"Officer!" said a muffled voice from the other side of the door, "This is a private club. Members only."

"I'm not here as a cop," I said. "I'm here to see someone who works here."

"Who are you looking for?"

"I'll show you when I see him."

Someone cranked a bolt back and the door opened. A light cloud of smoke poured over my face as I walked into the Tang San Cai gambling parlor. Taiwanese KMT money had set up the place, hence the Mandarin name. It was a pretty classy joint. Tang San Cai referred to the tri-colored glazed pottery of the Tang Dynasty, large replicas of which bookended the gambling tables. Cameras sat atop the urns, barely hidden by plastic shrubbery.

Blackjack, poker, dominoes, and pai gow tables spread out in the four directions. Smoke from cheap Chinese cigarettes swirled around the ceiling lights. Looking at the gamblers, mostly men in their 40s and 50s, I thought about my father. I thought about how he and his waiter buddies would hang out in these gambling joints to take the edges off of their 12-hour workdays. Every time these old men opened their mouths, they added to the overall reek of alcohol, which was strong enough to make my eyes go googly.

The two busiest tables featured attractive young female dealers with collared shirts that were open down to the third button. I might have liked them if they had showed some emotion, good or bad. The girls looked practically catatonic as they pulled in chips and tossed cards with the same unblinking efficiency as their male counterparts.

Nearly every block in Chinatown had a gambling den but they were all going to be shut down soon, and not by the vice squad. A referendum was going around in New Jersey to open legal casinos in Atlantic City later this year. The Chinese gambling joints were trying to hold on to their clients with Chinese culture and history.

"Uncle, you don't want to give money to those foreign devils, do you?" the coat-check girl would say.

The Brow would be on my ass in two seconds if he knew I was infringing on an area that was strictly for the vice squad. I was risking my shield to find that little hood. I caught the attention of one of the girl dealers and she gave me the evil eye. I recognized her as someone I'd once written up for moving violations.

I suddenly found the patterns in the carpet very interesting and sauntered away. I saw Paul at one of the dominoes tables. He was serving a drink with a cherry in it to a tubby old man.

I stepped in and said, "Paul, let's go home."

He held his empty serving tray over his crotch and said, "How did you find me?"

"I found a Polaroid of you walking out of here in one of those Asian youth books and I looked at the address on the back. Now let's go."

"This is my job. You're not my boss." Heads were turning in our direction. Pretty soon, some heavies were going to start making their way over.

"Paul," I growled, "do I have to stick my gun into your back to get you to leave with me?"

He sighed, set his tray by an urn, and followed me out, his head slightly bowed.

When we got down the block, he started whining.

"You know how much money I was making there? I was getting about $10 an hour with the tips! I can pay the midget back already."

"Where the hell were you last night? You never even called."

"I called at midnight on the dot."

"I don't answer the phone on the hour, you know that."

"I can't keep track of your stupid little habits."

"So where the hell were you?"

"One of the big bosses came in and took us out for a late dinner. Then after, he let us sleep over at his penthouse."

"Who are these guys, Paul?"

"The Hakka Charitable Association. They're businessmen."

"You're not stupid, Paul. You know they're a front for a gang."

"All I do is serve drinks, Robert. I'm not a gunman or something."

"Paul, you stay there long enough, they're going to ask you to drive cars out to abandoned lots in East New York and abandon them. You know what are in those trunks? The bodies of people who displeased the management. Yeah, think about that. Then before you know it, they'll have you beating up people who haven't paid back their loans. Maybe you'll have to cut up some girl for not sleeping with your boss. Then you'll be the one popping people, piling bodies into trunks, and telling younger boys to go abandon those cars."

"Really?"

"I see it all the time," I said. It was an improbable, worst-case scenario I was building, but what the hell. I had to scare this kid straight and for good.

"They told me it was a pretty clean business. They never said anything about killing people."

"No business is clean, Paul."

"I know the cops aren't clean. You know the clubs pay out bribes to stay open? I saw it."

"Those cops are going to get caught, and that gambling den is going to be closed."

When we got into our building, we went up the stairs. I continued up, past the floor of our apartment.

"Where are we going?" asked Paul.

"To the roof," I said.

"Why?"

"I want to show you something."

The roof-access door had a sign over it, saying "NO ENTRY" in both English and Spanish, so you know it had to be taken seriously. I picked the padlock with the sharp end of my key ring coil.

"Isn't this illegal?"

"I have the grandfather clause. I lived here before the sign was posted." Which was true. I got the lock open and the door swung back. We could see stars in the sky.

"Over here, by the water tower," I said. We went over.

"What do you see, Paul?"

"Chinatown."

"Look at those windows," I said pointing.

"They're bright."

"You know why they're bright? Those are fluorescent lights in there. That's where they've got women and children sewing clothes around the clock. See those restaurants down there?" I pointed to the 24-hour joints on Bowery. "That's where men are working 12-hour shifts. They're working for way below minimum wage. Those are the people your gambling den's taking money away from.

"My father worked as a waiter all his life. He didn't come over to serve uptown Chinese and tourists, but that's what he ended up doing because he didn't know any English and wasn't too smart. He wasn't an angel, either, but he did what he could for his family. Every buck he made was honest, and he lost a lot of that honest money gambling. Those motherfuckers who run the gambling prey on their own kind, and they take advantage of this entire community."

Paul looked out over Chinatown.

"Is that true about your dad?" he asked.

"What?"

"He jumped off the roof."

"He was drunk. He fell off."

"You know, you have to stop drinking, Robert."

"I'll stop drinking," I said, "if you just get an honest job."

"Okay," he said quickly. "You're on!"

"Hey, don't I get to have one for the road, at least?"

Paul shook his head.

"Son of a bitch, you fast-talked me into it!"

We went downstairs and poured out my last beers into the sink. I was pissed at myself for crying.

—

I woke up with a dull feeling in my head, as if a sack of marbles was pressing out from inside my skull against my forehead. I swung around, put my feet on the floor and my head in my hands.

All the alcohol in the apartment was gone, but I knew that if I went downstairs to a bodega and got a beer, the feeling would go away. I could forget all about trying to quit drinking. The thought made me drool a little bit.

My door opened and the midget strolled in. I looked up at him.

"Your bedroom smells funny," he said. "When was the last time you washed your sheets?"

"What time is it?" I asked.

"About 8:30 or so. I've been here for a while. Paul let me up. I didn't want to bother you until you were awake. You know, my brother quit drinking so I know what needs to be done."

"I don't need help."

He sniffed the air again and wrinkled his nose.

"That smell's definitely not good," he said.

"So what's the plan?" I asked him.

"Well, because you get unlimited sick days, you're going to start calling in."

"For how long?"

"As long as it takes."

"How long could it take?"

"Are you taking bets or something? Just call in sick, already."

I reached for the phone on my desk and picked up the receiver. Standing up made me feel like Elmer Fudd after he shot himself in the head with his rifle. I talked on the phone and didn't have to fake anything with regards to sounding woozy. It was irritating having a voice directly in my ear. I hung up at what I thought was an appropriate point and rolled back into bed.

The midget disappeared for a second and came back with a glass of water and what looked like two tiny dried flower blossoms.

"Drink this and take these," he said.

"No way, man. I don't go for Chinese medicine. Probably turn me into a diabetic."

"These are Flintstones vitamins! You probably won't be able to eat, so these should keep you alive."

I sat up in bed and put my back to the wall. I chucked back Dino and Fred and washed them down with half a glass of water.

"Are you hungry?" the midget asked.

"No."

"Then maybe you should sleep."

"I just woke up."

"Want to read the paper?"

"No way."

"Want to get up and watch TV?"

"I don't want to get up."

"Want to play a game of chess?"

"Not in the mood."

"Want to hear some music?"

"No."

"Do you just want to talk a bit?" he asked.

"About what?"

"Whatever pops into your head."

"Am I going to die?"

"Someday, yes."

"Hey! Seriously, is this cold turkey thing going to kill me?"

"No. Your body is going to feel like shit, but it's because you're struggling to live."

"What can I do to make it easier right now?"

"You can drink water or some lemon-barley tea that I brought over, eat Flintstones, and sleep."

"What about when I have to piss?"

"You can go to the bathroom, or I can get you a bottle to piss in."

"I don't piss in plastic bottles."

"You want a glass bottle?"

I closed my eyes and slid down off the wall until I was fully flat on the bed.

"This is funny," I said. "All this thinking and talking has made me sleepy. But you knew this would happen, didn't you?"

"Get some sleep."

I didn't hear the floor creak so I eased my left eye open.

There was nobody there. I guess the midget wanted the door open so he could hear if I started swallowing my tongue. I wasn't so sure it couldn't happen.

I let myself slip under into a world that was dark, dull, and throbbing.

—

A slight draft coming in under the sheets made me shiver. I opened my eyes and saw that I was lying in bed with no cover or clothes on. I was sweating.

Then it dawned on me that I hadn't actually left Vietnam. I'd been left alone in a GP while everyone else was on patrol. Because I'd overslept, they'd decorated it as a joke to look like my apartment.

"How the fuck did they know," I laughed, amazed at how good a job they'd done.

I could hear people walking around outside the tent, so I hoisted my M-16 onto my shoulder and covered my body with the sheet up to my neck. I was glad I had cleaned the barrel the night before.

I closed my eyes and my fingers made sure the clip was loaded properly. I set the rifle to rock and roll. I opened my eyes only halfway and stayed heavy-lidded. I didn't want Charlie to see the full light reflecting off of my eyes.

Someone was coming into the tent through a flap cleverly disguised as my door.

I closed my mouth tight and breathed slowly through my nose. I looked at the door and pointed the M-16 at it from under the sheet.

A tiny black head of hair slipped into the GP.

"Chieu Hoi!" I shouted.

The boy stepped in slowly, but in an authoritative way.

"Chieu Hoi!" I shouted again.

He got closer and I could see the holes in his shirt where I had shot him. He sat at the foot of the bed.

"What are you doing, Robert?" he asked.

"I could shoot you again," I said. "I'll fix you this time."

"Why would you do that?" He smelled of cigarette smoke.

"I have a rifle under here. It's pointed right at you."

"Is it loaded?"

"Yes, I checked."

"Well, if you're going to shoot me, you should at least let me see your weapon. It'll be easier for me to take."

"This is some VC trick."

"Just keep your eyes on me."

I pulled back the sheet and put my rifle in my lap.

"See this? I'm not fucking around," I said.

"So I see."

"Don't come any closer. I swear to fucking God, I'll shoot you, again."

The boy faced me with his shoulders square to me.

"You have to shoot me. Pull the trigger."

"I'll do it!"

"Then do it."

"Don't think that because you're just a kid, I won't!"

"I have a gun, too, Robert."

I saw that he wasn't fooling. There was something gleaming in his closed hand. He had quick little hands.

"Shoot me," the boy said.

"Shut up!"

"Shoot me, or I'm going to shoot you."

I pulled the trigger. I involuntarily jumped with the kick of the rifle. But there wasn't any rifle. I looked down. What I thought was the strap of the M-16 was my belt. My hands were empty.

"Illusions are funny, aren't they?" the midget asked. He eased a cigarette into his mouth and flipped the lighter in his hand. "Actually, I'm going to smoke in the living room. You need fresh air in here."

—

I was jerked awake by a sharp pain in my stomach. I turned on my side and pushed my hand into it. My arms and legs were cramping. I was hungry like I hadn't been since I was a kid. I rolled onto the floor and pulled myself upright on the dresser. One drawer wasn't closed all the way and my weight pushed it closed on the fingers of my right hand.

I howled out loud.

"Robert, are you OK?" shouted Paul from the living room.

My tongue felt like it was stuffed with dust, so I decided to open the door before saying anything.

I nearly blacked out on the 15-foot trek to the doorknob. I threw it open.

"I want chocolate," I said to the midget and Paul as they stared at me. "Something spicy, too!"

"Paul," said the midget, "go get some chocolate bars and a beef noodle soup to go." He tried to hand the money to Paul, who was still staring at me. "C'mon, Paul!"

Paul snapped out of it, took the money, and left. The midget looked up at my face and kept his eyes fixed on mine.

"Wash up, Robert," he said. "I think you had a bloody nose and it's dried on your face."

—

After I had eaten and drank about half a gallon of tea, I lay down on the couch. Lonnie had come over. The four of us watched TV and didn't say much.

The Taiwan channel was saying how ironic it was that nobody Chinese would be competing at the summer Olympics in Montreal. China was still boycotting and Canada, which had begun recognizing China diplomatically (and unrecognizing Taiwan) six years ago, wanted the Taiwanese team to drop the "Republic of China" suffix to their official name.

"We are the true Republic of China," the Taiwanese news anchor said, his head held stiff at a regal angle. "Over many centuries, there have been times when barbarians have overrun the mainland. But order will follow chaos and the country will come together again after this divisive period. It has always been so. It will always be so."

I had never felt so conflicted in my life. I was feeling a swirl of emotions. I was grateful to the midget and even to Paul, and something was really happening between me and Lonnie. But overriding all this was a general nausea and an incredible desire to tear myself away from everybody and get my hands on just half a fucking drink.

—

A couple days later, when my mind and body had reconnected, I stopped by the toy store on Mott. The sale signs were still in the window. The door was locked, but I could see Moy in the back pushing a broom. I pounded on the door. He shaded his eyes to look at me and waved me away. I pounded again, harder. He gave up, came over, and unlocked the door.

"What do you want?" he asked. He propped the door open with a shoulder and stood in the way, in case I had wanted to come in.

"I heard about your dad. I wanted to know how he was doing."

"He's going to be okay. I put him in a care facility in Queens." Dust bunnies quivered on Moy's sweatshirt.

"It was a stroke?"

"No. Turns out that it was only his back giving out."

"It wasn't because of me, was it?"

"Not directly," Moy said with a sigh. "He tried to lift some boxes on his own in the storeroom. You know, when you threw him out of the post office, that really broke his heart. You were like a son to him."

"I'm sorry about that."

"Sorry or not, it doesn't change anything."

"Can I visit your dad?"

"He put a curse on you. You should just stay away from him."

"What kind of curse?"

"The kind that wishes ill will in general."

"Seriously?"

"Yes. He got it done with a monk over the phone."

"He must really hate me."

"He threw away everything you ever gave him. Even his

nail clipper."

"Moy, you're not going to keep the store open?"

"I'm leaving with my collection, but someone's bought the store and the rest of the inventory." He looked up at the sky. Maybe it was going to rain.

"Who's buying the store?"

"The midget."

"He has that kind of money?"

"It's not that much. It's just a cheap store that sells cheap stuff."

"We had a lot of good times here. What are you going to do?"

"I'm going to move to Queens with Dori and open another store there."

"Where in Queens?"

"Somewhere."

"You're not going to tell me?"

"No. I'm busy now."

Moy stepped back, let the door close, and locked it. I thought about that entire collection of G.I. Joe dolls Moy had, including the incredibly hard-to-find Land Adventurer: Fight For Survival box set.

I stood and watched Moy move to the back of the store, out of the light. Then I left.

Chapter 16

Outside Jade Palace, some stool-pigeon waiters were cleaning up scraps of paper and ripping up posters the protestors had left. Willie Gee was supervising the cleanup.

"I heard you settled with the fired waiters, Willie," I said.

He turned and leered at me. "I gave them what they wanted, what this whole thing was about. Money."

"You could have let the whole thing go to court."

Willie dismissed the thought with his hand. "I was right, but it wouldn't have been cost-effective to allow them to continue to tarnish Jade Palace with their lies. It's always harder to be right than wrong."

A waiter came out with a garden hose. Two others pushed brooms on the sidewalk where the water sprayed.

"Have to get all their germs away from my restaurant," said Willie, smiling. "Officer Chow, are you coming to our benefit dinner?"

"Who are you benefiting?"

"The Asian-American Patrolmen's Association. They're a nationwide organization based in L.A."

"They're having their benefit here?"

Willie gave a smug smile.

"Our reputation precedes us, all the way to the other coast," he said.

"I wish they knew what was going on in this restaurant, about its real standing in the community."

"They know exactly where Jade Palace stands," said Willie,

chuckling to himself. "They know we offer the finest food at the best prices with the most attentive service. Also, I made a small donation to their organization."

"What happens when the money runs out, Willie? What happens when you can't pay out settlements or make donations to the right people anymore?"

"Money doesn't run out for a good businessman," said Willie, picking at his teeth. "Like my former guard down here. After he skipped town, I found out that he had been working for an old family rival in Hong Kong. He tried to play our competing interests against each other. He was nothing but a troublemaker."

From several stories up, thousands of dim-sum plates were clinking in sinks. It sounded like an air-hockey tournament.

The midget came up to us from behind.

"Tough break, Willie," he said.

"What makes you say that, little man? The labor settlement was in our favor," said Willie with a smile that could hide fangs.

"Well, if I'm not mistaken, Officer Chow has given you a parking ticket."

Willie swung his head around and looked at his Corvette halfway down the block. A folded ticket under the windshield wiper was clearly visible. The three eights in his license-plate number hadn't worked.

"No standing, 11 to four, just like the sign says," I said.

"You dirty, dirty bastard!" Willie seethed.

It couldn't have been sweeter if it were the last parking ticket I ever wrote.

—

I walked down to the park with the midget. It was a big deal because it was the last day for him to play games in the park. His toy store, like most of Chinatown, was going to be open every single day of the year.

"No more vacations for you," I said as we stepped into Columbus Park.

"I don't need vacations," said the midget. "Where would I go, anyway? I'm going to let the world come to me."

As we made our way to the stone tables, I was pleasantly surprised by the number of men and boys who had showed up. Nearly everybody the midget had ever played a game against was there. It was the biggest collection of losers in Chinatown. Someone was filling balloons with a helium tank.

"What's this?" asked the midget excitedly. I had never seen the midget surprised by anything before.

Two children hoisted up a large banner that read, "THANKS FOR PLAYING! BEST OF LUCK WITH THE STORE!"

"It's a celebration," I said.

Wang came up and pressed a coconut soymilk bottle into the midget's hands.

"Policeman Chow and Vandyne paid for everything," said Wang.

Men of all shapes and ages came up and shook hands with the midget and clapped his back. A sponge cake filled with cream and fruit with a Chinese chessboard design was ready to be cut by the guest of honor. I was glad I had ordered the largest size possible.

"How does it feel to be so loved by so many people?" I asked the midget.

He shrugged. "I've never known anything different." He poked a straw into the coconut soymilk and took a few sips.

"Are you sure you're not going to play in the park anymore?" I asked.

"I'm going to play in the store. I'm going to set up game boards so other people can play, too, like the American chess stores in Greenwich Village. I want there to be a place to go for games in the winter or when it rains."

"I'm going to miss seeing you out here."

"It's more important for me to be at my cash register! You think we came to America to loiter in the park or something?"

Two little boys pushed their way in and begged the midget for his autograph. He politely refused. "I'm not retiring!" he said. "Come into my store. Everyone's welcome to play against me or against someone else. I'll give you lessons, too. It's better than pinball!"

I saw Paul handing out flyers for the opening of the midget's toy and game store. He was employee #1.

"I hope you work hard," I said. "The midget's not going to take it easy on you."

"Do you see me goofing off? Look how many of these I've already given away," said Paul, pointing at a nearby garbage can that held a dozen crumpled flyers. I took one from him.

"Ten percent off all items, huh?" I said.

"It's a great deal."

"Paul, you know, you're not allowed to distribute these in public parks."

"Would you arrest your own roommate?"

"No, I'm off-duty right now." I read the piece of paper again. The Chinese name of the store was "Thirty-Six Strategies."

The English name was "Dragon Fantasy." "Who came up with the American name?" I asked Paul.

"I did. Pretty good, huh? We're going to sell this new American game, Dungeons and Dragons. It could be humongous."

"I believe you," I said.

I walked up behind Vandyne, who was caught up in a game against a teenager.

"Vandyne, the midget's here," I said.

"Yeah, be right there," he said vacantly, his hand bracing his chin.

"Not doing too bad here."

"Not bad at all. I took a page from the midget's playbook on this one. Say, Chow, who's the guy with the camera?"

"He's making a movie about the midget."

"He's not just a tourist, then."

"He's still a tourist," I said. "He ain't native like you and me." Then I whispered, "Look out on the left."

Vandyne flashed me an "OK" from under the table. His opponent glared at me and I went over to the filmmaker.

"I want to ask you something," he said. "How come only men are coming up to the midget? Why are all the women sitting at the sidelines? Is it some kind of unspoken sexist Chinese theme that women shouldn't interfere with men's affairs?"

"Naw," I said, watching men clumsily smear cake on their shirts. "Women just have more sense then men."

"I think that girl over there is staring at us."

"She's looking at me."

"You know her?"

"Yeah, her name's Lonnie."

"Wow, she's like Miss Chinatown."

"Yeah."

"Maybe I should get a shot of her kissing the midget."

I felt a twinge of jealousy jerk through my left arm. "Aw, just leave her alone," I said. "Here, read this flyer."

"'Dragon Fantasy'? What the hell's that supposed to mean?"

I went over to Lonnie. She was wearing a long-sleeved translucent shirt that showed a solid white blouse under it.

"Robert, it's so sad, isn't it?" she asked.

"It's not sad. It's a celebration of all the midget has done for Columbus Park. Now he's opening a store. It's like he's gone legit."

"He's been playing here for as long as I can remember."

"Before I knew him, he would play pranks on me. He'd throw peanuts at the back of my head."

"How did you get to be friends with him?"

"He helped solve a crime a long time ago."

"What was it?"

"It was this drug-smuggling thing," I said. "So, aren't you supposed to be at work?"

Lonnie beamed. "Not now, but I'm working a double shift tomorrow. You know, Dori is leaving to work in one of the Martha's in Queens? I have to train a new girl to take her place. She's so much nicer. Everything's going to be better."

"I'm glad Dori's gone. Now you won't have to bring your whip to work anymore."

Lonnie laughed and her neck and upper chest grew red.

"That's a nice outfit you got there. It's, ah, very sexy."

"Thank you, Robert. I've never heard you say anything like that before." Just then I saw Paul giving me a sour look from his post at the park entrance.

"Are you warm enough in that thing?" I asked Lonnie.

"It's very warm," she said. The redness was spreading to her face. Something made me turn and look over my shoulder. I saw the filmmaker pointing his camera at Lonnie and me. I could see him smiling.

"Who's that?" asked Lonnie.

"He's making a film about the midget," I said. "Lonnie, let's go get some cake." I did some breaststrokes through the crowd and put people between us and the camera.

—

When the party was over, the midget, Lonnie, and Paul went over to help set up the toy shop. I decided to take advantage of a few hours of privacy while Paul was tied up.

I went looking for some fruit juice at the Hong Kong supermarket but I didn't want to walk by the beer section. I had to keep fluids moving through my body, the midget said. I cut across the back where they kept the incense and packs of Hell Bank Notes.

People would burn these notes in metal buckets at gravesites to give their loved ones money in the afterlife. Everyone goes to "hell" when they die, but it isn't bad if you have enough money to throw around. Burning Hell Bank Notes was a ritual that had lost all religious significance over the centuries, but it remained as culturally Chinese as pouring everyone else's tea before your own. Even Chinese Christians burn Hell Bank Notes.

A bundle of notes stuck out of an opened package and some bills were strewn around the floor. The smallest denomination was $1,000. The plastic had been torn away in small rips as if some rat had chewed it open. I looked around and saw a little girl grinning at me mischievously from the next aisle.

"Did you do this?" I asked her.

She smiled wider and shook her head. Her two front teeth were gone. I bent over and put my hands on my knees.

"You're a bad girl," I said.

The little girl scampered over and tried to free some more notes. I put down my basket and watched her. She pulled out a bundle of notes and waved them over her head. A minute later, her grandmother came around the corner.

"You stupid little girl! Don't touch those! You want to give yourself bad luck! They're for dead people! Now you're going to die, too!"

The little girl started to cry as her grandmother lifted her up roughly by the elbows. All over Chinatown, other kids were in various stages of having the culture scared and beaten into them. I thought about the belt-whip marks on Paul's back, and how I would never let that happen to him again. I felt a little good about myself. It wasn't a feeling I was used to.

I picked up a newspaper aligned with Hong Kong, along with a carton of orange juice and some cans of lychee juice.

At home, I flipped through the paper. Vietnam was going to hold elections for a newly unified government. Protests were being held in Beijing to oppose the demotion of Deng Xiao Ping, a protégé of Chou En Lai. The prince of Cambodia had resigned. Big changes were coming to Asia in the first week of April.

A tiny item near the back mentioned that a Chinese man with a large frame had been found murdered in a hotel room in Vancouver's Chinatown. Shot twice in the back of the head. He had come in from New York. It was the kind of thing that didn't make it into the American newspapers.

—

I was nearing the end of my first dry week since early Nam. I told Paul not to do anything for me. I was cooking, cleaning, and eating fruit. It felt good in a painful kind of way, and I noticed that I could smell and taste things better.

I had gone to a Chinatown Democrats fundraising event. I was in the pictures, but I didn't stay for dinner. When I saw the wine glasses they were putting out, I'd given the ridiculous excuse that I had to do laundry. After I'd gotten home, it actually made sense to bring a couple of loads of dirty clothes down to the basement machines.

I sat in a brittle plastic chair by the dryers and ate two bruised pears.

I picked up a pair of slacks that had come out of the dryer and turned the pockets inside out. The remains of some Tic Tac mints were stuck to the pocket lining. I had to scrape them off with the flip-out emery board of a nail clipper.

In my palm, they looked like little eggshell chips.

Or paint.

Those weren't eggshells in Yip's coffee-bean grinder. They were paint chips. Lead paint.

—

The midget was behind the counter of the toy shop. Paul

was sweeping the floor. It had been completely redesigned and looked like a brand new store.

"You're out a little late!" said the midget, following my gaze around the store. "See anything you like?"

"Look what you did to the store! You move pretty quick," I told him.

"I move smart," he said. "That means you have to move quick sometimes and hire the right people."

"I'm glad you've got a decent job now, Paul. How come you can't clean up the apartment floor this good?"

"I have to clean around you," he said with a tight smile. I turned back to the midget. "You know where Moy's moved to?"

"Somewhere else."

"OK, fine. But I need to ask you about something else." I looked at him square.

"Let's go have tea." The midget flipped the store keys to Paul and we went to a tea place on Mott. We sat down in the back against a wall of wood paneling.

"You know I've been beating everybody that filmmaker can dig up for me to play," the midget said. "He flew out American-chess players from San Francisco and Chinese-chess players from L.A." There wasn't a trace of smugness in his voice. "He wants to film a final showdown in the store."

"Anyone come close to you yet?" I asked. The dainty teahouse table was low, but it was just a little too high for the midget.

"This one woman I played against, she had good instincts, but poor execution. She could tell what was going to happen, but she couldn't come up with a good strategy."

"She Chinese?"

"She is, but she doesn't speak."

"That's too bad. She could have been the love of your life."

"I found the love of my life years and years ago."

The waitress brought over a pot of black tea and two heavy ceramic cups. She was about 22 and wearing the restaurant uniform, a bright green tracksuit with a bastardization of the Adidas logo.

"Would you like some honey or sugar?" she asked.

"No," I said.

"Um, would you like a phone book for your chair?" she asked the midget.

"Only if it has your number in it," he said with a wink. She frowned and skittered away.

"You never miss a chance to harass women," I said.

"I never miss a chance to harass stupid people, on or off the game board. So what's going on?"

"Have you seen Yip around?"

"As a matter of fact, I saw him dragging two new suitcases in the street the other day."

My heart sank.

"Did he leave town?" I asked. "I stopped by his apartment, but no one was there. All his stuff's gone."

"He hasn't yet, but he will. Wouldn't you if you murdered your wife?"

"How do you know Wah was murdered?"

"How could there be lead in a can of preserved bamboo

shoots? There isn't a factory in the world that still uses lead in their cans."

"Maybe it fell in somewhere," I said.

"The lead fell in that can, after it was opened," said the midget. "The British colonial government in Hong Kong would never allow lead to end up in a manufacturing plant. China, maybe, but not Hong Kong."

"So someone from the restaurant wanted Yip to kill his wife, and he did — by grinding lead paint in a coffee grinder and sprinkling it into her food."

"Not just someone from the restaurant — Lily, Wah's old boss. Of course she wanted Wah dead. Getting a potential union organizer out of the way meant a big promotion for her back in Hong Kong, where the parent company is. It's owned by an old pro-communist general who was friends with Willie Gee's dad."

"Isn't it a little weird, that communists want to bust unions?"

"The old men gave communism to the students and have them preach it to the peasants. All those big company owners in Hong Kong, they live like royalty. They get the biggest houses with the best feng shui — on the top of a mountain by a river. Nice places. They could also probably get their friends very similar places. Even set up someone like Yip in China — out of reach from American authorities."

"Why would Yip want to go to China?"

The midget rolled his eyes. "Yeah, why would he want to go back when he's got it so good here? Living in a beat-up apartment and sharing a common bathroom with all the other dying old men on his floor." The midget took a sip of his tea. "You don't understand because you were born here, Robert. When men came over, they only intended to be here temporarily, even if it ended up being years or decades."

"Wah was the one who became an American citizen, not Yip," I said.

"They used to argue because Yip wanted to go back and Wah wanted to stay here. Lousy as it was, she loved living here in America."

"Couldn't Yip have just left, without murdering his wife, if he wanted to go back so badly?"

"Well, he could have. But he wanted to go back with a certain degree of comfort — a fat wallet to take up the slack in his pants."

"Where is Yip now?"

The midget took a deep breath. He reached into his waistband and pulled out a ball-point pen. He scrawled something on a napkin.

"This is the address of a vacant apartment. Nobody knows who owns it. He's probably there."

The midget whistled at the waitress and said, "Hey tall girl, let's get the check here. We're in a rush."

"I'm not that tall," she said.

"Are you kidding?" said the midget. "You're a freak!"

—

I tested the front door and luckily the lock was broken. I had pushed my way half in, but pressed the apartment buzzer anyway.

Static came over the speaker.

"Yip," I said into the dented microphone, "it's me, the cop."

He didn't buzz the door open, but it didn't matter.

When I got up the stairs, Yip was standing in the apartment doorway wearing a thin t-shirt, shorts, socks, and slippers. He looked frail and old.

"Officer Chow, this is a surprise."

"You seem a little nervous, Yip. What's going on?"

"It's just that I wasn't expecting you." He managed to break his face into a smile. "Hey, come in, sit down."

"You've got a teapot boiling and some butter cookies on your table. You were expecting someone."

"I'm just having a snack."

"Maybe I'll have one, too," I said, strolling into the apartment.

Yip leaned against the sink and shifted uncomfortably. The rickety kitchen table held a paper plate with assorted Danish butter cookies. A pack of playing cards lay next to the plate.

"What does she see in you?" I asked him.

"Who?"

"Lily," I said, taking a cookie. He rubbed the back of his neck and smiled.

"I don't understand what you're talking about," he said, hiding his hands in his armpits. He remained standing. I sat in a chair next to his two suitcases and knocked them over with my knee.

Yip cringed as the luggage tumbled.

"I'm so clumsy," I said. I picked up the pack of cards. "How about a game of blackjack, Yip?"

"I'm feeling a little tired, maybe we could play tomorrow."

I glanced at the suitcases.

"I've got a funny feeling you ain't gonna be around tomorrow."

He came over and sat at the table. "Maybe one quick game," he said.

"I think we should play for a while," I said. "I'm feeling real lucky." We played about a dozen hands. I was the dealer and busted on nearly every hand.

"Now it's your turn to deal," I said.

"I'm an old man, you can't let me get too tired," Yip said weakly.

"Come on, I know how you like to gamble. Please don't be so polite. You shouldn't feel bad about winning."

He dealt me the ace of spades, but my second card was a four. Two cards signifying death. There was a knock at the apartment door. Yip shuffled the cards and didn't move.

"Someone's here," I said.

"Yes, but it must be the wrong apartment."

"You shouldn't ignore it," I said.

"I shouldn't have answered the door all day," he said, glaring at me. I jumped up and pulled open the door.

"We've met," I said. "Lily, right? Thought you were in China."

Her face, already powdered to the hilt, went even paler.

"Why Officer Chow, I didn't know you'd be here. What a surprise."

"Come in, come in! What are you doing here, Lily?" I said. She took tentative steps inside, as if she expected the floor to give way. Yip set the cards aside. He looked as if he had a mild fever.

"Wah had arthritis, didn't she Yip?"

"Yes, she did. You know that. Everybody knows that. It was a struggle every day for her to work."

"My grandmother had arthritis and it was always worst for her when she woke up," I said. "She couldn't do anything. I had to turn on the water, tie her shoes, open cans."

Yip sat back and folded his arms. "What are you getting at?" he asked.

"I know you ground up lead paint to spike that can of bamboo shoots, but I still don't understand how you could do it. Kill a helpless old woman whose only mistake was loving you and living with you."

Lily inched along the wall, looking for a crack to slip into.

"Why would I want to kill my wife?" Yip cried out. I felt anger rumble in the back of my head.

The lights went out. I lunged and had Lily by the throat. I threw her on the floor. I snapped the lights back on.

"That was a childish thing to do!" I growled. Lily was on the floor, choke-sobbing. "What did Jade Palace's owners promise you to get rid of Wah? How big a raise did you get from Willie Gee?"

"You're so stupid," Lily mumbled to the floor.

"You're nothing but a lousy, drunk policeman!" sneered Yip. He turned, bared his teeth at me, and sprayed saliva when he talked. "You only got your job to fill a racial quota. You're a no-good son of a no-good man who committed suicide in disgrace!"

I looked over at the table. I kicked it over and pulverized the nearest cookie with my heel.

Then I calmly clicked my radio. It wasn't working. I looked around the apartment. There was no phone.

"I'm going downstairs to call the precinct on a payphone," I said, handcuffing Yip's hands behind his back. "Don't even think you can go anywhere," I warned Lily.

I left the apartment and found a phone next to a rusted garbage can across the street. Before I got to it, I heard a scream and a crash back at Yip's building. I put my hands in my pockets and let out a whistle.

—

A few days later, I was sitting in the Brow's office.

"I am ordering you to stay away from Lily Leung, Mr. Chow," he said. "She's an upstanding member of the community and you're harassing her."

"She's going to sneak off to China and never come back, sir."

"I don't blame her. She saw her friend jump out a window. I'd be traumatized, too."

"Sir, do you know where those marks on her face came from? She pushed him out and he tried to bite her."

"He pushed her back and jumped out. He was grieving for his recently deceased wife."

"With his bags packed, sir?"

"Son, why are you holding on to this?"

"Sir, Yip's wife, Wah, was trying to organize the workers. Lily paid off Yip to kill her. Then she killed Yip to cover up her trail." The Brow squinted at me and stomped his foot.

"That's absolutely brilliant, Mr. Chow! That's why you're our most experienced detective!"

"Sir, maybe you're not treating these deaths as murders because the *Times* and the *Daily News* ignored the story."

"I call that exercising good news judgment."

I sat back and crossed my arms.

"Don't be unhappy Mr. Chow, we're giving you an EPD for keeping the peace during the chaos of the Chinese New Year parade."

"Excellent Police Duty. That's great, sir," I said. EPD was the lowest citation you could get. Boy scouts could qualify for it.

"Also, it seems that the Chinese community got wind of your citation. They're setting up a dinner in your honor, Mr. Chow. Think of all the times you've attended these events, and now you're the honoree! Look at the progress you've made."

"Who's putting on this dinner, sir?"

"It's going to be at Jade Palace. Willie Gee is arranging everything. You're going to make the front pages of the Chinese papers. Congratulations, Mr. Chow."

He stood up and shook my hand, although I was too shocked to get up.

"You realize, sir, that Willie Gee is Lily Leung's employer?"

"This dinner shows that there's no hard feelings! I think you're reaching a moment of truth, Mr. Chow. Now you can see how highly you're regarded in the community."

—

English was waiting for me in the hallway.

"So you're getting a dinner thrown for you, Chow. Momma

must be real proud of her boy."

"Don't call me 'boy.'"

"You're a really funny guy, Chow. You know, I didn't understand your sense of humor before, but now I think I get it. Anyway here's a little something I got you. Welcome aboard. I'm giving you an investigative assignment." He pressed something smooth and plastic into my hands.

"You're giving me a Polaroid camera?"

"You know the drill. You're not that dumb. When you're making your rounds, take pictures of any suspicious youth you see. Let's see how you do with that."

"How do you define suspicious?"

"Anyone who looks smarter than you."

—

I walked down to the street and stretched my arms. The sun felt warm.

There were about a dozen people in the toy store. The midget was behind the counter, playing a game of Chinese chess with Vandyne. Paul was restocking the shelves with little bottles of enamel paint.

I held up my camera. "Got you something, Paul," I said.

"What am I going to do with this?" he asked.

"Take pictures of cops," I said. I turned to Vandyne and the midget. "They're throwing a dinner to honor me. I'm getting an award for stopping the parade disturbance."

Vandyne put one hand on my shoulder. "All right," he said.

"That filmmaker's coming by here soon," said Paul. "He

wants this to be the finale to his movie. A guy goes from playing games in a park to buying a toy store. He wants all the midget's friends in it, too."

"Well, I better get my hair cut," I said. I left for the barber's on Doyers.

"Hey!" yelled Law the barber when I came in the door.

"Law, I'm going to give you a break and let you take your time on this one. I'm going to be in a movie. I want a haircut, shampoo, and a shave," I said.

"I'm going to make you look like a star," Law said, laughing. "I'm going to put your picture on my wall."

I had time to read some of the Taiwan-biased paper before he could get to me.

The Wells Fargo armored car robbery in New York was possibly an inside job; a couple of gunmen had gotten away with $851,000. Jimmy Carter had won the Wisconsin Democratic primary for the presidency. The KMT Chinese were worried about him because it was rumored that if he were elected, he'd establish ties with the People's Republic and cut off Taiwan. He'd been a farmer, and was therefore a communist sympathizer.

"Hey you, right now," Law said to me, patting an empty chair.

He delicately pulled a sheet around my neck and placed a steaming cloth over my face. It was like being wrapped in a womb. Then Law sprayed my hair with water and snipped around for a while. I felt wet hair clips brush by my ears.

The bell on the door suddenly went off and someone ran in.

"Robert!" yelled Paul.

"What?" I said, yanking the towel off my face.

"The filmmaker's at the toy store now and he brought in this guy from Japan. The midget's losing! Everyone's there!" He was out of breath.

I jumped up and pulled the sheet off. Law scowled, jerked his drawer open, and chucked his scissors into it.

"I'll be back, Law. I'm sorry about this. I'm so sorry," I said on my way out.

We pushed our way into the store. People were crowding the sidewalk, trying to see inside. With a stage light set up in the store, it was brighter than the first day of summer vacation. The filmmaker had shoved his fist into his mouth.

The Japanese player folded his hands in front of him as he stared at the board placidly. It was looking bad for the midget, who had a far-off look of wonderment in his eyes.

We got there just in time. The game was over in only a few more moves.

The midget won, of course. It had only looked like he was losing.

—

Willie Gee must have had some really good info on me, because seated with me at the first dining table in Jade Palace's banquet hall were the midget, Lonnie, Vandyne, Rose, Wang, and coach Teeter. And my mother. Paul had to watch the toy store. I'd see him at home later. Another entire table was taken up by community-relations officers that you never actually saw in the neighborhood and their wives. They all needed forks.

It was a nice dinner, one of the fancy Chinese ones where every dish is a kind of meat, and no rice or vegetables are served. A long stretch of seafood and meats slipped in and spun on the large lazy Susan in the middle of the table. Sliced jellyfish, cuttlefish, stewed snakehead fish, steamed flounder, Peking duck, sliced dried beef, sliced dried pork, lobster, and shrimp were all reduced to bones, shells, and colorful smears.

For the presentation portion of the evening, I was seated on a platform between the chairman of the Pearl River Businessmen's Association and the head of the Kwangtung Province Business Alliance. A dozen other businessmen were up there with me. I had on my uniform – for the last time, I told myself.

A banner hung over our heads. In English it said, "Chinatown Supports Police Department." In Chinese it said, "Congratulations, Happiness, and Longevity." Photographers from three Chinese-language newspapers snapped pictures. One was supported by the KMT. One was working for a Hong Kong conglomerate. The third was backed by money from the communists.

Businessmen gave speeches in Chinese at the fixed microphone stand at the center of the stage. The Chinese people were surely making progress in America, they said, and Policeman Chow was such a hard worker that the foreigners couldn't help but promote him. It wasn't really a promotion, but I knew better than to interrupt an elder.

One guy from the Hong Kong business alliance gave a speech encouraging the Chinese people to continue to fight the communists. He ended by giving a dirty look to the communist photographer.

Right before he went up, Vandyne came up to me at the table and said, "I'm only doing this because my nephew loves that stamp book you got him."

"I figured he'd like it more than me," I said. Vandyne toyed with the tuning pegs on his guitar. He stooped slightly at the mike.

"Hello," he said awkwardly. He put his hands together and nodded his head. Then he played and sang "I'm Walking" by Fats Domino. The singing was a little off, but the playing was spot on. He gave off a good vibe and even got the Chinese people to clap in time.

He came off and I gave him a hug. Then I went up to the mike. I had a three-paragraph speech ready about how my dad was a waiter and how he'd suffered at the hands of a place like Jade Palace. I was also going to talk about how more Chinese had to come forward to report crimes in the community. Paul had helped me with the prepositions.

But the microphone was turned off. I tapped it a few times, but nothing came out of the speakers. The dinner was winding down and people had already broken away from their assigned places to talk at other tables. I was worried I wouldn't have a chance to have my say.

I stood at the podium and leaned on my elbows. For the most part, the Chinese people were talking amongst themselves and the cops were doing the same. It brought home how I was just an instrument. I was the dummy who made both sides look good. It didn't matter what I thought or said for myself. In fact, nobody even cared to listen to me.

"Willie!" I yelled when I saw him passing by. "Tell them to turn on the microphone."

Willie Gee was dressed in a red suit with gaudy lace trim on its oversized lapels. He smiled and said, "One second!" He ducked into a bar at the side and came back with a bottle of Heineken and a glass. "You wanted a beer, right?" he said as he popped the cap off and poured it.

The smell of alcohol made my eyes water. I felt like I was

drinking it already. I could have just one beer, couldn't I? Willie put it on the stand and pushed it closer to me.

"It's cold," he said, smiling.

Lonnie's hand came crashing in and swept the bottle and glass into Willie's chest.

"I'm sorry, I'm so clumsy!" she said.

"Stupid girl!" growled Willie Gee. He slipped off to the kitchen, but not before snapping his fingers at one of the older waiters and pointing at the broken glass on the floor.

"This dinner isn't really your style, is it?" Lonnie asked me. She had on a red chiffon dress that made her look like she was stepping out of a rose.

"No, not at all." I came out from around the microphone stand and stepped down from the platform. I put my hands around her shoulders while keeping some distance between our bodies. People were slipping on their coats and leaving.

"Are you going home now?" she asked.

"I'm pretty much done here," I said. I asked the newspaper reporters if they wanted to talk to me, but they all declined. They already had the story written, they said. They only came to take pictures.

"You're going to do just fine," said Vandyne, clapping my back.

"You look so handsome tonight, Robert," said Rose.

"Chow," said Vandyne as he came in closer. "I want you to know that we still need to brainstorm business ideas together. This guitar playing isn't going to support the both of us."

"You still got 16-odd years, right? Twenty and out?"

"I got a lot of odd years left," Vandyne said.

Teeter came in. "They didn't even let you talk, huh?"

"No, but I guess I shouldn't have been surprised. It wasn't exactly a crowd-pleasing speech I had planned."

"So congratulations on getting some investigative assignments."

"Teeter, how in the world did you know?"

"I know this guy high up in the department. He was pretty impressed after watching you in the hockey game."

"Is he high enough to get me out of doing stupid public-relations assignments?"

Teeter smiled. "As a matter of fact, it's over for you."

"Over?"

"This is the last one. He's ordering you to be removed from the public eye. It doesn't behoove a future detective to have his face all over the place."

"Who is this guy, Teeter?"

"You'll know later on. He's a really good guy who keeps a low profile, but he's a powerful name."

My mother and the midget came up to me at the same time. She looked him over.

"Hey, you must be the poor little man who plays games in the park," my mother said. Her voice sounded like she didn't think the midget could count to five.

"I'm not poor," said the midget.

"I told Robert that I couldn't believe that a grown man would waste so much time just playing games."

"Mom, the midget is going to be the star of a movie."

"Is it a children's movie?" she asked.

The midget cleared his throat. "I'm going out for a smoke," he said. Wang left with him.

"That's a rather rude exit," said my mother.

I was about to say something mean when Lonnie cut in.

"You're Robert's mother?" she asked.

"You Robert's girlfriend?" asked my mother, pointing her right elbow at Lonnie.

"Yes, I am," said Lonnie, taking her hand.

"When are you two getting married?"

Lonnie laughed like Chinese people do when they're ready to move onto the next topic or leave. We left.

—

At the bottom of the escalator, Wang and the midget were sitting on a stone bench. The midget had taken his name tag off and was folding it over and over.

"You have a minute, Officer Chow?" asked the midget.

"Sure."

"I wanted to talk to you in private," he said.

"Wang, can you escort Lonnie home?"

"Sure. It would be a pleasure."

"Oh," said Lonnie. "Robert, I'll see you later, then." I gave her a tight hug. Then I sat down with the midget and watched them swing out through the glass front doors.

"Officer Chow, I want to offer you my heartiest congratulations. Even though this award's bullshit."

"Thank you, and let me apologize for my mother. I'm sorry for the way she treated you."

"Don't feel sorry for me," he said. "I've got more than everything I've ever wanted. But what about you? It looks like the police are changing your duties."

"You know what they want me to do now? Go around and take pictures of Paul and his friends because they can't even tell the good ones from the bad ones."

The midget smiled and cracked his neck.

"Speaking of bad ones, how about that Yip?" he said.

"Yeah, he tried to get close to me just to find my blind spot."

"I think he genuinely liked you."

"I don't know how to take that."

We stood there a little while, listening to the slurping sound coming from the rubber handrails on the escalators.

"I was thinking," the midget said, "that I still need one more person in the store. I know it's far beneath you, but even just a few hours a week would be really helpful to me and Paul. I'll give you partial ownership."

I looked at the midget.

"You're just trying to keep tabs on me," I said.

"Well, that's not the only thing. Consider it a standing offer." The midget slid off the bench. I went over to the glass doors.

"Don't hold the door for me," the midget said. "You're the one who just got feasted." He leapt ahead and got the door for me.

Chapter 17

I was leaning against the subway exit at East Broadway and Essex. Paul had given me a plastic bag of raisins, peanuts, and chocolate chips. I reached in, grabbed a handful, and threw it into the back of my mouth.

The evening rush of commuters stepped out. First came the men who would take two steps at a time ahead of the general trudging foot soldiers. I took another too-big handful of mix and chewed slowly. Constant eating of snack foods was supposed to help, the midget said.

The midget had told me a little more about his alcoholic brother. He hadn't made a clean getaway from the bottle. The midget didn't know where he was now.

I looked at the backs of the heads of people coming up and out. Women lagged behind the men, probably because their shoes hurt and they couldn't walk as fast. One girl coming out looked great from the backs of her half-oval calves to the curved tips of her straight black hair.

She came up the stairs and made a U-turn and faced me directly.

"Robert?" she asked.

If my mouth weren't full, I would have said "Barbara." As she looked at me expectantly, I realized how fortunate I was to have run into her.

After I chewed and swallowed, I tried to look nonchalant.

"How are you, Barbara?"

"I'm doing good. Kinda busy, of course. You know."

"I know."

"Have time for a drink?"

"I have the time, but how about coffee instead?"

Her jaw swung out of joint.

"You're on the wagon!" she said.

"Yes."

"You're in love?"

"I am seeing somebody."

"Is she younger?"

"Yes."

I felt a little good when Barbara winced.

I took her to an over-rice place close by, a place that had Jewish characters in the cornerstone because it used to be a deli. They made some pretty mean Malaysian ice coffees.

"You're not going to get far with any woman, taking girls to the places you do," Barbara said. She put her purse on a chair next to her.

"Flirting with me will embarrass us both, Barbara. Anyway, I don't want to go to a place that has a liquor license. If I even just smell it, who knows what might happen."

"It's that bad?"

I nodded.

"Barbara, could you do a favor for me?"

"Depends. What did you have in mind?" She was smiling as she pulled her hair behind her ears. Barbara, I thought, you'll be 80 years old someday and you'll still be beautiful.

"I know this boy, he's smart as hell, maybe as smart as you were back then. The family situation is a mess and they don't have any money. He's kind of a wise guy, too, but he needs help. I'm no use to him. He needs to talk to someone who understands what it means to have that ticket out of Chinatown."

"Look at me, I landed back in it. What good am I?"

"You only live here. You have a job, an office job. You went to college on a scholarship."

"I feel like my life is so screwed up. . .I feel like I don't know how to love."

"You were married, you do know how to love. You took vows."

She put her elbows on the table and put her head on her closed hands.

"Barbara, you're already a success, you just have to allow yourself to be happy. Helping this kid, Paul, will make you happy. Think of how good you'll feel spreading the message of opportunity. He needs someone smart like you."

"I wish I were stupid," Barbara said.

"Not you, too!"

—

I was sweeping cardboard-box crumbs down the aisle and out the toy store's front door. The midget was sitting on a barstool behind the counter, looking over a sheaf of order forms.

I had called in sick again. It was nice having unlimited sick days. But I needed time off to figure out what to do with the Polaroid camera and how I was going to get out of implicating potentially innocent boys. Pushing a broom was better than scratching my chin.

"You know," I said to the midget, "I'm not getting anywhere in life. This is the same broom I used almost five years ago when I worked for Old Moy."

"Are you sure?"

"My initials are still on it, see? Old Moy was too cheap to buy a new broom. Surprised he didn't take it with him when he left."

"He wasn't such a bad guy. You know he loved you?"

"He didn't love me."

"He called you his second son."

"Then he hated me. The second son always gets the shaft. Don't you know kung-fu movies? The second son gets killed and the prodigal first son returns to the village to avenge him."

The midget looked back to his clipboard.

"Kung-fu action dolls," he said to himself. "They even have some black ones. Jim Kelly from 'Enter the Dragon.'"

"Order two. I want one and I think Vandyne will want one, too."

"I'm going to order a bunch for the store. I think the kids are going to be into it."

"Maybe you should ask Paul. Shouldn't he be back, already?"

"Well, if he's there a while, the interview's going well."

"It takes 45 minutes to get to midtown, 45 to get back, so he's been in the interview for more than an hour?"

"He can handle it."

I put the broom aside and fidgeted with the bandage on my left hand. I had sliced myself lightly with a box cutter.

Just then Paul walked in, his long coat already fully unbuttoned to show his dark suit and bright tie.

"Hey, what happened?" I asked, coming up to him.

"What happened to you?" he asked, pointing at my hand.

"I cut myself."

"With a box cutter?"

"No, with the broom. C'mon, tell me what happened!"

"Well, that Barbara, she's really nice looking. Smart and classy."

He saw me frowning and cleared his throat.

"So after talking with Barbara a little bit, I met her boss and we talked some more."

"What did you talk about?"

"Talked about the brain drain from China and Taiwan. When people from Taiwan finish grad school in America, they apply for citizenship and bring the rest of their families over. When people from China finish grad school in Russia or Japan, they're going to go back to China. In the long run, eventually, China's science and engineering will surpass Taiwan's. They also have more natural resources."

"So what's that mean?"

"It means that someday, China will be a superpower and Taiwan businesses will be investing in it. And combined, they will import goods to all over the world faster and cheaper than anyone else."

"No way. The KMT would rather have the island go up in a mushroom cloud before working with communists."

"Just wait a generation or two. People will let that go. The next generation in America's not going to give a damn about Vietnam."

The midget said, "The current generation doesn't give a damn about Vietnam."

"I don't even give a damn about Vietnam," I said. "So, anyway, what happened, Paul?"

"Well, we just talked a lot. Never talked so much in my life."

"Did the boss like you?"

"I think so. He offered me an internship."

"That's great! When do you start?"

"I told them I couldn't do it."

"What!"

"This internship doesn't pay for the first three months!"

"You're taking that fucking internship!"

"Well, then I can't pay rent, okay?"

"Yeah, yeah. Get on the fucking phone right now. Apologize and everything!"

"Okay, okay."

Paul went around the counter and picked up the receiver.

"Ah, Robert," said the midget. "Can you watch your language? This is a toy store."

"Oh, man, I'm sorry about that." I waved to some kids staring at me.

"Another thing."

"Yeah?"

"Who am I going to get to replace Paul here?"

"Just get another kid!"

"What kid can you count on to work in a toy store?"

I took a deep breath and thought.

The midget tapped the clipboard against his thigh.

"I know a lot of people who'd love to work at a business that they had partial ownership of. Business does well, your ownership is worth even more. It's better than a pension. There's nothing like being your own boss. You take pride in your work," he took a breath. "Do I have to beg you to work with me?"

"What are the hours?" I said.

—

The early evening seemed as good a time as any to go see English and quit, particularly while I was in civvies.

He was sitting in the detectives' lounge, watching Bugs Bunny and Elmer Fudd.

"Chow, you got any pictures yet for the mug books?"

"Yeah, here you go," handing him a stack of Polaroids. "I took them last night."

He put them face-down on his stomach and continued to watch TV.

"You're not even going to look at them?" I asked. "I put a lot of effort into the stakeout."

"I'll look at the end of the show. I know this is your first assignment and all, but don't get too anxious."

"I'll be out by my locker," I said.

—

It took me longer to pack than I thought. I kept finding

stupid little things that brought up memories that I was immediately forced to live through again.

The puck from the hockey game I'd scored two goals in. Where were those firemen now?

Baseball caps from Chinatown associations and clubs whose dinners I'd gone to. I tried a few on. Kinda tight.

A picture of me and Vandyne the first week we were partners. We both looked tired.

"Is this some kind of fucking joke!" thundered English, throwing the pictures into my box.

"Hey, I don't want to take those with me!" I protested. "That's police property."

"What are you trying to pull here, Chow? You took pictures of your feet!"

"You have to admit that that right big toe does look like it's up to no good."

"What the hell is this!" English said, surprised as if my box had just materialized. "You're cleaning out your locker? You're quitting?"

"Now I get why you're the top detective, English."

He nodded a few times and sucked in his lips.

"Come over here, Chow," he said quietly, walking over to a window by the landing.

"What is it?"

"Just come over here!"

I went over to the window, which started at about knee level and went up a foot above my head. There was chicken wire running through it and some paint had dripped onto it before being sloppily wiped off, but you could still see the street pretty well.

English opened the window a few inches so we could hear the noise from the street.

"What do you see out there, Chow?"

"Chinatown."

"No! Look at those kids over there, crouching on the corner. What are they doing?"

"Just waiting for something or somebody. Maybe a bus for a field trip."

"Over there. Why are those two boys yelling at each other?"

"Sounds like yelling, but they're just talking. Those three girls down there. They're not in school because they're going to work in a sweatshop. They all have one small container of barbecued meat from a restaurant because the sweatshop has its own rice cooker."

"They get the rice for free?" asked English.

"Benevolent of them, isn't it?" I kept looking out the window. I focused in on a skinny kid crouched on some stairs in front of a door. He was looking up and down the street. "That kid," I said, pointing. "He could be a lookout for a gambling outfit up in that association building."

"Are you sure?"

"I don't know for sure. He could be."

"Chow," English said turning to me. My upper right arm was growing warmer and I realized it was because he had his hand on it. "The guys I have taking pictures now would have shot all of those kids."

"Why?"

"Because they all look the same to the cops. You know what

I mean," he said. I did know. He went on. "Those good kids don't deserve to be lumped in with the bad ones. They should get some credit. And you're the only one who can give them that."

"So it's a good thing that we only single out the kids who might be troublemakers."

"You know the deal, Chow. We get a victim who identifies someone in our unofficial mug books, they could land in a world of trouble. And they could be completely innocent, too."

"They're all innocent until proven guilty. Aren't they?"

English stood his ground. "Don't tell me how it's supposed to be. You know how it is."

"I suppose you're going to beg me not to quit."

"I'm not going to beg you anything, Chow. I mean, either way, I don't care. Innocent Chinese kids going to jail won't mess my sleep up at all. I just want to know if you care. I think you do, because you took out Paul's picture.

"What's going to happen if Paul or someone like him gets tagged on a bullshit charge? He can kiss college goodbye and any chance of having a real job."

I thought about Paul at my age, years from now, sitting in a chair in Martha's, smoking a cigarette and looking for trouble.

"I was just cleaning my locker," I said, kicking my box. "I wasn't going to quit."

"Oh, and another thing. Who do you know, Chow?"

"What are you talking about?"

"We got orders from the top that because of your investigative assignments, you can't go to those opening-day ceremonies anymore. Too high-profile. You're strictly going to be on plainclothes duty going forward."

"Doing more than just taking pictures, right?"

"Yeah, don't worry. We've got more action than you can handle. You can even work with Vandyne, again. Anyway, the Brow wants to see you. He's ready to take your head off."

"I don't want to see that guy. It's bad enough hanging out and talking with you."

"Let me tell you something, Chow," said English. "I think you have a bad attitude and lousy hygiene, but I wasn't the guy holding you back from detective track."

"Like hell," I said.

"Hey," he said, crossing his arms. "It was the Brow. He kept telling me I couldn't put anything else on your plate."

I thought about that for a moment. Another thought hit me.

"English," I said. "How did you know it was me who ripped out Paul's picture from the mug books?"

He smiled. "The other guys, if they found out that someone was really a good kid, they wouldn't have bothered to take out his picture."

—

The Brow was cleaning out the bowl of his pipe with the sharp end of a metal envelope opener. His blue eyes flashed up at me and went off to the side.

"I suppose your banquet was your last public event for us, Mr. Chow."

"Now I know why I never got those investigative assignments."

"Given the easiest most mindless task in the world," he said through gritted teeth. "Eat, drink, and make merry for the cameras. Still, you managed to make a mess of everything."

"I've been your little soldier boy long enough," I said, pointing to the woodcut print of Andrew Jackson on his wall. "I'm not shining your boots anymore."

He threw his pipe into the corner and pointed at me menacingly with the letter opener.

"You're nobody, Chow! You think you're above and beyond walking a simple beat now! You think you're going to get a gold shield!"

"Someday, yeah."

"You'll not see smiling eyes ever again from this mick! When I see you, you'll get nothing but hate, and more than you can stand!"

"When I'm in civvies," I said slowly and evenly, "you won't even recognize me from the other chinks in the street."

—

On the street, the smell of freshly laid-out garbage hit me. You could see the drizzling rain against the glow of the streetlamps, but it was almost too light to feel.

I shifted the box I was carrying from one side to the other. I had decided to take home all the baseball caps that had been crammed in my locker. Paul might like them.

The rain got harder. I put the box down on my feet and zipped up my coat. A wet cat ran by.

The light was on in my apartment window. Paul was home.

I had to call Lonnie and tell her I wasn't going to be going to any more dumbass dinners. The pay would still be the same in the near term, but it was still a step up for me. Probably my first step up ever.

I got into the lobby and looked for my mail on the radiator, but there wasn't any because Paul had already grabbed it.

I raked some fingers through my soaked hair. Then I hoisted the box onto my shoulder and went upstairs to see if I had gotten something good.

Photo: Cindy Cheung

Ed Lin's first novel *Waylaid* was based on his childhood of renting out rooms to johns and hookers at his parents' sleazy motel. Published by Kaya in 2002, *Waylaid* was universally praised in a broad range of publications including *Booklist*, *Asianweek* and *Playboy*. *Waylaid* also won the Members' Choice Award from the Asian American Writers Workshop in 2003.

Lin, who is of Taiwanese and Chinese descent, lives in New York with his wife, actress Cindy Cheung.

This is a bust : a novel